"Carly."

His eyes were bright, alm... ...feverish as they gazed into hers.

"Trace, what is it?"

"Are you still willing to help me keep Danny?"

"Of course I am. Whatever you need—"

"Then, will you marry me?"

"M-marry—"

"Marry me." He stepped inside and closed the door. "And before you call the hospital and send for two big guys in white coats to haul me away, please give me a chance to explain."

Stunned, Carly watched him walk across the room. For several moments he gazed at the toes of his boots, as if they might hold the answer to world peace.

"I know my proposal came out of left field, but believe me, I am not stark raving mad, nor am I drunk."

When she started to speak, he held up a hand to silence her. "No, wait. I've got to say this before I lose my nerve. When I'm finished, you can ask all the questions you want, or just tell me to get the hell out."

Dear Reader,

I hope you enjoyed last month's new authors, and I know you are looking forward to this month's lineup of books. What better way to begin the month than with one of your all-time favorites, Nora Roberts? Nora is back with a sequel to *Night Shift* entitled *Night Shadow*. This is a very special—even magical—book, with a hero you won't soon forget. I don't want to give anything away, so let me say only that everyone who reads this book is going to be clamoring for a "Nemesis" of her very own.

The rest of the authors this month are terrific, too. Mary Anne Wilson's *Child of Mine* deals with a wrenching custody suit and a man who has to prove his right to raise his own son. You'll be on his side right from the start, pulling for him to win his child—and the woman he loves. Lynn Bartlett's *Heart and Soul* is set on a university campus where there's a lot more than learning going on. High-level espionage and very adult passion are certainly ingredients that were missing when I went to school! Finally, try Sandy Steen's *The Simple Truth,* the story of a mother searching for her lost son—and running head-on into love, along with a little boy who *might* be hers but is absolutely adorable no matter what.

In months to come, look for Dallas Schulze, Marilyn Pappano, Ann Williams, Heather Graham Pozzessere and more. In fact, starting later in the year, we'll bring you two stories you've waited a very long time for—those of the remaining Marshall brothers, from talented Kristin James, who has been missing from the line for far too long.

There's always something exciting happening at Silhouette Intimate Moments, so join us every month for the best in contemporary romance fiction.

Leslie Wainger
Senior Editor and Editorial Coordinator

SANDY STEEN

The Simple Truth

SILHOUETTE·INTIMATE·MOMENTS®

Published by Silhouette Books New York

America's Publisher of Contemporary Romance

SILHOUETTE BOOKS
300 East 42nd St., New York, N.Y. 10017

THE SIMPLE TRUTH

ISBN: 0-373-07375-5

First Silhouette Books printing March 1991

Books by Sandy Steen

Silhouette Intimate Moments

Sweet Reason #155
Past Perfect #202
The Simple Truth #375

Silhouette Special Edition

Vanquish the Night #638

SANDY STEEN

spent many an hour daydreaming while growing up in the Texas Panhandle. Later, inspired by her husband of more than twenty years and her two children, Sandy decided to put her dreams on paper.

Although her family had some doubts when they first observed her method of plotting her stories, they are now her staunchest supporters. Sandy herself is sure that if she can make a reader believe in the wonder of fantasy and feel the joy of falling in love, then she has, indeed, succeeded.

For the missing children.
And for all the people who love them,
pray for them
and wait with open arms.

ACKNOWLEDGMENTS:
Fran Reich, R.N.

Julia Caughey Cartwright,
Director Media Relations,
National Center for Missing and Exploited Children

Chapter 1

Consciousness returned not with a whimper but with a roar. The instant Trace's eyes opened, a blinding, skull-splitting headache—and reality—slammed across his brain.

Crashed!

The word skittered through his mind, disjointed electric impulses attempting to validate the glare of white that was all he could see. He blinked, trying to focus his eyes, and realized that the colorless expanse was framed by the plane's broad windshield.

The jet's nose was completely buried in snow.

The final terrifying moments before the crash streaked across his mind. In less than five minutes, first one engine, then the other, had coughed to death. The jet had dropped like a stone, and only scraps of luck had provided a snow-covered meadow large enough to land the fatally wounded plane. Trace absently massaged his temples. He had no idea how long he had been unconscious, only that they were on the ground . . . and alive.

When nothing but the wind's cold moan whipping over and around the downed plane confirmed his assessment, live wires of fear snaked into every corner of his mind, taking priority over pain. He didn't hear the others! Why couldn't he hear the others? The unwanted answer came quickly, and just as quickly Trace refused to accept it, refused to believe....

"Matt!" The sound exploded in his head, and his vision doubled, then blurred into a haze of colors.

There was no response.

Woozy as a punch-drunk sailor, he forced himself to focus on the executive jet's instrument panel to verify the automatic locator signal. Instinctively he reached for the battery switch, and a roar to rival Niagara Falls filled his skull. Momentarily his eyes squeezed shut against the pain; then he silenced the radio and shut down the electrical system, all the while telling himself that if he had made it, then the others must have, too. But even as hope dealt a hand of optimism, the eerie, unanswering quiet inside the aircraft called its bluff.

"Matt! Jenny!" The frightened ring of his own voice did nothing to stem his rising panic or the pounding in his head.

"For God's sake, Matt. Answer me!" His fist smacked the release on the shoulder harness while his other hand flipped open the seat belt. Another blinding pain lanced through his skull, threatening to plunge him back into unconsciousness. One hand grabbed for the control yoke; the other went to his head, fingertips pressing one throbbing temple. Trace steadied himself as a wave of nausea and dizziness threatened to drag him back into darkness.

No sudden moves. Won't be any good to anyone out cold.

Realizing that he probably had a concussion, Trace gasped for a full breath and paid for half-empty lungs with more agony. Some pain-free right brain function told him that a couple of ribs were undoubtedly broken, but he ignored the message. He pulled himself from the seat as quickly as the crescendo in his head allowed, careful to hang on until the spinning cockpit slowed, then came to an unsteady stop. As the rest of the Holden Enterprises corporate jet settled into focus, he forgot the ache in his head.

The cabin was wrecked. Furniture was overturned, papers from Matt's briefcase scattered everywhere; cushions had been tossed against the wall, bits of their stuffing exposed, and the place was empty of passengers. No sight of Matt, Jenny or Danny. . . .

Some fifty feet from the jet's body, the tail section, ripped from the fuselage as if it were the victim of some giant child's temper tantrum, lay discarded in the snow.

Struggling for every breath, his head roaring mercilessly, Trace found his way through the debris to the jagged gaping hole at the rear of the plane.

"Matt!" His brother's name barely carried beyond the branches of an enormous fir tree that had severed the two parts of the aircraft.

"Oh, God, Matt, answer me," Trace yelled, leaping into swirling snow.

Unmindful of the subzero wind whipping his body and the knee-deep snow impeding his progress, Trace worked his way around the tree, praying as he never had in his life. *They have to be alive! Have to be!*

He begged God not to punish him for his many sins by taking the only people on earth he loved. And who loved him. He prayed for one more of Jenny's lovingly delivered scoldings about finding a good woman and settling down. He prayed for one more chance to be worthy of Matt's undying faith in him. Trace prayed and kept on praying.

He didn't stop until he found them.

Pinned beneath the tree, Matt's body lay facedown, shielding Jenny's. His head and shoulder covered her face, an arm protectively hooked around her waist while one of her hands rested on his shoulder. They might have been embracing or in the midst of some macabre dance but for the circle of darkening red haloing their heads.

Eyes squeezed shut, Trace tried to deny reality. He summoned a vivid mental picture from the past of Matt laughing, Jenny smiling, her hair ruffled by a breeze.

Trace opened his eyes.

One side of Jenny's always neat page boy fanned in an angel's wing against the snow. A crimson-tipped angel's wing.

Crimson. Bloodred. Blood...

"No-o-o-!"

Frantically ripping branches aside, he finally scrambled over the deadly weight keeping the two people he loved most from help. "No! No! Dear God in heaven—"

He lifted Matt's wrist, searching, praying for a pulse. Then Jenny's. Nothing. Nothing. Reality refused to be denied.

His anguished roar rent the air.

Frigid wind snatched the raw, primitive cry from his lips and flung it around the small, snowy, mountaintop meadow turned cemetery. Nothing escaped the sound of his agony. It touched every leaf, assailed every rock, filled every snowflake with pure, inconsolable desolation.

In anguish's cruel grasp, he sank to his knees beside the still forms of his family, unmindful of the snow or blisteringly cold winds. Streams of tears formed crystal streaks ending in icicles that clung to his jaw. He never noticed as he plucked a sprig of fir needles from his brother's hair.

"Why d-didn't y-you hang on, Matt? You s-should have j-just hung on for... for a few more minutes. You knew I'd come. Why...?"

But Matt couldn't answer, and from some deep well of untapped emotion, anger and denial twisted into a ball of fury, rolling over Trace, threatening to suffocate him.

"Damn it, Matt." Two doubled fists hit the offending tree limb. "You c-can't do this. I won't let you, d-do you hear me? You and Jenny and Danny are all I—" Trace gasped. "Oh, no, D-Danny...not Danny." His teary gaze searched the area for his nephew's small form, with no results.

Desperation again drove him plowing through the branches. This time his efforts were fruitless. Against all reason Trace clung to hope, but even while his gaze scanned the white-cloaked meadow, his mind deliberately shut out the horrifying possibilities of how the force of the crash might have dealt with the child's light-as-a-feather frame.

"Danny!" Even though Trace didn't expect the four-teen-month-old to call out, he prayed for some sound of response. The ever-present whistle of wind through snow dusted fir and cedar was his only answer.

"Danny! Danny, can you hear me?" *Oh, God, please let him be alive.* "Danny!"

A faint keening sound reached his ears. The wind? The noise came again, and Trace was certain it wasn't the wind. Heart pounding wildly, he listened until he was able to pinpoint the direction. *It was coming from inside the plane!*

Hands and arms bracing his battered ribs, Trace staggered into the main part of the cabin. He waited, listened and prayed. From beneath a tattered cushion resting against the bulkhead the sound came again, a muffled whimper. Trace snatched the cushion away.

"Danny!"

As he knelt beside his nephew, Trace's wide hands cradled the small head. "Thank God. Thank God you're alive." Barely conscious, but definitely alive. On Danny's forehead a bruise, already dark blue, drew his attention. Concussions were serious business in adults, but even more so in children. With trembling hands and occasional blurred vision he gently inspected Danny's tiny body and found multiple bruises, contusions and a compound fracture of the left leg. The towheaded toddler cried out at Trace's slightest touch to the injured leg.

"It's okay, Danny Boy, it's okay. We'll have you in a nice clean hospital before you know it."

Utilizing every scrap of first-aid information his memory could provide, he carefully examined Danny's head. With the aid of a pocket flashlight he checked the boy's eyes and was relieved to see they weren't dilated, but he still couldn't be sure there was no concussion. Nor could he be certain there was no internal bleeding, but he prayed luck was with them. "Don't worry, partner. Uncle Trace is with you. I'm going to keep you warm and—"

Danny started to cry, jerky, pitiful, hurting sobs. "Don't...don't cry. I'm here, and I'm going to take care of you. But you've got to be very still, okay, sport?"

Trace longed to clutch the boy to him, to feel the warmth of his little body, know the reassuring beat of his heart, but he dared not for fear of causing further damage or pain.

"Ma-a...ma-a," Danny wailed from his limited vocabulary.

"Sh-h-h, sh-h-h." Trace left Danny only for the few seconds required to grab the first-aid kit from the cockpit. As he sorted through the contents, he talked continuously to Danny, hoping his voice didn't betray his own fears. Fortunately the medical kit contained everything he needed, including a recognizable pain killer. Another short frantic search turned up Danny's diaper bag with two full bottles of milk. Using a small pocket knife, Trace cut one of the capsule-shaped pills into pieces, certain Danny couldn't take the drug full-strength. Using a cap from one of the bottles he crushed bits of the medication and mixed it with milk, then managed to get most of it down Danny. Making sure to reserve enough pills to help Danny, he spared two for himself, swallowing them with small sips from the flask of water he'd found in the first-aid kit.

"Ma-a-a," the child pleaded between sips.

"Sh-h. Listen, sport. Mama's not here now. But you're gonna be fine."

Tear filled blue eyes begged, while small arms reached to be held. "I know it hurts, sport, but you can't move around, okay?"

The rejection brought fresh sobs, and it was all Trace could do not to give in to his own tears. But he was Danny's lifeline; he had to do whatever was necessary to keep the toddler calm and immobile until help arrived. The first order of business was tending the injured leg. Applications of antiseptic and antibiotic cream brought on another round of crying and Trace fought to work and hold Danny still at the same time. Soon he realized Danny remained motionless as long as he talked to him. The sound of a familiar, calm voice seemed to reassure the boy, so Trace talked about anything and everything, pausing only long enough to refill depleted lungs and moisten dry lips.

"Hey, sport, remember that bear we saw at the circus? The one with the ball on his nose? What color was that ball? Red. Yeah, it was red, and it was right on the tip of his nose, wasn't it?" He made a face and playfully touched the boy's nose. "Funny bear, huh?"

Trace tucked a blanket around Danny and kept on talking. Big blue eyes tracked his every move, growing wide with alarm if Trace drew too far away, darting anxiously if his voice stopped.

"When I was a kid the clowns were my favorite. But I think Mr. Bear was better than the clowns, don't you? Remember how he waddled around and everybody laughed?"

Rambling like an idiot, animating his face to suit the conversation, Trace talked about clowns, talked of ships and string and sealing wax, anything to keep Danny's mind off the pain and the encroaching cold—but most of all, to keep the boy from focusing on the absence of his parents. Thank God Danny was too young to fully comprehend the situation.

Gradually, with the help of splints, the effects of the drug and nonstop chatter, sprinkled liberally with loving assurances, Trace immobilized the injured leg and Danny quieted, even dozed. Keeping the boy in a long-term state of semisedation was not feasible, but Trace knew the injury would worsen if Danny moved about too much.

Knowing the plane's automatic emergency signal was functioning and had probably been intercepted already, Trace scavenged the plane, gathering whatever clothing, blankets and food he could find, checking for flares and flashlights. If push came to shove, there was enough food to stretch for two days, maybe three if he cut back and saved most of it for Danny. With the pint of distilled water from the first-aid box and melted ice from the serving compartment, Trace estimated the total water quantity at possibly a quart, plus Danny's two bottles. Maybe, just maybe, it would be enough to last until they were rescued.

A further search revealed a tarp stored in an overhead compartment. Working quickly, he draped and fastened the tarp, successfully sealing the jagged hole that had exposed them to the elements. Not exactly weatherproof, he thought, but it would keep out the snow and most of the wind and cold. Satisfied—at least temporarily—that he had done what he could for the living, he turned up the collar of his leather flight jacket and stepped outside to tend to the dead.

Thirty minutes later, numb clear to the bone from subfreezing cold, Trace entered the plane. A signal fire blazed in the center of the meadow, and Matt and Jenny...

He hadn't been able to force himself to leave them lying in the snow, unsheltered, so he had gently covered their bodies with fallen cedar branches, marking the spot for rescuers. In his heart, Trace knew that, of all people, Matt and Jenny would understand. Danny came first now.

Trace glanced at his fitfully sleeping nephew. The boy was innocently unaware that his life had changed so drastically. Stepping close, Trace squatted beside the makeshift bed and touched the child's forehead. Danny's skin was already hot and dry. Another search of the diaper bag turned up a box of plastic bottle liners. Hardly ideal, Trace decided, but sufficient to improvise ice packs. Within minutes he had filled the bags, cut swatches of fabric from cushions, then wrapped the snow-filled liners inside, first placing one across the boy's feverish brow, then two bracketing the injured leg. Danny cried out but didn't wake fully, slipping back into sleep as the snow packs began to do their job.

Trace sighed, easing himself to the floor of the airplane's ruptured cabin. *Now we wait.*

He prayed the temperature wouldn't nose-dive. Weather reports he'd picked up before they left Canada had indicated that a minor storm was due to sweep the Pacific Northwest before noon the following day. He and Danny had to be rescued before then or they might never be. At this altitude, an overnight snow, even a light one, could force rescue operations to a standstill.

But would a rescue party arrive ahead of the storm? How would he keep Danny alive if they were forced to stay on this mountain until a storm blew over? What if the injured leg became infected? What if...?

You'll "what if" yourself into hysteria if you're not careful.

Checking his watch, Trace was shocked to discover how little time had passed since the plane crash. His and Danny's whole lives had changed in less than an hour. As dusk clothed the ragged peaks, Trace knew there would be no rescue attempt until morning.

Danny whined, and instantly Trace was there, readjusting the snow packs, talking in low, soothing tones. At his first soft-spoken reassurance, the whining subsided. Carefully, Trace lifted Danny's hand; his thumb gently stroked chubby little baby fingers. Another whimper halted the motion, but again Trace's voice calmed the boy. Even consumed with fever, Danny instinctively responded, linking the voice to someone who cared about him. Each time Danny roused, Trace talked. The words, he soon discovered, were unimportant as long as voice offered comfort. As the cold, interminable night crept toward a faraway gray dawn, Trace kept up a steady pace of refilling the liners and talking.

"There you go, sport." Trace adjusted the fourth—or was it fourteenth?—snow-stuffed pack, then retucked the blanket around Danny's narrow shoulders. Trace felt as if his skull was being hammered to pieces from the inside out, and time had dissolved into a fuzzy uncertainty. The only clock he recognized ticked off the intervals between fresh snow packs. And memories.

"Did you know I broke my collarbone once.... No, wait. That time it was Matt. He fell off a swing and cried like hell. 'Scuse me, heck. Swore it didn't hurt, but I knew he was just saying that because I was scared. He w-was like that, you know. Always thinking about other people. I hope you're just like him when you grow up, Danny. He was . . ." Tears stung his eyes. " . . . the best. Your mom, too.

"I'm ashamed to admit I was jealous when Matt told me he was in love. Jeez, I was scared. Afraid we wouldn't be c-close anymore. But your mom . . . sweet as sunshine. One smile from her and it was easy to understand why your daddy loved her so. What they had was special . . . just between them, but it sorta spilled over, touching everyone else. And they loved you. God, how they loved you. I only saw Matt cry twice in his whole life. The day our folks died, and the day they got the call to come and get you." Fat teardrops splashed unnoticed onto the large hand holding the much smaller one.

As the darkness wore on, the one-sided conversation became cathartic. Trace barely heard his own voice, now raspy from use, unaware he no longer spoke to Danny but to himself—to his own pain, grief . . . and guilt.

"Everything happened so fast. Number-one engine went. . . . I yelled for Matt to secure everything, but . . . then number two cut out."

Replaying the minutes before impact, Trace racked his brain, trying to pinpoint the source of the aircraft's trouble, praying it hadn't been pilot error, yet even willing to accept the blame if it would help answer the ultimate unanswered question—why?

"I checked the plane like always. Swear to God, it was clean as a whistle. Sure we'd make it when I saw the meadow. Thought we *had*. If I hadn't passed out, maybe... And why weren't they buckled in? Why? Why? Why?

"Oh, God, Matt. You raised me . . . gave me so much . . . b-believed in me when no one else could. I...m-miss you," Trace rasped as the pearl-gray light of a new day seeped into the broken cabin. He gazed at the patch of light brightening the plane's interior and tried to feel hopeful. Soon, probably within hours, they would be rescued. Intellectually, he knew life went on, and so would he and Danny, but his heart ached with the knowledge that there was nothing he could do to bring Matt or Jenny back, no matter how hard he prayed, denied or mourned.

But there *was* something he could still do for his brother. Carefully brushing a wisp of blond hair from Danny's small forehead, he felt the fine strands sift through his fingers. In a voice as raw and parched as his soul, Trace vowed, "I promise you, Matt, I'll take care of your son. And I'll teach him to be the kind of man his daddy was. You'll be proud of both of us."

Carly was proud of herself. She had gone a whole five minutes without thinking about the two survivors, especially the child. According to the helicopter paramedic's report, the pilot and child were in fair condition, and the rescue was "routine." But for Carly, from the moment she had learned that one of the expected patients was a twelve-month-old boy, nothing had been routine.

As she waited for the first sounds of the helicopter's approach to disturb the quiet of the hospital lobby, Carly warned herself repeatedly to keep her emotions in check. She was officially off duty, and a fully staffed and prepared emergency team was standing by. Practically speaking, she wasn't needed.

"Thought I told you to go home."

Turning from the entrance to the emergency room, Carly came face-to-face with Linc Garrison's familiar scowl. Visually sidestepping his keen gaze she asked, "Is that an order as my boss?"

"As your friend."

"Well, friend, I did exactly as you instructed, and now I'm back."

"Liar. Since your shift ended three hours ago, you've been to pediatrics twice, checked a half dozen patients and worked on next week's schedule, but you have *not* left this hospital."

Carly glanced away, her slender fingers brushing a truant wisp of hair from her forehead. She smiled, still avoiding eye contact. "Has anyone ever told you that you're a bully?"

Linc swung a chart from beneath his arm, flipped open the cover and began to scribble notations. "Has anyone ever told you you're a workaholic?"

Carly shrugged. "Must be a flaw in my character."

"No argument there. If you weren't the best damn nurse to walk through the doors of Community General Hospital since I became chief of surgery, I'd fire you for insubordination."

"You can't fire me. No one else around here will put up with you."

"True." The aluminum chart cover slapped shut. "But if you don't stop living in this place twenty-four hours a day, I'm gonna tie you to one of these beds until you get at least eight straight hours sleep."

"Had our vitamins this morning, did we, Doctor?"

"*We* haven't had anything but that sludge produced by the Coffeemaker from hell." Linc didn't miss her repeated glances toward the emergency-room doors.

"You're not gonna be much good dead on your feet."

"I just wanted to see—"

"Yeah. I heard about the little boy. Compound fracture of the left tibia. What about the pilot?" Linc asked.

"Concussion, probably broken ribs. Who knows what else? It's a wonder they survived," she answered, unable to sustain the game of visual keep-away.

"I understand the kid's parents didn't. We're gonna have one traumatized little boy on our hands."

"I know." Carly gnawed at her bottom lip for several seconds, then added, "Rescue said before the pilot lost consciousness he identified the dead passengers as the boy's parents and himself as the child's uncle." She met her friend and co-worker's gaze. "They also said the boy was so scared he screamed bloody murder when they tried to separate him from the pilot."

Gazing into eyes so blue they needed a poet's words to do them justice, Dr. Garrison marveled at the woman who literally ran Community General Hospital between the hours of 11:00 p.m. and 7:00 a.m. Beauty, brains, compassion—a powerful combination in any woman, but in Carly McShane the composition was extraordinary. Add softly feminine curves in a delicate five-foot-five-inch frame, the face of an angel, the soul of a saint and the package was almost...spiritual. Linc often lamented the fact that they had become friends instead of lovers, but he never ceased to cherish their warm and open relationship.

"And you just want to make sure that baby knows he's got one friend in this big bad place, right?"

"Something like that." She gave him a you-know-me-too-well smile.

Linc understood Carly's need to comfort, not only as a nurse, but as a mother. Ever since the night he had found her in tears, crouched in the hospital's chapel after an emergency operation on a small child had gone badly, he had understood a great many things. Why she haunted the pediatric ward, often working long hours after her regular shift ended. Why she empathized with the parents who sat in the waiting room, powerless and praying. And why she was so drawn to solitary children, particularly little boys.

"All right," Linc said, knowing he was fighting a losing battle. "But as soon as we get the two emergencies stabilized, I'm kicking you out of here. And I don't want to see your smiling face until time for your shift. You get my drift, Nurse McShane?"

"Got it."

The anxiously awaited *wop-wop-wop* of helicopter rotors cut short their conversation, and in seconds the emergency room doors burst open.

Four hours later a tired but pleased Carly gazed at the sleeping form of little Danny Holden and marveled, as always, at the stamina and resilience of a child's body. The boy was going to be all right. Not perfect, but all right. There would be a scar from the surgery Linc had scheduled for a later time, and Danny would have to learn to walk all over again, but in time he would be good as new.

Thank God the boy's uncle had been ingenious enough to pull a few emergency "tricks" from his hat. Still, the subsequent swelling would delay, until tomorrow or the following day, the surgery needed to properly set the boy's leg. All in all, little Danny had survived the ordeal extremely well, physically *and* mentally. Aided by a stuffed dinosaur, Carly had even coaxed a hint of a smile from him just before the mild sedative took effect. She longed to see the promise of that smile fulfilled.

Danny stirred. Carly touched his forehead, thankful it was simply bruised and nothing more, then tucked the serviceable but soft hospital blanket around his tiny shoulders.

"Don't worry, sweetheart. Carly's here."

Gently, so as not to waken him, she lifted his little hand and held it. The child sighed and quieted.

With every caress of his baby skin, Carly was asking for trouble, and she knew it. Each time she looked at Danny Holden, the need to hold him, to care for him, escalated. The moment the paramedics wheeled him into the emergency room, Carly had taken one look at the pale, drawn precious face and felt her heart break. And when he opened his eyes and looked at her for the first time, the fractured pieces of her heart melted right down to her toes. After that, nothing on earth could have forced her from Danny Holden's side.

Transference, psychologists called it, and she had been warned of the hazards, particularly as a nurse. Nurses were supposed to be compassionate and giving, unable to stand idly by while others suffered, yet remain professionally objective. But Carly wasn't objective. Where children were concerned, her objectivity had vanished eleven months ago.

Nine months, five days and seventeen hours ago—the day her nine-month-old son had been kidnapped.

How could she *ever* be objective about any child after losing Brian? How could she *ever* look at another little boy who was even remotely close to Brian's age and not wonder if her son's smile was as sweet? Or if his baby-fine, natural blond waves had given way to curls? Or if fuzzy green dinosaurs made his eyes sparkle? Or...

A thousand other questions invaded her mind every time she saw a fair-haired toddler. Not a day, not even an hour, passed without thoughts of Brian. Was he safe, warm, secure? Did he have someone to tuck him in? Make him smile? Hold him when he cried? A thousand—no, a million—unanswered questions plagued her, haunted her, refused to give her peace.

Her only solace, then and now, was her job—giving, helping others, especially the children. And out of the many children she had seen or cared for since Brian had been taken, none had stolen her heart as Danny Holden had. None had managed to slip past the protective barrier she tried so hard to maintain.

But today, more than usual, Carly desparately needed to keep busy, to feel useful.

Today was Brian's birthday.

No one, not even Linc, knew how important this day was, so no one could understand what Danny's presence meant to her. And no one could convince her that he wasn't heaven-sent to help her past a painful milestone.

Danny stirred again. Unable to stop herself, Carly began humming a tune. A soft, caressing melody. The same melody that had been part of the nightly bedtime ritual she'd shared with her own son.

Trace drifted, floating toward the surface of the strange pool of blackness surrounding him. The notes of a lullaby, comforting, like a memory from his childhood, compelled him, drew him upward. Slowly he opened his eyes and turned his head in the direction of the sound. Instantly, the singing ceased, and a figure moved toward him. He was unable to focus his eyes, but the blurry vision appeared to be a woman dressed in white. A nurse? Memories strung together in painful sequence instantly linked him to reality. Nurse . . . hospital . . . rescue . . .

"D-Danny?" At first he didn't recognize the croaking sound as his own voice; then he decided it had to be, because the word was thumping around in his head like a muffled sledgehammer.

Soft, warm fingers gently touched his arm. "Danny is all right, Mr. Holden. He's in the next bed, resting quietly, which is exactly what you need to do."

Trace tried to push himself upright, but his body failed to respond. "Danny . . ." He had to be sure Danny was all right, but the sledgehammer was no longer muffled, and his head felt too big and heavy to lift. When the hand on his arm applied the slightest pressure his body offered no resistance, yet his mind struggled for control.

"Wait." He heard the squeak of rubber-soled shoes on an uncarpeted floor as she walked away. A light snapped on, throwing soft illumination over a white metal crib. "See for yourself," the woman in white said. "Danny is going to be fine."

Carefully lifting himself up to rest on one elbow, Trace was able to see into the crib. Dark blond lashes fanned against plump baby cheeks, and Danny's blanket-covered chest rose and fell with the rhythm of sleep. Relief flooded Trace's heart as he focused on the nurse's face. Some rational part of his mind cataloged big blue eyes and a sweet smile. No, an angelic smile. His initial thought was how perfectly the smile matched the voice. His second was that the blond hair heartwrenchingly reminded him of Jenny.

"Did they find...?" He wanted to be certain the rescuers hadn't overlooked the snowy grave of pine branches. The thought of Matt's and Jenny's bodies alone on that mountaintop was too much to handle.

"Don't try to talk." Carly lifted a glass of water and held the flexible straw to his mouth.

The wet, cool liquid sliding down his parched throat didn't soothe the burning ache of grief. "Matt? Jenny?"

"Please don't worry, Mr. Holden," Carly assured him, realizing what he was trying to ask. "You brother and sister-in-law are in the hospital's..." Even after years in nursing, she loathed the word morgue. "They've been taken care of."

Trace sighed, sinking back into the pillow. His tortured mind tried to fit the world into some semblance of order. The crash. The rescue. He and Danny alive. Safe and in a nice clean hospital. Matt and Jenny...

So much for order.

Unwilling or unable to trust his voice, Trace nodded his comprehension.

"You need rest. Close your eyes."

He did as she asked only because the pain beating against his temples threatened to rip off the top of his head. Still, a part of his brain refused to submit to his body's weakness, and he protested.

"Have to be with Danny—" He tried to hang on to consciousness, but it slipped steadily beyond his grasp.

"I'll be right here...." Carly rested her hand against his forehead. Her fingertips caressed Trace's cheek, then smoothed the hair at his temple. "I won't leave Danny for a minute."

Trace wanted, needed, to trust her promise. But somehow the need to ensure that Danny was cared for got all mixed up with his own needs. Childhood memories of his mother at his bedside during an illness crept from the past and wove their way into the present. Offering long denied comfort, the nurse's voice flowed over him, balm for a wounded spirit. He wanted to tell her not to stop, to keep holding his hand, stroking his cheek, but a mind-stealing drowsiness hindered speech.

"Don't..." he rasped. "Don't leave...him."

"I promise." Carly watched his body relax and knew, at least temporarily, that his fears concerning Danny were assuaged. And judging from Trace Holden's violent behavior when his nephew had cried out during emergency-room treatment, that was no mean feat.

At the boy's first response to pain, the hard-muscled pilot had sprung from the examining table like a tiger on a kill, shaking off the restraining hands of a doctor and two orderlies. Wobbly but determined, he had then announced, in profane and extremely precise terms, the exact consequences anyone could expect who kept him from his nephew's side. The ensuing argument amid the child's wails and Trace's bellows had resulted in Linc bending hospital rules to allow them to share the same room. Now, as he rested quietly, Carly decided that Trace Holden looked about as fierce as a cat dozing on a sun-soaked windowsill.

His face was strong, the kind of face that pleased women and intimidated some men. She wondered if the color of his eyes—maybe blue or deep green—might temper that strength without softening it. He needed a shave, she thought, remembering the bristly feel of his whiskered cheek against her hand. Perhaps in the morning she should offer to shave him, at least until the tenderness of his broken ribs subsided. Then again, perhaps not. Her nursing experience had shown her that male patients were usually as particular about their grooming as female patients—worse, in some cases. Maybe he was the kind of man who liked to do his own shaving. Or maybe he was into fashionable stubble. She studied his jawline, which was set with determination even in relaxation. On him, stubble looked good. Better than good.

The fine lines webbing the corners of his eyes proclaimed him to be either a worrier or big smiler. *A worrier,* Carly decided, basing her decision more on instinct than on his reactions in the emergency room. The same instinct that prompted her to add, *and a loner.* There was an aura of tension about Trace Holden. Even in sleep, he wasn't completely relaxed, as though he were trying to hold himself...separate. Yet the image of a loner conflicted with the man who had jumped so fiercely to Danny's defense.

He mumbled several words in his sleep, and Carly leaned close.

"Don't..."

"Sh-h-h, Mr. Holden."

"...leave me."

The hoarsely whispered request tore at Carly's heart. When it comes to needing comfort, we're all still children, she thought. She readjusted the blanket, remaining beside the bed until she was certain he slept. Then she crossed the small hospital room and resumed her vigil.

She stayed there through the afternoon and early evening, sleeping intermittently in a semicomfortable chair. Only the need to shower and change for work finally forced her from the room. During her night duties, she spent every second she could spare checking on Danny and his uncle. As her shift drew to a close, she slipped into Danny's room, stealing a full five minutes to gaze at the sleeping child.

He looked so small and helpless lying in the crib. So precious. *Brian would have been about the same age if . . .* Her heart swelled with a bittersweet ache so deep, it hurt to breathe. Carly forced her mind to obliterate *would have been* from her thoughts. *IS. Brian is about the same age. Somewhere he's alive and happy and well cared for. I can't stop believing. Not for a minute. Not for a second.*

Outside the hospital window, welcoming dawn pressured the night into retreat. Sunlight made believing easier. Night, with its loneliness and chilling nightmares, sometimes made hanging on to sanity almost impossible. But hang on she must. Rubbing her arms as if to ward off the darkness's chilly imagery, Carly wondered if she would ever feel secure again.

Danny whimpered, and across the room Trace was instantly awake. Still woozy, but definitely stronger, he threw back the covers and had one foot on the floor before he realized someone else was already at Danny's bedside. He recognized the "someone's" soothing voice. As both bare feet touched shockingly cold tile, the first thought through his aching head was that she had kept her promise. The second was how Danny responded to her touch and immediately quieted.

"Is he all right?"

Carly jumped; her head whipped around at the unexpected sound of a harsh male voice inches from her shoulder. "Mr. Holden! What do you think you're doing out of bed?" Even whispering, her voice was softly authoritarian.

Trace clutched his rib cage and fought vertigo. "He's in pain."

"Some, but he's going to be just fine."

"You're a nurse, aren't you? Can't you do something? Give him something?" His head screamed with pain, but he had to make certain Danny was truly all right.

With deceptively small but capable hands pressed against his upper arms, Carly attempted to guide her patient back to bed. "We have, Mr. Holden. And I promise you—"

Ignoring her efforts, Trace pushed forward, taking the well-meaning nurse with him. His eyes widened at his first close look at Danny. An IV tube was taped to one small hand, and both legs were splinted. And he was so still. Frighteningly still.

Trace felt his life's blood drain away. "He's not—"

"No," Carly rushed to assure him. "He's fine. We're giving him antibiotics intravenously—"

"But there's no cast. Why isn't he in a cast? My God, didn't you people—"

"Please stay calm, Mr. Holden."

"Stay calm! His leg is broken, and you haven't done anything for him. This is a hospital, for God's sake! Where the hell is the doctor?"

"Mr. Holden! Calm down or I'll have an orderly put you in restraints or remove you from the room altogether."

Her voice was velvet-covered reinforced steel, the words forceful enough to banish any doubts about her authority. Trace yielded. Reluctantly.

"Just tell me why there's no cast on his leg. There should be a cast."

"Yes, but not until tomorrow."

"What happens tomorrow?"

"Dr. Garrison will stop by on his rounds this morning and explain—"

Powerful fingers punished her delicate wrist. "*Now.* I want to know *right now.* What happens tomorrow?"

"All...all right, Mr. Holden." Carly struggled to free her arm, but she knew his hold had more to do with grasping for reassurance rather than hurting her. "The fracture in Danny's calf will require an incision in order to set—"

"Surgery?"

"Minor, but yes, surgery."

"Why didn't they do it right away?"

"Because of the swelling. By tomorrow the doctors will be able to set Danny's leg properly."

"And what about his head? There was a big bruise." He motioned toward his own head.

"He had a mild, and I stress the word *mild,* concussion. Because of the concussion, plus the need to keep him calm, he's been lightly sedated." She eased her agitated patient back onto the side of the bed. "He'll be ready to go home before you know it."

Home.

The word hit Trace with all the power of a double-fisted blow to his gut. Memories of the crash, of finding Matt and Jenny, came rushing at him from all sides. Matt and Jenny had been the only home Danny had ever known and the last scrap of family Trace had left. No Matt and Jenny. No home?

Carly realized he was looking through, not at her, and her heart chilled at the suffering reflected in Trace Holden's eyes. He didn't even realize his grip had restricted the flow of blood to her hand. "Mr. Holden," she said softly, a firm but gentle tug finally snaring his attention as she escaped his hold.

His gaze dropped to delicate fingers massaging the red welt encircling her wrist. "I didn't meant to hurt . . . it's just that Danny's so little and—"

"Don't apologize for caring, Mr. Holden."

Seeing her at close range for the first time, he understood why her blue eyes stood out in his memory. They dominated her face and gave new meaning to the expression "wide-eyed." And then there was her smile. He remembered mentally tagging it angelic and decided only his temporarily dulled mind could have formed such an understatement.

"Thanks." His gaze dropped to the metal name badge pinned to her uniform, fully expecting it to read Angel, First Class instead of the Nurse C. McShane he saw.

"No thanks are necessary. You and Danny have had a tough time. Believe me." She smiled as she gently helped him to lie down, careful to avoid straining his ribs. "In his own way Danny was just as adamant in his concern for you. The staff in emergency had their hands full keeping him restrained long enough for Dr. Garrison to do his job. Every time Danny caught sight of you across the room he started yelling his protests."

"I didn't . . . hear him." Guilt washed over Trace. *I should have heard him. Danny is my responsibility now.*

Carly recognized and understood the guilt in his voice. "You sort of passed out just before Danny really got going."

"Was he . . . Did he cry a lot?"

"Well, I wouldn't say he was thrilled, but Linc managed to get him calmed down."

"Linc?"

"Dr. Linc Garrison, our chief of surgery and one of the finest orthopedic physicians on the West Coast. I assure you, Danny is in excellent hands."

"He's a great kid. His leg must have hurt like hell, but he didn't give me a minute's trouble on the mountain," Trace said, as if to apologize for the child's behavior. "Almost as if he knew I couldn't cope with his crying and survival all at the same time." His voice and expression softened.

Carly adjusted the pillow beneath his head. "Children have an incredible sense of empathy. They instinctively know when we adults have reached our limit."

"I've never been around any kids but Danny." His eyelids drooped, struggled to stay open, then closed completely. "Matt always says he's hell on wheels, but . . ."

Carly saw the muscles in his jaw tighten, saw his eyes squeeze tight and recognized the body language of denial. She wanted to tell him the pain would lessen. But then she would have to add that it would never completely disappear. Whether triggered by death, divorce or abandonment, the stages of grief, stages Carly knew intimately, were inevitable. First came denial and the all-consuming need to shut out the pain, to isolate one's self from the situation. Anger followed, fueled by the need to blame someone, anyone, for the loss. Then bargaining. How many times had she promised God her own life in return for her son's? Thousands? Then came depression, and endless nights of blackness and despair. Then, finally, acceptance. With acceptance came hope. And Trace Holden would have hope again, but at the moment Carly knew he was probably having difficulty believing in anything as nebulous as the simple truth of hope.

Trace opened his eyes, scrubbed his face with his hands, then raked long fingers through his coffee-brown hair. "How long since ...?"

"The rescue team brought both of you in yesterday morning."

"Where are we, Seattle?"

"Union City, Community General Hospital." At his puzzled expression, she clarified. "Not far from the Snoqualmie Summit ski area."

He tried to pull himself higher in the bed and winced from the effort.

"Do you want something for the pain in your ribs?" she offered, knowing full well that no drug on earth could effectively dull the ache in his heart.

"No."

One syllable. Definitive. There it was again, that aura of aloneness stating unequivocally: back off. Carly decided that Trace Holden was not a man who let discomfort of any kind demand his attention. Pain, like all other feelings, connected the sufferer to someone or something else, and she sensed that he avoided connections like the plague. She straightened the bed covers across his broad shoulders and walked away.

At the door, Carly glanced back at the man in the bed. Trace Holden looked like the ragged end of nowhere—scruffy, sad and alone. Too well, she understood his look and desperately wished she could ease his hurting. But she couldn't. Sooner or later he would find a way to deal with his grief. Not necessarily because he wanted to, but because, like death, sometimes life doesn't offer choices.

Assured that both her patients were as comfortable as possible, Carly slipped quietly from the room. She quickly finished her necessary end-of-shift chores, then dragged her weary body to the staff lounge and collapsed onto a couch whose ancient stuffing could easily have passed for a cloud at that moment. She was asleep before her head settled on a lumpy cushion.

Chapter 2

Trace was startled awake, and several seconds lapsed before he realized that the disturbing noise came from across the room and not from inside his head. Danny's sudden cry yanked him fully alert.

"What the hell's going on?" Trace demanded, propped on one elbow.

"Ah, Mr. Holden," said, a tall, plain-faced nurse whose no-nonsense attitude matched her voice.

"And who—" Trace pointed a finger at the white-clad man grasping the foot of Danny's crib "—is he?" The sound of a recognizable voice brought a whimper from Danny.

The nurse stood aside to allow the man to roll Danny's bed toward the door.

"Take your hands off that crib." The look exchanged between nurse and orderly sent Trace to his feet, ready for battle.

Nurse Plain Jane and her sidekick both halted. "Now, Mr. Holden. You get yourself right back in that bed!"

"I'm not moving and neither are you until you tell me where you're taking my nephew." Danny's crying picked up in tempo, and so did Trace's determination.

"To X ray," she said, dividing her attention between the agitated child and the antagonistic adult.

"They took X rays in the emergency room!"

"Well, yes, but—"

"There's something wrong and you're not telling me!"

"No, but—"

"Danny's not leaving this room until I talk to the doctor."

"Really, Mr. Holden, such hostility—"

"Lady," Trace's eyes narrowed, "you don't know the meaning of the word until you push that bed one more inch—"

"Is this a private war, or can anyone enlist?"

"Oh, doctor. Thank goodness," the nurse said, turning toward the door.

Looking more like an L.A. Rams linebacker than a surgeon, the doctor strolled into the room, removed a chart from beneath a bulging bicep and extended his hand to Trace. "Mr. Holden, I'm Linc Garrison, chief surgeon in this war zone."

"The name's Trace, and maybe you can tell me what the hell is going on and why my nephew needs more X rays."

"Because yesterday the swelling prevented a one-hundred percent clear shot of Danny's injury. Today the swelling is down, and we need another look-see."

"Then I'm going with him."

It was patently clear to the doctor that Trace Holden was a man who operated with a hands-on, meet life head-on straightforwardness that demanded the same from the people he encountered.

"Suit yourself," Linc said. "But you won't be allowed inside the radiology lab and, to be perfectly honest, the presence of a parent or relative often creates more problems than it solves." Linc placed a hand on Trace's shoulder. "I can personally vouch for our first-class pediatric staff. They'll have Danny back safe and sound before you know it."

When Trace didn't respond in the negative, Linc gave the go-ahead sign to the orderly who, followed closely by the nurse, tugged the squeaky bed out the door. Danny's whimper dissolved into distant sniffles, then faded altogether.

Trace knew the doctor was right, but waking up to find Danny being handled by strangers had been unnerving. "Where's Danny's nurse? The one that was here..." *This morning? Last night?* The pain in his head had lessened but Trace couldn't remember the time sequence since the rescue. "...earlier."

"Petite?" Holding his hand at chest level, Linc measured an imaginary line. "Short blond hair?"

Trace nodded, the motion causing his head to pound. *The Angel,* as he had come to think of Nurse C. McShane, had been here each time he had opened his eyes since the crash, and he realized that he had expected her to still be here. Unaccountably disappointed because the soft-spoken caretaker was absent, Trace tried to reconcile his disappointment with equal parts of embarrassment over his pleading behavior of last night.

"You must be talking about Carly."

So that's what the *C* stands for, Trace thought.

Linc flipped open the chart and scanned the top page. "She's off duty. And if she took my advice, which rarely happens, she's home sleeping." Linc glanced up from the chart to find his patient massaging his temples. "Still got a headache?"

"A real son-of-a-bitch."

A chuckle vibrated from Linc's broad chest as he set the chart aside and slipped the stethoscope from around his neck. "That's to be expected with concussions."

"Doc, about Danny—"

"Question-and-answer session in a moment. Lie back."

Reluctantly Trace submitted to the examination, gritting his teeth as Linc's knowledgeable hands probed and pressed his tender ribs.

"Your concussion was serious enough to keep you fading in and out for the last couple of days. You've got three broken ribs plus assorted bruises and lacerations thrown in for good measure, but I'd say you're over the worst of it. Now, what do you want to know?" Linc asked, looping the stethoscope back around his neck.

"How bad is Danny's leg?"

"Semibad. By that I mean it's a nasty compound fracture, but as soon as the bone is set, he'll heal just fine. Kids are resilient little buggers."

"When will you set his leg?"

"This afternoon. Actually, we'll cast both legs and hips, then place a stabilizing bar between his feet. And just so you won't panic when you see him, the whole thing appears much worse than it actually is. The casting material is lightweight and porous enough not to hamper circulation. After Danny's had a few days to adjust, he'll be sitting up and turning over, probably even regaining a big part of his mobility."

"How long will we have to stay in the hospital?" Trace asked.

"You'll be free to go tomorrow, or the day after at the latest. Danny we'll need to keep for three, maybe four extra days. Like you, he's got some bruises and a couple of lacerations I want to make sure don't become infected. Not that I expect any complications," he hastened to add, seeing Trace's alarmed expression. "Besides, I'd like to keep him as inactive as possible for a few days to give the bones a good start on healing."

"I'm staying with him."

"You mean, in the hospital?"

"Yes. I'm not leaving Danny alone."

"I can understand your concern. Right now, you're the only person he knows and trusts completely, so it's important to have you near. He needs all the reassurance and affection you can give him, but you don't have to be at his bedside every minute."

Trace knew that need. Intimately. "I, uh, haven't had a lot of experience with kids, but I intend to...to take care of Danny."

Linc smiled. "Judging from the way you fought half the staff to get to him when they brought you in, I'd say you have the one essential qualification necessary when it comes to caring for your nephew."

A grin teased the corner of Trace's mouth in spite of himself. "Bullheadedness?"

"Love. Without it, you haven't got a chance. With it, all things are possible. By the way, your business partner called, and I assured him you were in good shape. Is there anyone else we need to contact. Other family members?"

"You're looking at all the family there is."

"What about—" Linc glanced at a note attached to the top page of the chart "—Danny's aunt and uncle? A Mr. and Mrs. Andrews. They phoned several times while you were in Emergency and, according to this note, they've called to check on both you and Danny regularly."

"What did you tell them?"

Sarcasm fairly dripped from Trace's voice, making Linc wonder if he had stumbled across a family feud of some kind. "Well, since this hospital has a policy not to give specific information over the phone, Danny's condition was given as satisfactory. But Mrs. Andrews called again early this morning asking about Danny. As a matter of fact, she and a Mr. Nathan Borell are due here," Linc glanced at his watch, "any moment."

Trace frowned. His headache was back. If he'd had a list of people he *didn't* need to see, Jenny's snooty sister and Matt's lawyer would have been numbers one and two. Actually, he could handle the lawyer. At least he knew where Nathan Borell's allegiance lay. Deirdre Andrews was a different story.

"Is that a problem?" Linc asked, noticing the frown. "If you're not feeling up to visitors, I can have the duty nurse restrict—"

"No. No, that's all right. Mrs. Andrews is Danny's aunt." Trace knew he couldn't put off seeing these particular visitors for long. He might as well get it over with.

"Trace." Linc placed a hand on the other man's shoulder. "Would you mind a bit of observation carved from experience?" At the other man's nod of permission, he continued. "You and Danny have suffered a crushing blow, one that will take a while to overcome. But regardless of how trite it sounds, time does heal most wounds, and the pain will diminish. In times of crisis, family, even extended family, can be vitally important."

Trace's frown furrowed deeper. As far as he knew, Deirdre Thorpe Andrews rarely acknowledged that she had a family, much less recognize its importance. He could never understand how Jennifer Holden and Deirdre could have been bred from the same parents. The personification of warmth and caring, Jenny had had a generous spirit and loving heart that had touched everyone who knew her. Deirdre, on the other hand, was a remote, passionless woman, rigid and obsessed with being in control. Trace couldn't remember ever seeing her exhibit a genuine smile.

Not that there had been many opportunities to witness such a phenomenon. Deirdre and Walker Andrews seldom came to the Holden home when he was visiting, and when they did, the occasion was always social mixed with business. Walker, as a vice president of Holden Enterprises, and Deirdre, as sister-in-law to the president, were the consummate corporate animals. Snubbing the boss's brother, even one they considered as common as Trace, was simply not done. No, Trace decided, Deirdre wanted something, and the fact that she would be arriving in the company of Matt's lawyer was anything but coincidental.

"Thanks, Doc," Trace said flatly. "Is there a hotel or motel around here close?"

Obviously, as far as Trace was concerned, the subject was closed.

"The nearest one is at least a mile away, and I'm afraid it's not exactly The Ritz," Linc admitted. "There's the ski lodge, and some condos, but those are a good twenty minutes away."

"Then maybe there's a boardinghouse or apartment I can rent by the week?"

"He can stay at my place."

At the softly spoken offer, both men turned to stare at the petite woman standing in the doorway.

Seeing their startled expressions, Carly realized how her offer must have sounded. "I, uh...I mean my house..." She stumbled over the words, her cheeks an attractive shade of pink. "What I meant was, my *boarding*house has two vacancies...."

Linc's grin was instantaneous, warm and . . . friendly. "Trace Holden," he said with a nod in her direction, "meet the lady you were inquiring about, Carly McShane. One of the best nurses and most stubborn women the good Lord ever saw fit to create."

"A left-handed compliment, but I'll take it." Walking across the room to join them, she flashed Linc an angelic smile before turning to Trace. "How are you feeling, Mr. Holden?"

"Better. . . ."

"Carly is our night charge nurse," Linc said, returning his attention to the chart. "And the one you have to thank for all the tender loving care you and Danny have received. She's stayed late and came in early to make sure you two were well taken care of."

In the cold light of day she was even better than Trace remembered. And he remembered her very well. Had he actually begged her to hold him, not to leave him? He had, and the realization sent heat flashing up his neck until his ears tingled. "Thanks . . . uh, for staying with Danny."

"My pleasure." This time her Angel First Class smile was all his, along with the wink of a dimple, minuscule and only on one side of her mouth, as though God had intended to give her the standard pair, then changed His mind at the last minute. Trace told himself she was probably married and had a house full of kids and he had no business admiring her dimple. Deliberately, he avoided eye contact. "It, uh, meant a lot to me knowing Danny didn't wake up . . . alone."

He's embarrassed about last night, Carly thought, remembering the way he had held her hand. "All part of the service," she said softly, reassuringly.

Her tone snagged Linc's attention, and he glanced up at Carly, then Trace, and had the uncanny feeling that they were sharing some sort of secret.

Trace gazed at her, trying to shake the uncomfortable sensation that he was sharing an uncomfortable level of intimacy with a woman who was a stranger, yet...not a stranger.

His eyes weren't blue or green, Carly realized, but an unexpected shade of brown. No they weren't exactly brown, more like cinnamon or sherry.

"We're going to spring Trace from this joint tomorrow, so as usual, Carly, your timing is perfect. Wanna bet Fitz falls in love with him on sight?"

"What?" She forced her gaze to Linc. "Oh, yes. You're absolutely right. She'll adore him."

"Who?" Trace asked, grateful for the change of subject.

"My landlady, Mrs. Fitzpatrick," she answered.

Linc's eyebrows danced in an exaggerated wiggle as he twirled an imaginary mustache. "Fitz has this *thing* for fliers."

"And doctors..." Carly added.

"And lawyers and Indian chiefs," they said, finishing together.

They were obviously close friends, and as Trace watched them, he wondered if their friendship extended past working hours. He envied the camaraderie he sensed between Garrison and his lovely nurse.

"Fitz likes men, in case you hadn't guessed," Linc volunteered. "All men."

"You're making her sound like a man-chasing hussy, and that's hardly accurate," Carly countered.

"If you ask me, she's seen *A Streetcar Named Desire* once too often."

For the second time in the last hour Trace smiled. A definite accomplishment, considering his somber mood and the events of the past few days. He looked at Linc. "Just what does this unique woman look like?"

"Ah," Linc grinned. "You're intrigued. Well, Fitz could stand to drop a few pounds, but she's got it where it counts, if you know what I mean. And she's not exactly what you might call fashion conscious, but—"

Carly gasped. Hands on hips, she shook her head. "Linc Garrison, you should be ashamed of yourself." Then, to Trace, she said, "Mrs. Fitzpatrick is a sweet, kindhearted woman with a gentle soul. She's a bit eccentric, but—"

"*Eccentric?* The woman is an eighty-year-old fruitcake. She sips Napoleon brandy, gives every male over the age of ten the eye, and refuses to wear any garment made after World War II, at which time, according to her, they stopped producing quality women's wear. She's got a clothes closet that would shame any movie studio's wardrobe department."

"She's sweet," Carly reiterated.

"She's certifiable," Linc amended.

Turning to Trace, she said, "Don't let Linc give you the wrong impression, Mr. Holden. Mrs. Fitzpatrick runs a clean, respectable place and treats her boarders like family. Besides," Carly glared at Linc, "her granddaughter lives with her and keeps her out of trouble."

"Now, *there's* someone to be intrigued by." Linc's eyebrows danced another jig. "Eighteen—"

"Seventeen."

Linc shrugged. "Okay, seventeen, gorgeous and—" At Carly's look of disapproval he cleared his throat. "But we digress."

"*We* certainly do." Carly flashed him a you-should-be-ashamed-of-yourself grin.

"When can I meet this classic femme fatale posing as a mere landlady?" Based on nothing more than the warmth in their voices as Linc and Carly described the exotic Fitz, Trace had decided to take whatever vacancy was available.

"I can give her a call right now, if you like," Carly offered.

Trace liked and said so. He also liked the way Carly moved gracefully across the floor and the way she cradled the telephone between her ear and shoulder. An image of her cheek snuggled against his shoulder popped out of nowhere, then streaked into oblivion so fast he wasn't sure if the reality had ever existed.

"Well," Linc remarked on a sigh, "I've got work to do, and you're in the best of hands. I'll check with you after your visitors leave, and we'll give you a final once-over, then tomorrow you're a free man. Oh, by the way," he said, turning to leave. "A couple of men from the FAA will also be around this afternoon."

The mention of the arrival of Federal Aviation Agency personnel brought Trace crashing back to reality. For a few moments, listening to Linc and Carly go on about the screwball Mrs. Fitzpatrick, he'd forgotten the reason he needed the rented room in the first place. How could he have forgotten for even an instant that Matt and Jenny were gone? Remorse pierced his soul, and the relentless questions that had plagued him through sleepless nights rushed back into his thoughts. Trace had gone over the events of the crash so many times he had lost count. What had gone wrong? What would the FAA investigation show as the cause? No matter how often his own review of the crash indicated otherwise, the words *pilot error* were always in the back of his mind.

Turning back to Trace's bedside, Carly couldn't fail to notice that her patient's mood had taken a downward slide. "She's delighted at the prospect of having a new boarder."

"Pardon?"

"Fitz." She motioned toward the phone. "When you're released, I'll be happy to introduce you."

"Thanks," Trace said, concern over a place to sleep having been superseded by the impending FAA investigators' visit. Recounting in detail the incidents before, during and after the crash was not something he looked forward to. In his own mind, he had done everything humanly possible to save his passengers and plane, but his heart was still plagued with guilt.

All too well, Carly recognized and understood the emotions flickering across Trace Holden's face. Shame because he was alive when someone he loved wasn't. And guilt, always guilt, at the unanswerable question. Why?

"Has Danny started to talk yet?" she asked, hoping to lighten his mood.

"What? Oh, he can pretty much say Mama but the rest is mostly garbledee-goop."

"That's about right for his age. Wait until he really gets going. I've seen some in here you'd think were into marathon jabbering."

The conversation was so *normal* it was bizarre, as though this were any ordinary exchange between nurse and parent. But Trace wasn't Danny's parent. Danny's parents were lying somewhere in this very hospital, dead.... Trace closed his eyes briefly.

"Is your head still hurting?"

"No."

"Can I get you anything?"

"No."

"Perhaps you'd like for me to leave—"

"No!" His gaze met hers. "I mean . . ."

Carly's heart went out to him. "Mr. Holden, I know what it's like to . . . to lose someone. And if you need to talk or just don't want to be alone . . . I'm here."

Every instinct told him the offer was genuine and so was she, but trusting didn't come easy. Hadn't he already given her his trust, albeit unconsciously? She had seen a part of him no one, not even Matt, had witnessed. She was warmth in a cold world. As he looked into her incredibly blue eyes, he realized that until now he'd thought such women existed only in some poet's imagination.

"Are you for real?" He didn't realize he'd spoken his thoughts out loud until it was too late. "I'm sorry, that sounded rude, and I didn't mean for it to."

"Don't apologize. Sometimes it's hard for us to accept the offer of a lifeline even when we want to."

"I don't need a lifeline."

With the exception of Matt, if he had depended on lifelines he would have drowned long ago. Every connection he'd ever made in his life had ended in loneliness. The equation was simple: caring for someone, becoming part of someone, inevitably equaled suffering. First with his parents, and now Matt and Jenny. The cost was too high, and Trace had already paid too many times. Cancel out caring—he couldn't bring himself to use the word *love*—and you cancel out pain.

Carly longed to tell him that she empathized with the emotions he was experiencing, to tell him that his feelings were perfectly natural. Even though his earlier response had warned her that he might not be receptive, the desire to comfort him was too strong to be subdued, and before she realized her intent, she reached out and placed her hand over his.

The warmth of her touch seeped into his body like a hot toddy after a December day in the Rockies. While his conscious mind fought the need, fought for control, his subconscious struggled to draw closer to her welcome fire. Against his will, Trace's fingers curled around hers just as the sound of a throat being intentionally cleared drew their attention.

A woman wearing a mink coat opened to reveal a high-fashion black dress, and a cold expression stood in the doorway. A short, balding man carrying a briefcase stood beside her. The woman's sharp-eyed gaze darted to Trace and Carly's entwined fingers.

"Hello, Trace. You seem to have responded quite well to treatment," she said with an undertone of sarcasm. "One would hardly know you had barely escaped death."

Tension so imperceptible that Carly thought she might have imagined it, tightened Trace's grip a second before he jerked his hand away. A brittle silence followed before he acknowledged the new arrivals.

"Deirdre."

No greeting, no cordiality, just the name. His tone barely implied civility, while his body language and the hard expression on his face stated clearly that he was not pleased to see the woman. Carly glanced from Trace to the immaculately coutured Deirdre and wondered at the palpable hostility between the two. Since the fateful day when Carly had gone against her instincts and allowed her ex-husband to see Brian, she had learned to trust her intuition. And right now all her instincts fairly screamed that this woman was trouble.

The balding man shoved his wire-framed glasses back into place on the bridge of his nose, then hurried across the room and shook Trace's hand. "My boy, we're all so relieved you're in good shape."

The female visitor hadn't moved, and Carly suspected she was waiting for her to leave.

"I'll check and see if Danny is finished in X ray," Carly said. Unreasonably, she felt as if she were deserting Trace. The notion was absurd, yet persistent, and before she could stop herself, she offered as much nonverbal support as her warmest smile contained.

"Thanks."

As she maneuvered past the other woman, Carly caught the unmistakable scent of outrageously expensive perfume. The door clicked shut a second after she stepped into the corridor. Carly stopped and turned to gaze at the closed barrier. A shiver skated down her spine, and again her intuition warned her that the woman was trouble for Trace Holden and for Danny. Carly didn't understand why she knew that; she simply *knew* her impression was right, and she forced herself to resist the urge to stand between Trace and the enigmatic visitor. *This is insane. You barely know the man. You can't mother the entire world, Carly.* On a sigh, she resolutely turned toward the bank of elevators that would transport her to radiology.

Inside the hospital room, Nathan Borell smiled broadly. "You're looking remarkably fit after such an ordeal, Trace." The aging attorney's warm smile transformed his round face from merely pleasant into friendly, even jolly.

"I was lucky."

"Indeed. You and little Danny were both extremely fortunate. For a while we feared everyone on board..." Nathan Borell glanced away. "Well, we're all relieved you and Danny are safe and sound. Aren't we, Deirdre?"

"Absolutely." Deirdre Andrews' cool voice and even cooler gaze drifted over Trace. Perfectly shaped and tinted lips formed a harmless-looking smile that didn't fool Trace for a minute.

"Your concern is touching." Trace forced himself to remember that she, too, had suffered a loss. For a fleeting moment he even allowed himself to feel sorry for her, to share the pain of their mutual bereavement. But he couldn't trust her facade of grief any more than he could trust any of the emotions she always manipulated to get what she wanted. Deirdre Andrews gave new meaning to the word

self-serving, and Trace had witnessed enough of her mach-
inations concerning Jenny over the years to know better
than to trust her.

"Of course I am concerned," she said.

*About the terms of the will, maybe, but you couldn't care
less about me or Danny.*

"Walker sends his best and asked me to say that he knows
you will understand why he was unable to join us today.
Since Matt and Jenny... Since the accident, he has had his
hands full with the company."

Trace stared into Deirdre's frosty gaze. "Yes, as Vice
President of Holden Enterprises I'm sure he has." *And
while he's as it, I'm sure he's busy looking for some way to
gain control.* The first to admit his dislike of Walker and
Deirdre was based on a past misunderstanding, Trace had
tried, for Jenny's sake and the sake of family, to put his
personal feelings aside. He had never succeeded. Based
more on gut instinct than on actual fact, he was convinced
the "deadly duo," as he had dubbed them, were ruthless in
pursuing their ambitions—namely, to control Holden Enterprises.

The snap of briefcase locks cut into the conversational
lull. Nathan turned to Deirdre. "If you'll excuse us for a few
moments, Deirdre, I need to discuss some details with Trace,
privately."

Annoyance tightened the perfectly shaped lips. "Of
course."

When the door closed behind her, Nathan's expression
sobered. "Before we begin, I just want to tell you how much
I ... Well, your brother was one of the kindest, most caring
men I knew. Matt was my friend as well as my client." He
swallowed hard. "Everyone who knew him and Jenny was
richer for the experience. I'm...going to miss them...very
much."

"Thank you." Trace had a clear picture of himself repeating those two words endlessly for the next few days. Matt and Jenny *were* loved, and a lot of people's lives had been touched by their passing.

"Uh, Trace, I need to talk to you about the funeral."

Trace sighed. "You mean, place, time, that sort of thing?"

"No, I mean the services that took place late yesterday afternoon."

Trace stared at Nathan Borell as if he had suddenly grown two heads, a hot rage building from the depths of his soul.

"I know you must be upset, but everything was done according to Matt and Jenny's instructions. There was a note attached to their will specifically requesting that should one or both ... They wanted to be buried as quickly as possible, with very little fuss in order to spare family and friends."

All the anger slowly seeped away, leaving Trace feeling drained and empty. As usual, Matt's concern for those he loved had priority, and perhaps, Trace thought, it was for the best.

How could he tell the lawyer he needed no prayers or services or mourners to pay homage to Matt and Jenny's memory, because he had already done so? How could he explain that in those long hours on the icy mountaintop he had held his own private memorial service? While cold winds buffeted the fractured jet that had plunged what was left of his family to their deaths, Trace had privately memorialized his brother and sister-in-law in a way not even the most righteous minister could.

He had simply remembered how much he loved them. How much he had always and would forever love them. During that long night, in his heart, Trace had gently, lovingly laid two of the three most important people in his life to rest. For him, at least, a funeral service was unnecessary.

Noticing the attorney's anxious expression, Trace said, "Thanks for taking care of everything, Nathan."

Clearly relieved, Nathan managed a weak smile, then cleared his throat and removed a legal-sized folder from his briefcase. "Matt left two legal documents. One is a meticulously detailed instrument regarding the structure of Holden Enterprises, in which Mr. Andrews figures prominently. The other was his and Jenny's joint personal will. As you know, your brother was extremely careful, never leaving anything to chance if he could avoid it. A formal reading will take place in a few days, but in preparation for just the kind of situation we now face, Matt and Jenny left explicit instructions, including a proviso that you be informed of the content of the will within seventy-two hours of their...demise."

Intellectually, Trace had known Nathan's visit would mean talking about the will, listening to instructions and even probable decisions, but emotionally... Now, face-to-face with Matt's last wishes, a dull, heavy ache gripped his heart.

After removing his glasses, Nathan pulled a handkerchief from his breast pocket and wiped the lenses for what seemed like endless minutes. Trace realized that this man he had viewed for years as merely a businessman was himself genuinely swamped with grief. When the glasses were once again securely fitted to his face, Nathan met Trace's gaze.

"There's no point in dragging this out by reading a bunch of legal verbiage I know you couldn't care less about. The bank is appointed executor, and there will be a formal reading of the will. You'll receive a copy. Suffice it to say, Matt took care of every detail. As far as a division of assets is concerned, fifty-one percent of the company stock goes to Danny, twenty-five percent to you. The remaining twenty-four percent goes to Walker and Deirdre, jointly. The house in Seattle is yours, along with a section of land in Colorado. There's a sizable trust fund when Danny turns twenty-one, until such time...you are appointed his legal guardian. He...he also left this for you," Nathan said, his voice wavering as he drew an envelope from the briefcase.

Trace stared at the plain white rectangle with his name scrawled across the front in Matt's recognizable bold handwriting.

"If you'd like some privacy to read—"

"No!" Trace's head snapped up. His voice sounded strained and unfamiliar to his own ears. "No, thanks, I'll...wait." He wouldn't, couldn't, read it now. Maybe later, when he was alone. But then, he would be alone from now on, wouldn't he?

No, he had Danny.

Stunned, and more than a little awed, by the news of his guardianship, Trace again stared at the envelope. His index finger absently stroked the edge.

"Well—", Nathan heaved a sigh "—there are a few more minor items, but those are the important points. All of the documentation, the necessary signature requirements, can be taken care of as soon as you're up to it. Of course, you will probably want your own attorney—"

"No, I'd like for you to handle everything."

"Very well." He shook Trace's hand. "If you have any questions, don't hesitate to call me. I always thought Matt and I made a good team, and I look forward to working with you."

"Thanks. I can see why Matt depended on you so much."

Nathan smiled. "Shall I admit Mrs. Andrews now? She'll have to be apprised of the situation."

Seconds after Trace agreed, Deirdre sailed into the room.

"Thank you for waiting," Nathan said, closing the briefcase, then launching into a summary of all he had told Trace. When he finished, Deirdre Andrews looked from one man to the other.

"There must be a mistake," she said calmly.

"A formal reading will take place within days, at which time you will be welcome to read the official—"

"Obviously, this document is outdated. I am sure Matt intended to be more generous. There *must* be a mistake. Walker has poured his heart and soul into that company. We always assumed..." As she twisted her black leather gloves in her white-knuckled grip, her gaze narrowed. "No. I refuse to believe Matt Holden would leave a corporation he spent years of his life building in the hands of an...an irresponsible...jet jockey!" With each word her voice rose steadily.

"No one is denying Walker's valuable contribution to Holden Enterprises, Deirdre—"

"Do not patronize me, Mr. Borell. This...this," she gestured wildly toward the briefcase containing the will, "is nothing but a sham!"

"Now just one moment, Mrs. Andrews—"

Ignoring the lawyer's shocked expression, she turned to Trace. "If you think Walker and I are going to stand by while you take control, you had better think again. We have no intention of allowing you to ruin a company we helped build."

Trace had expected Deirdre to be upset, angry, but he hadn't expected such vehemence. Understandably, from her and Walker's point of view, running Holden Enterprises was a prize to be sought above all others. And even though it held no such attraction for Trace, Matt had entrusted him with at least part of the company, and he would not betray that trust.

"I don't see that there's a damn thing you can do about it, Deirdre."

A red-faced Nathan glanced from one to the other. "Please, Mr. Holden, Mrs. Andrews—"

Trace waved him silent. "Save your breath, Nathan. Obviously Deirdre isn't satisfied with the terms of the will."

"You're damn right I'm not satisfied. And neither will Walker be. I cannot believe my sister never saw you and your brother for what you are. Common, low-life...and now to leave *you* in charge of a child's upbringing, not to mention control of a multimillion dollar corporation, is sheer lunacy."

"Enough, Deirdre."

"Oh, but it's not nearly enough, Trace. Do you honestly think I'll hand you Holden Enterprises on a silver platter?"

"You have no choice—"

"You're wrong. I have *lots* of choices," she practically squeaked as she pivoted to face Borell. "You'll be hearing from my attorneys."

"Give it up, Deirdre," Trace hoarsely demanded.

Her head snapped around. "Advice you might do well to take yourself, Trace, since I intend to break this will." Without waiting for a response, she turned on her heel and left the room.

"Can she make good her threat?" Trace asked a stunned Nathan Borell.

"Uh, well, as I told you, Matt was extremely thorough. Her chances of breaking the will aren't good, but that probably won't keep her from trying. There are a lot of lawyers who would jump at the opportunity to handle a case involving an estate the size of this one."

"But can she succeed?"

Borell looked at the empty doorway, then back at Trace. "In my professional opinion, no...."

"But?"

"Even though she may not be able to have the provisions of the will set aside, there is one avenue..."

"What?"

"Regarding, uh, guardianship of Danny."

"Why don't you cut to the chase, Borell?"

"Stated bluntly, whoever has Danny, controls your brother's company. If the Andrews were to consider a custody suit, it could very well affect the balance of power at Holden Enterprises."

"I don't give a damn about the balance of power. They can't have Danny."

"All I meant—"

"Can they do that? Sue for custody?"

Borell swallowed hard. "Yes."

"Can they win?"

"Well, they would have to prove you're unfit to raise a child. Then there's the fact that Matt *and* Jenny named you guardian—"

"Can they?"

"It is possible, but unlikely."

Trace glanced at the envelope in his hand. "I hope to God you're right."

Downstairs in the hospital parking lot, Deirdre slammed the driver's door of her Jaguar, picked up the mobile phone and punched in a number, careful not to damage her manicure.

"Andrews," came the response after only one ring.

"Oh, Walker, you were absolutely right about the will!"

"Deirdre, for God's sake, calm yourself and tell me what happened."

"Trace receives twenty-five percent of Holden Enterprises stock, Danny holds fifty-one percent, while you and I wind up with a measly twenty-four percent."

There was a long pause at the other end, then a terse, "Are you sure?"

"I was *there,* Walker. Borell told me himself. Oh, you retain your position as vice president. The board of directors may even promote you to president with an appropriate salary increase. But we will *never* have controlling interest. We will *never* be able to run the company the way it should be run." Quick, warm breaths of anger filled the car, clouding the window.

"Oh, and not only were we practically last in line—" she flipped the switch marked Defrost and warm air hissed into the interior "—but the will named Trace as Danny's guardian." The toe of one expensive Italian black leather pump thumped the car's carpeted floor.

At the other end of the line, anger flattened Walker Andrew's mouth into a thin, hard line.

"Walker, have you heard a word I said?"

"Every damn syllable."

"Well?"

"Well, what?"

"Do something!"

"And just what would you have me do, Deirdre? This situation is going to require more than one of your world-class tantrums. What did you say to Trace?"

"I told him in no uncertain terms that we would not stand by and see the company destroyed."

Walker uttered a very unchairman-of-the-boardlike obscenity. He would be the last person on earth to deny that Deirdre was self-indulgent on a grand scale, but he had never considered her a fool.

"Deirdre, if your outburst has forewarned Trace to expect a battle for control of Holden Enterprises, I will throttle you."

"Did you expect me to allow that—"

"I expected you to have enough sense not to tip our hand before we could stack the deck."

"Walker—"

"Now listen to me." His voice hardened. "Our objective is still the same. After working toward a takeover for more than a year, we are not going to allow Trace Holden to stand in our way. You're not getting cold feet, are you?"

"No."

There was another moment of silence before he spoke again, his voice now softer, deceptively enticing. "Darling, I know you are upset, but everything will work out just as we planned. You trust me, don't you?"

"Of course, Walker, but—"

"Good, then let me take care of everything." When he heard her sigh of acceptance, he said sweetly, "Drive carefully, darling. I'll see you at dinner."

Walker Andrews replaced the telephone receiver, then swung his chair to face the bank of windows forming one wall of his plush tenth-floor Seattle office. Elbows propped on thickly padded armrests, fingers tented, he gazed out over Elliott Bay without actually seeing the view.

Poor Deirdre. If you only knew how well I pull your strings.

Deirdre prided herself on being an intelligent woman, always in control of every situation. She would be a vengeful hellcat if she ever learned the truth. But so long as he continued to play on her fear of being alone, prefacing his own opinions with words such as "we" and "our" and tossing in an occasional "sweetheart" for good measure, she would do exactly as he wanted.

Now all he had to do was present the idea that little Danny should be removed from the influence of a freewheeling bachelor's life-style and placed in the care of a stable married couple such as themselves, and Holden Enterprises would fall into his waiting hands like an overripe apple on a windy fall day. So far as he could see, the only real drawback to his new strategy would be living with a noisy, smelly kid until he was old enough to be shipped off to boarding school.

Walker smiled to himself. *Yes, I think an intimate dinner for two would be the perfect setting to put my new plan in motion. By the time I finish with my dear, malleable Deirdre, she'll be on her knees begging to adopt that whiny little brat.*

And once he had Danny, he would have it all.

Chapter 3

"Hiya, handsome," Carly whispered, leaning over Danny's crib as he blinked sleepy eyes. She touched her index finger to her lips, then transferred the invisible kiss to a sweetly soft baby cheek. Her reward was the biggest smile he could manage around the pacifier's rubbery bulb. Definitely a smile of recognition and one that melted Carly's heart right down to her toes. "One of these days you're going to break a lot of hearts with that smile." The pacifier popped out of his mouth, and the smile widened into an oh-yeah-well-watch-this, ear-to-ear grin.

"Why, you little flirt," she teased, brushing a lock of hair from his forehead.

From the doorway of the pediatric ward Trace watched Carly lavish praise and sweet words while skillfully maneuvering a dry diaper under and around Danny's cast. She fastened the disposable diaper securely, then changed his clothes. Listening to the sound of her voice, watching her gentle handling, he easily understood why Danny absorbed her softly spoken flattery like a thirsty sponge. Carly Mc-Shane had a special gift for making frightened people less afraid, less lonely. That thought both reassured and distressed Trace.

She had a Florence Nightingale disposition and an angel's smile, a combination that somehow made her dangerous in a way he couldn't explain. But he was just honest enough with himself to admit that part of his discomfort stemmed from knowing she had witnessed his vulnerability at close range. The fact that she hadn't reminded him by word, expression or gesture of his weakness, but rather had gone out of her way to put him at ease, was both pleasing yet puzzling. And irritating.

He moved away from the door. "You seem to have the magic touch." The words came out more brusquely than he intended.

Carly and Danny jumped. Instinctively patting Danny's tummy, she glanced up as Trace approached dressed in running shoes, jeans and an unzipped, worse-for-wear bomber jacket over a teal-green shirt. A navy-issue duffel bag swung over his shoulder.

Avoiding her gaze, Trace stopped beside a small combination chest of drawers and changing table. He swung the bag down, and Carly saw him wince as his upper body twisted with the effort. His free hand automatically went to his bruised ribs.

"Here, let me help." Hand outstretched, she took a step toward him.

"I can manage."

Her hand dropped as he sidestepped both her and her offer and bent over the side of the crib. "Hey, sport," he said, capturing a small waving fist. At the sound of the deep, familiar timbre of Trace's voice, Danny responded with an unqualified squeal of delighted recognition and a toothy grin.

A few hours earlier Trace had been released from the hospital, and his mood—the same mood born with the arrival of his two visitors the previous afternoon, a mood that could only be described as a shade lighter than a moonless midnight—hadn't changed.

Carly never listened to the ever-busy hospital grapevine, but she couldn't seem to help herself where the handsome pilot and his nephew were concerned, and the grapevine said there were plenty of reasons for his dark temper. Even though both visitors had departed by the time Carly and Danny returned from X ray, gossips had quickly tagged the paunchy man as a lawyer and the woman as Jennifer Holden's sister. They had also wasted no time in detailing the aunt's huffy exit and a request for Linc to witness Trace's signature on an unidentified legal document, followed within the hour by a lengthy visit from two Federal Aviation Agency investigators. On top of everything else, Matt and Jennifer Holden's funeral had taken place the day before yesterday without Trace, and now he had to face leaving Danny in the hospital. If anyone was justified in being in an ill humor, Trace was.

"He, uh, was a bit cranky yesterday, but that was probably due to his new surroundings," Carly said, referring to the move from the room the two had shared to the small but well-staffed pediatric ward.

Trace nodded, his attention focused on Danny. "Yeah. Yesterday was a bitch."

Red-eyed from lack of sleep, shoulders hunched as his hands strained against his jean pockets, he resembled a man badly in need of absolution.

"Please don't feel guilty about about leaving Danny." She wanted to tear out her tongue for blurting out the very thoughts she had tried to avoid. *Great, Carly. Just what the man needs, a little armchair psychology.* "I'm sorry. It's none of my business—"

Immediately, his expression closed, his body language changed. "You're right," Trace said, dragging a hand to his waist in a posture that would have been cocky under different circumstances but now defined self-protectiveness. "It is none of your business."

Embarrassed, Carly half turned away before he added, "But you're also right that I don't like the idea of leaving him one damn bit."

Stretched to its limit, "don't like" barely covered the anxiety he experienced whenever he thought about the possibility of losing Danny. *Anxiety, hell. Be honest with yourself, Holden, you're scared right down to your toes.* "Sorry if I was rude."

Carly had the feeling he seldom offered apologies, and she accepted this one graciously. "You were just concerned."

Gazing down at his nephew, Trace swallowed a lump in his throat. "He's . . . he's mine now. I mean, legally, I'm his guardian."

As soon as the words left his mouth, Trace realized two things. On some level he had recognized Danny as his from the moment he had found Matt and Jennifer's lifeless bodies in the snow. The document in Nathan Borell's possession was only a necessary legality to satisfy the rest of the world. As far as he was concerned, Danny was undeniably, and forever, his. Joy swelled his heart at the thought, yet at the same time his mouth went dry at the awesome responsibility inherent in his admission. The second realization was that he had again shared something very personal, no matter how small, with a women he had known only a few days.

At a loss for the right response, Carly stammered. "That's...n-nice." Nice? Having a child wasn't *nice*. It was everything.

"Just you and me now, sport," Trace said, giving Danny's hand a gentle squeeze.

Carly gave him credit. Given the trauma of the past several days, she suspected Trace was close to the last of his reserve of strength. Assuming full-time responsibility for a child's life was tough enough when two people had nine months to prepare, but the quantum leap from bachelorhood to fatherhood in one day had to be breath-stealing, hand-trembling scary.

"I have a feeling the two of you will do just fine," she said, giving Danny's tummy another caress.

Trace glanced up. Her face was close enough for his breath to tease the fringe of golden highlighted, honey-blond bangs slanted across her forehead. Gazing into her eyes, he suddenly wondered why, even in a state of semi-sleep, he had thought those same eyes merely blue. They weren't just blue, but *blue,* like the North Atlantic sprinkled with summer sunshine. *Sunshine.* The word was expressly suited to Carly McShane, because every time she was near, he felt warmed. He was warm now. And getting warmer.

At such close range Carly couldn't help but stare. There was just no way to get around it, she thought. Trace Holden was as handsome as sin, and just as tempting. The kind of man a woman could easily fall in love with. The admission shocked her. Was she tempted? Since her divorce and the subsequent kidnapping of her son, she had given little, if any, thought to allowing another man in her life. But Trace was a temptation. Not so much physically—although she couldn't discount the flutter of butterflies in the pit of her stomach—but emotionally. The feeling of being connected to this man grew stronger each time she saw him. And the dark shadows of her loneliness grew lighter.

Trace straightened to his full height and took a step back. "I, uh, had someone bring a few of his things from Matt and Jenny's house in Seattle." He gestured toward the discarded duffel bag. "You know, clothes, toys and stuff."

"Great," Carly said on a shaky breath. "He'll feel better with his own things around him."

She smiled up at him, and for the first time in his life Trace understood what it meant when they said someone lit up a room. Carly McShane represented light and warmth in a way he had never experienced. It felt good. Good and scary.

Nervously running his fingers through his neatly combed brown waves, Trace glanced at the clock above Danny's bed. "You've been off duty for over an hour," he said without thinking.

"I wanted to stay." And she had. For Danny and for Trace. And for herself.

The simple statement did strange things to Trace's sense of balance, like righting his otherwise unsteady world. Compassion was part of her profession, he reminded himself. Yet, somehow, he sensed that her attentions had been above and beyond the call of duty, and the thought distressed him . . . and pleased him more than it should have.

"Thanks," he said, feeling the necessity to respond, yet not sure of what to say. She kept bestowing little kindnesses, and he kept expressing his gratitude. Normal, expected social amenities, yet with each indulgence and appreciation he experienced a growing connection, less social and more personal. "Is, uh, your offer still good?"

"My offer?"

Glancing at her perplexed expression, he explained, "To introduce me to your landlady."

"Oh, yes . . . absolutely. Whenever you—"

"Would now be convenient? Unless you have other plans . . . or something."

"Right now is fine. Why don't I meet you in the main lobby after I check out, say in ten minutes?"

"Fine. And thanks . . . Carly."

"You're welcome."

Carly quickly logged off her shift, collected her coat and hurried to catch the elevator. While she waited, she again cautioned herself not to get emotionally involved with Trace Holden and his nephew, particularly since she would be seeing them every day. Knowing her own susceptibility, she mentally enumerated the reasons why she *shouldn't* get involved. Such relationships were unprofessional, emotionally unhealthy, she told herself. And the last thing she wanted in her life was additional emotional turmoil.

But she couldn't forget the look of fear and confusion in Trace Holden's eyes. He needed a friend, whether he was willing to admit it or not, and Carly doubted he ever would. For men like Trace Holden, the greatest need was control, not friendship; perhaps not even love.

And then there was Danny.

She had only to see his smile or clasp his tiny hand to understand her feelings for him. Feelings that were becoming far deeper, far more important, than she had intended. She rationalized those feelings by telling herself she would probably be similarly drawn to any little boy so close to her son's age. Besides, Danny was so sweet, warm, real, while Brian was . . .

No! Carly caught her breath at the mere thought. *No one can ever take my son's place! Danny's just a hurt little boy who needs me.* But even as she tried to convince herself that Danny was nothing more than a special patient, Carly knew it wasn't true. She had already spent more time thinking

about him, worrying about him, than she had a right to.
And all the while a tiny voice inside her head whispered,
*You're fooling yourself. And not doing a very good job, at
that*. Now her concern, and a great many other emotions,
had spilled over onto Trace.

He was prompt, and she was nervous. In addition to the
self-disciplinary speech she had given herself, Carly suddenly realized this was the first time she had been alone with
a man outside of work since Brian had been taken. Not that
she was *alone* with Trace, she reminded herself.

"I suppose you'll be taking Danny home to Seattle when
he's released," Carly said as they walked the three blocks to
the boardinghouse.

"No. I mean, I don't know. I can't quite bring myself to
stay at Matt and Jenny's place, but I can't take Danny to my
place, either."

"What's wrong with your place?"

"Let's just say a sofa bed crammed into a corner of an
efficiency apartment that can only loosely be described as
clean is hardly the right environment for a toddler."

"Oh," Carly said, a mental picture of his bachelor ac-
commodations forming in her mind.

"I spend ninety percent of my time in the air, so..." He
shrugged. "I figured, why spend big bucks on a place I'm
only in ten percent of the time? Besides, every penny went
back into my business."

"I thought you worked for your..." Carly could have
kicked herself for reminding him of his brother and the accident. She glanced up to find him watching her anxious
expression.

"It's all right. Until six months ago I operated an air-
freight business, but when Matt offered me a job as Holden Enterprises' chief pilot, I decided to sell half interest—
the operating half, in my company." He smiled again, and

Carly promptly decided it was a shame he didn't do it more often.

What a bizarre twist of fate, Carly thought, that had put Trace at the controls of that plane. But then, she understood better than some just how bizarre fate could be.

When he glanced down at her, Carly smiled back. For several moments after he looked away, she stared at him. Trace Holden had two things guaranteed to draw women like bees to honey—good looks and a touch of mystery. He gave the impression that no matter how long someone knew him, they would never know all of him. It was a surefire brand of attraction most women couldn't resist. She was on the verge of congratulating herself for not being one of them when she realized she had almost allowed him to walk past Mrs. Fitzpatrick's house.

"We're here," she said abruptly.

They stopped in front of a white clapboard house trimmed with green shutters. Trace decided it undoubtedly reflected the owner's reputation for conspicuousness, because a flagpole stood in the middle of the yard, flying a rendering of the stars and stripes large enough for several post offices. The instant Carly's finger touched the bell, the front door flew open.

"We've been worried sick about you." A wisp of a woman sporting an outrageous shade of red hair and a put-upon expression hovered in the doorway. "You should have been home and in bed hours ago. I told Bridget when she left for the university, I said, 'She's going to put herself inside that blasted hospital she thinks so much of, if she doesn't start taking better care of herself—'"

"I'm sorry, Fitz—"

"Don't keep normal hours. Don't eat enough to keep a bird alive." A delicate, age-spotted finger waggled beneath Carly's nose. "All you ever do is work, work, work."

"Fitz, I have someone I want you to—"

"I'm telling you right now, one of these days you're just going to—"

"Mrs. Fitzpatrick!"

"You don't have to shout, Carly, dear. I may be old, but I'm not deaf. Who's he?" A thinly penciled eyebrow arched as the fine-boned finger shifted direction.

"This is Trace Holden. You remember, I mentioned yesterday that he might be interested in a room."

Sparkling green eyes set in a small and delicately wrinkled heart-shaped face scanned Trace from his sneakers to the part in his hair. The green-eyed gaze sharpened considerably as it came to rest on Trace's ruggedly attractive face.

"Carly, I would most certainly remember if you had mentioned even one word about such a handsome gentleman."

Carly glanced sideways in time to see Trace restrain a surprised smile. "Trace, may I present Mrs. Margaret Katherine Fitzpatrick. Fitz, this is—"

"Yes, yes, Carly, dear. Come in, come in, before you both catch cold."

Before Trace or Carly could protest, they were hurried inside, relieved of their coats and ushered into a cheery kitchen, cozy despite its turn-of-the-century spaciousness. Although she normally treated all her boarders like extended family, Fitz had all but adopted Carly, fussing over her like a doting parent. Without asking, the landlady went straight to the stove, poured two cups of hot cocoa and set them in front of Trace and Carly as they seated themselves at her table.

"There. That ought to warm you right up."

The rim of the cup barely touched Trace's lips before she added, "How about a shot of brandy in yours, young man?"

"N-no, thanks."

Trace and Carly exchanged looks. His said, *Is she for real?*

Hers answered, *You ain't seen nothing yet.*

"Now, Mr. Holden—"

"Please call me Trace."

"Of course, and you must call me Fitz. Everybody does. Or... you may call me Margaret, if you prefer." A coquettish smile accompanied her offer; then her hand gestured with a flourish. "Whatever."

Carly released an exasperated sigh. As usual, trying to maintain a conversation with Fitz was like trying to watch a three-ring circus without getting dizzy. If she wasn't stopped, Trace would think the ditzy landlady and everyone connected with her was a menace to society, and that he would be better off in a pup tent than exposed to such lunacy.

"Uh, Fitz," Carly said, "Trace would like to rent a room for a week."

"Can't."

"Can't? But just yesterday you assured me—"

"There aren't any. I rented my last vacant room just this morning. If you had come home at the usual time, Carly, dear, I would have introduced you. Such a well-mannered young man. His parents must be so proud."

Carly sighed. She opened her mouth to apologize to Trace for bringing him on a wild-goose chase, but Fitz's typically roundabout way of getting to the point stopped her.

"Of course, dear Trace could have the carriage house. I don't normally rent the carriage house, because it has two bedrooms and most everyone just wants a room and a bath, but occasionally... You remember, Carly, the Halverson family rented it when the husband broke his leg skiing." Fitz frowned. "Or was that before you came? Oh, well," she prattled on, "no matter." Abruptly, Margaret Katherine Fitzpatrick turned and swept her four-foot-eleven-inch body through the door as regally as a queen exiting her throne room, leaving behind two bemused expressions.

"I thought you and Garrison were putting me on." Trace chuckled. "She's a conversational merry-go-round."

Carly laughed. "Still interested in living here?"

"Why not?"

"Well, look at it this way," she said, carrying their cups to the sink. "Your stay is only temporary and...if the men in white coats show up, which I fully expect to happen any day, we can all go on the group plan."

"I hesitate to ask, but what is the granddaughter like?"

"Normal, thank God." Wiping her hands on a nearby tea towel, Carly turned to find Trace standing less than two feet away, smiling broadly. "You should do that more often."

"Do what?"

"Smile."

As the smile in question dissolved, he stuffed his hands into the pockets of his jeans and glanced at the floor.

"And before you decided smiling is in bad taste under the circumstances, think about all the beautiful memories you have."

"There's not much future in memories."

Gently, she laid her hand on his forearm. "You're wrong, Trace. Memories give the future color and texture. And hope. Without our yesterdays, we could never fully appreciate our tomorrows."

Gazing into her blue eyes, Trace thought that tomorrow sounded worth a hundred smiles as described by Carly. He had never in his entire life met anyone who better personified hope. She was a welcoming fire on a winter's day, and he desperately needed her warmth. Hesitantly, he covered her hand with his.

A heated radiance, like sunshine slowly filling a room on a June day, tingled from the spot where her hand lay trapped beneath his. His hand was wide, strong, with long slender fingers. Dark brown hair swirled up his arm and disappeared beneath his shirtsleeve. Her gaze inexorably trailed up the sleeve, over broad shoulders to meet eyes darkened to mahogany.

Her hand is so small, he thought, the pad of his thumb gently stroking the back of her hand. Small and delicate as a dandelion in a spring breeze. And he felt less afraid, less...

Lonely. Strange, Carly thought, but with just his touch, she didn't feel quite so lonely.

At that moment Fitz stuck her head around the kitchen door. "You want to see it or not?"

Carly and Trace jumped apart. Trace cleared his throat and answered in a husky voice, "Yes. Yes, I do."

"Well, then, don't just stand there. My yoga class meets in thirty minutes, and I hate tardiness."

"You better go," Carly said, clasping her hands together. She made no move to join them.

"Aren't you coming?" he asked, wondering why the spot on his arm where her hand had been seemed suddenly colder than the rest of his body.

"No, I... If I don't get some sleep, I won't be worth much when seven o'clock rolls around."

"Oh, yeah." He had been so grateful to have her with him that he had completely forgotten that her night-shift hours required her to sleep during the day. "Fitz is right. You should be in bed."

His words affected her like stepping outside an air-conditioned building on a scorching summer day. As before, she shoved such thoughts to the back of her mind, but physiologically she wasn't as successful. Her body tingled with a warmth she hadn't experienced in longer than she cared to remember.

"Will we see you later?"

Carly blinked. "We?"

"Danny and I."

"Oh, uh, of course. Yes. I'll stop by before I go on duty."

With that, Fitz stamped into the kitchen, took Trace by the hand and led him away.

As Carly climbed the stairs to her own room, the thought crossed her mind that having Trace Holden within smiling distance for a week would be an extremely pleasant experience. Very pleasant indeed.

Ten hours later, refreshed and ready for work, Carly strolled into the pediatrics ward to find Trace in an anything but pleasant confrontation with Deirdre Andrews and a stranger.

"From now on, you ask me before you just *pop in* to see Danny." As he leaned possessively against Danny's crib, Trace's thunderous expression amplified his ready-to-take-on-all-comers stance. The set of his jaw and the look in his eye said, *This is my territory. I am in charge. Hands off.*

"We only have Danny's best interest at heart," Deirdre Andrews insisted.

"Like hell! You don't have anyone's interest in mind but your own."

"That is simply not accurate, Trace." She slipped her arm through the stranger's. "Walker and I care a great deal about little Danny. And we want to make sure he grows up with all the advantages he should have."

"While the two of you reap the advantages Danny's stock in the company provides for his legal guardian is more like it."

"Absolutely not!"

"Cut the crap, Deirdre."

"There is no need to be crude, Trace. If you are honest with yourself—"

"Honest? I'll give you honest!" Trace's icy voice escalated as he pushed himself away from the crib and straightened to his considerable height. "If Matt had left controlling interest of Holden Enterprises to me, you'd be all over me like a cold sweat, licking the drops right now, with Walker giving instructions on technique."

Deirdre gasped, stepping closer to her husband. Walker Andrews eased his indignant wife to one side. "Stop right there, Holden. I won't stand by and allow you to insult my wife."

"Get out, both of you," Trace said with a sneer.

"Not until you understand the necessity of removing Danny from a clearly unsuitable life-style."

"Walker, if you don't get out of my sight this minute, I won't be responsible—"

"Lower your voices this instant!" All three antagonists turned at the sound of another voice. With one hand resting territorially on the rail of Danny's crib, an unsmiling Carly gave them her best nurse-in-charge glare. "There are other children and parents in the ward, and I will not allow them to be upset. Please take this *conversation* outside!"

"I apologize for the disturbance, Nurse...." From the other end of the bed, Walker squinted at her nameplate, waiting for her to supply the last name.

"McShane."

"Nurse McShane." He smiled a little too sweetly for Carly's taste. "My wife and I merely wanted to check on our nephew's progress. To be sure he had everything he needs. What about a specialist? I can assure you that money is no object when it comes to Danny's welfare."

"Community General happens to have one of the foremost orthopedic staffs you'll find anywhere in the Pacific Northwest, Mr...."

"Andrews. Walker Andrews. Quite honestly, I don't understand why Danny wasn't flown directly to Seattle instead of this...rural hospital."

"Why should he have been flown to Seattle, Mr. Andrews, when this *rural* hospital *specializes* in orthopedic medicine? Due mostly to skiing accidents, we see more broken bones through here in a month than Seattle sees in a month of Sundays. *We* don't send cases to Seattle, *they* send cases to us. So I can assure you that we are doing everything medically possible for your nephew and that he is receiving the finest care available. As for any change in arrangements, you'll have to check with Mr. Holden, since, according to our records, he is Danny's legal guardian."

Carly didn't like the look of the husband any better today than she had the wife yesterday. From Deirdre Andrews' haute couture suit and tasteful gold jewelry to her husband's expensively tailored overcoat, the Andrews were the picture of refined wealth. But judging from their behavior, Carly wondered what kind of hearts beat beneath the costly clothes. Admittedly, she was predisposed in Trace's favor, but she had a feeling her loyalties were well placed.

In the midst of the hostility-charged atmosphere, the object of concern happily cooed and ahhed to himself, completely oblivious to anything but a line of small mirrors and brightly colored shapes strung across his crib.

"You were in Danny's room yesterday." Deirdre Andrews stepped from behind her husband. "As a matter of fact, if memory serves, Trace was holding your hand." She glanced from Trace back to Carly. "How nice for two old...*friends* to run into each other." The emphasis on the word "friends" left no doubt that it was intended as an insult.

Trace covered the distance from his end of the bed to Carly's in one stride. He placed a protective hand on her shoulder. "Carly *is* a friend. She's also the night charge nurse, and she's been kind enough to give Danny a great deal of extra time and care." He looked down into her clear blue eyes. "I don't know what I would have done without her."

"To be sure," Deirdre said sweetly.

As stunned by Trace's defense as by Deirdre's stinging remark, Carly simply stared as Walker took his wife by the arm and led her away.

"I'm sorry," she said as soon as they were out of earshot. "My behavior was very unprofessional, but..." Her voice trailed off when she noticed that Trace's attention was riveted on the departing couple. When he turned to face her, Carly almost caught her breath at the anguish in his sherry-colored eyes.

"Trace?"

"They want Danny."

"What do you mean?"

"They're going to sue for custody of Danny."

Chapter 4

Trace's announcement of the impending custody suit had twisted and turned in Carly's mind the way she had tossed about in her bed throughout a restless night. This morning, with the consequences of such legal action still heavy on her mind, her attempt to finish a Fitz-assigned task was halfhearted at best, not to mention precarious. Holding a curtain rod in one hand, she tried to maintain her balance as she scaled the aged wooden ladder. Carly looked up just as Trace entered the carriage house carrying a large cardboard box stuffed with an assortment of clothes and books, and wearing a scowl on his face.

"What the hell do you think you're doing? Trying out for a high-wire act?"

"Subbing for Fitz. She tore out of here on one of her errands and asked me if I would hang the curtains she seems to feel you can't live without."

"Well, I can damn well live without you breaking your neck." He quickly set the overloaded box aside and offered her a hand down.

"Thanks," Carly said, more than glad to have both feet on something more stable than the rickety ladder.

"I appreciate what you and Fitz are doing to make me feel comfortable, but I'm not going to be here long enough for you to bother. It's just temporary."

Temporary. Carly had forgotten—or, more accurately, purposefully ignored—the fact that in a few short days Trace would be leaving. And so would Danny. *Oh, Carly, you're a fool! You know better than to get emotionally involved with a patient.* And his uncle? *Now you're in for more heartache, and you've got no one to blame but yourself. You'll never learn.*

"It's..." They were standing so close that Carly was forced to tilt her head back in order to gaze into his eyes. "It's no bother."

Seconds crawled by before they realized, at the same time, that Carly's hand was still tucked inside his.

Trace was the first to break contact and take a step away. "I, uh, stopped by the hospital, but you had already left," he said, sliding both hands into the back pockets of his jeans.

"Yes." Why was her hand tingling? And why did she suddenly feel out of breath and unreasonably warm? "I looked in on Danny when my shift was over, and he was sound asleep." Carly brushed her bangs back from her forehead. "I, uh, hope you don't mind, but I bought him a present."

"You didn't have to do that."

"Oh, but I wanted to," she insisted. She crossed to a shopping bag leaning against the arm of a couch and pulled out a stuffed, multicolored dragon. "It plays music," she announced, smiling. Her delicate fingers twisted the key, and the tinkling notes of "You are My Sunshine" filled the room.

Carly's delight over the gift was surpassed only by Trace's delight at watching her. Her face glowed, and the child inside her fairly danced in her sparkling eyes. She would make a wonderful mother, he thought.

"The way you love kids, I'm surprised you don't have some of your own to shower with gifts. You'd make one hell of a mother for some lucky kid. Fitz told me you—"

"It's none of Fitz's business!"

The abrupt and totally unexpected response took Trace by surprise. "I didn't meant to—"

"Intrude? Well, you did. And so did Fitz. She has no right to...to go around talking about my personal life. She, she..." The words wedged in Carly throat. She knew she was being unreasonable. But then, so was her pain. That pain, coupled with the knowledge that Trace and Danny would soon be gone from her life, sparked a desperation she couldn't handle.

"Fitz only mentioned that you gave a lot of your off-duty time to the kids in the hospital." He stepped closer, concern etched across his face. "You give so much to Danny, I thought it was a shame you didn't have your own child to love."

Carly's breath lodged in her throat, and for a moment she swayed as if buffeted by a powerful force. *I do. I do,* she wanted to scream. *But I can't hold him. Can't buy him presents.*

Trace watched her fight to regain control of her emotions and realized he had inadvertently triggered some unnamed demon. The thought that he might have caused her pain, no matter how unintentional, was unbearable. "Carly, I'm sorry if I said something wrong.... Whatever it was, I could kick myself.... I wouldn't hurt you for the world.... God, I'm so sorry...."

Hugging the wildly colorful toy to her chest, she lifted her teary-eyed gaze to his. "It's ... all right."

"The hell it is." *Thoughtless, Holden. Next time, think before you speak.* He hesitated only a second before touching her cheek. A tear trickled over his fingers.

"No. Really. I had no right to..."

"You had every right."

"I should have known Fitz would never gossip. It's—it's..." She couldn't bring herself to tell him how his innocently spoken words had hurt. Trace wasn't responsible for asking what outwardly appeared to be perfectly normal questions. "I guess I'm more tired than I realized."

"And I didn't help." He reached into his hip pocket and withdrew a clean, neatly folded handkerchief. "Here."

She accepted it, drying her nose and cheeks with the soft cotton square.

"Please forgive me." He took the cloth from her and dabbed a damp spot she had missed, then handed it back.

"Nothing to forgive," she sniffed. "I overreacted."

"As we've established you had a perfect right to. Just as we've established I was rude and insensitive—"

"No," she protested. "You've never been rude." Glancing down at the handkerchief, she twisted the thin material between her fingers. "I—I don't talk about my ex-husband very often."

"You must be..."

She looked up. "What?"

"Nothing. Forget it. This time I would *definitely* be rude."

"I must be what?"

"Still in love with the guy."

"Because of the way I reacted, you mean?" He nodded. Carly took a deep, cleansing breath. "No. I'm not."

They stared at each other. She, still twisting the handkerchief, wishing she had the nerve to tell him the rest, to confide all her feelings of despair and loneliness. He, watching her torture the helpless fabric, wished that nothing, including himself, would ever again cause her pain.

"Well..." Carly said after an interminable silence. She handed him the musical toy, then nervously rubbed her palms along the side seams of her jeans. "I guess I'd better get out of here and leave you to get settled in. If you need anything, anything at all..." She turned and headed for the door.

"Carly?"

She turned. "Yes?"

"Would you have dinner with me?"

The question caught her off balance, leaving her without a plausible reason to decline. "I...I..."

"It's the least I can do to repay all the time and care you've given Danny." *And for causing you even a moment's grief,* he could have added, but didn't.

"Repayment's not necessary, Trace."

"Yes, it is. Besides," he admitted with a grin, "I hate to eat alone, and I happen to know this is your night off. We both have to eat, so...please."

Her own better judgment warned her against accepting, not because she feared him, but because she was afraid of her own fragile emotions. She should decline.

"All...all right," she said, blatantly disregarding her saner side. "But nothing fancy. My wardrobe can't handle fancy."

Trace glanced down at his worn jeans and jogging shoes. "It's not even in my vocabulary. Will you be up by seven o'clock?"

"Up? Oh, yes. I'll . . . be wide-awake."

"Then I'll see you at seven."

This is not a date, Carly told herself for the tenth time since waking up from her few hours' sleep. If one could call a series of catnaps sleeping. Besides, attributing her nervousness to lack of rest was certainly easier than admitting that thoughts of Trace's hand tenderly caressing her cheek had been an underlying cause of her restless afternoon.

After going through her limited wardrobe, she finally settled on her only dressy outfit. From the front, the two-piece knit looked like a simple skirt and matching top, but the back dipped enticingly low to reveal a tantalizing view of her bare back and shoulders. Kitten-fur soft against her skin, the outfit was Carly's favorite and her only concession to vanity despite the necessity of traveling light in her search for Brian.

The buzzer on her door sounded at exactly seven o'clock, and Carly dropped the plain gold hoop she was trying to clip to her ear.

"Hi," she said, slightly out of breath in her rush to answer the door after scrambling for her jewelry.

"Hi."

Trace was dressed in a pale blue shirt, open at the neck, and coffee-brown slacks that fit better than they had a right to, and Carly was pointedly reminded that Trace Holden was an extremely attractive man. She recalled him telling her that he often loaded freight as well as piloted the plane, and decided that accounted for the muscles in his shoulders and arms. He had the kind of build a lot of men spent hundreds of hours and dollars trying to achieve, the kind of body a lot of women spent hundreds of hours admiring.

Brushing back one side of his cream-colored raw silk blazer, he slipped a hand into his pocket and said, "I'm not crazy about ties. Hope you don't mind."

"No. You look..." *Handsome, gorgeous, wonderful...* "...fine."

A cab waited outside the boardinghouse, and before Carly realized it, almost twenty minutes had passed and the taxi pulled up in front of Ivar's Salmon House. Over plates of delicious alder-smoked salmon and pleasant conversation, Carly's nervousness gradually eased, and she was able to enjoy both the meal and Trace's charming company.

"Your dragon was a rousing success," he said as the waiter brought dessert and coffee.

"I'm glad."

"As a matter of fact, I think the nurses were as happy as Danny was to have the distraction. They told me he'd been fussy all day."

"Maybe the cast is irritating him," Carly replied, making a mental note to call the hospital as soon as she got home.

"If you want my opinion, he misses you."

A tiny thrill shot through her, until she realized she shouldn't be pleased that Danny missed her. She knew the emotional bond forming between her and this child was unhealthy, yet she was powerless to stop it.

"Danny and I owe you a lot, Carly." When she started to protest, he stopped her by quickly adding, "And don't tell me you were just doing your job. You've gone above and beyond your regular duties, and you know it."

Carly dropped her gaze, embarrassed by his praise.

"For you, nursing isn't just a way to earn a living, it's the way you live. One of the things that gives your life purpose."

She glanced up to see Trace absently toying with a half-empty coffee cup. "Yes," she whispered.

"That's the way I feel about flying. It's been the most important thing in my life, and until a week ago I thought it always would be."

"And now?"

"Now, flying is the second most important thing in my life. Danny is the first." Carly saw his fingers tighten around the china cup and feared it would shatter under the pressure. "And he's going to remain my top priority."

Now that the subject they had both unconsciously avoided had been broached, some of Trace's tension eased. He took a deep breath and released his stranglehold on the cup.

"You mean the custody suit?"

"Yes."

"But you told me Danny was legally yours."

"I thought he was. And he is. For now."

"But Mr. and Mrs. Andrews want him, too."

"Deirdre and Walker want control of Holden Enterprises, and they'll do anything to get it. Including using Danny."

"Why would they need Danny—"

"Because according to Matt's will, Danny's fifty-one percent of the stock gives controlling interest in the company."

Carly had to admit that she was operating on pure instinct where Deirdre and Walker Andrews were concerned. And her instincts told her that even if the couple was at least partly sincere, Danny could never mean as much to them as he did to Trace. "They don't seem to be the parental type, do they?"

"Bet on it. I've known them both for a long time. Deirdre's spoiled and Walker is greedy. Oh, I'm sure they'd give

Danny the best of everything. The best governesses, the best boarding schools, abroad, of course—''

''But not much love.''

Trace pinned her with his gaze. ''No. And *things* can never substitute for warmth and caring...for real love. If Deirdre and Walker win, Danny loses.''

Carly looked into his eyes. Even though she had known him only a short time, her heart told her that Trace was honest and fair, with solid values. But, most of all, he loved Danny. ''Then you have no choice. You have to do whatever it takes to keep Danny with you.''

Touched by her simple expression of faith, Trace reached out and took her hand. ''Thanks.''

''What are you going to do?''

''Whatever I have to. I intend to devote every ounce of my energy to retaining custody. Everything else takes second place. I'm not a rich man, but I'm prepared to spend every dime—and more—to see that Danny grows up a happy, well-adjusted kid, not some lonely, pampered, brat. And anybody who says otherwise better be prepared for one hell of a fight.''

His voice carried the same tone of determined finality she had heard before. It was a brand of determination Carly could identify with, admire and support. How often had she been told the search for her son was hopeless? But she had refused to listen, would always refuse.

''I have an appointment with my lawyer in the morning to discuss 'strategy,''' Trace said, staring into his cooling coffee. ''What he doesn't know is that I'm not talking strategy, I'm talking battle plan. This is one war I intend to win, no matter what it takes.''

''Would it help if I testified, or gave some sort of a deposition? I mean, I could tell the lawyer how well Danny responds to you and how he seems to have bonded with you already. Surely those are the kinds of things a judge would consider.''

Astonished at her offer, Trace shook his head. "I couldn't ask you to do that."

"You're not asking, I'm volunteering."

"This isn't your problem, Carly. There's no reason why you should get involved."

That word again. How could she tell him that she was already involved beyond her intentions, beyond the point she knew was good for her? How could she explain something she herself didn't clearly understand?

Trace stared at Carly and thought of how much Matt and Jenny would have liked her. He could almost see his brother's smile of approval. Part of him wanted to accept her help, while another rejected it and her. She was everything he didn't want to need, yet here she was, offering.... "I've never met anyone like you, Carly McShane," Trace said, awed by her generosity.

Perhaps his life and viewpoint had become too narrow, or perhaps he'd simply been too busy over the last few years to appreciate such honest emotions. Whatever the reason, looking into Carly's stunning blue eyes, Trace knew he had missed a lot.

Back in Union City a short time later, the thought of facing a barrage of legalese didn't unnerve Carly as much as Trace saying he had never met anyone like her. Long after he had delivered her to her room, she pondered their unusual...relationship? No, she couldn't exactly define it as such, but neither could she deny that they had some kind of connection. And regardless of whatever tag she chose, or whatever the emotional cost to her, Carly knew the decision to support Trace in the custody suit was the right one.

"Good morning." A smiling Nathan Borell's gaze bounced between Trace and Carly as they entered his appropriately stodgy office. His expression indicated that he had expected Trace to be alone.

They dispensed with introductions, and, as usual, Trace got straight to the point. "I want you to pull out all the stops, do whatever it takes to make sure Danny doesn't wind up in the hands of those two mercenaries."

"Trace, this is real life, not the movies. The law may often grind slowly, but I assure you, for the most part, it is fair. You have a legitimate claim, verified by Matt and Jenny's will. Deirdre and Walker will have to prove you are unfit to care for Danny in order for a judge to grant them sole custody. Proof, I might add, that will be difficult to get."

Morning sunlight reflected off his balding head as Nathan peered over his bifocals. "Unless, of course, there is something in your past they could use against you."

His mouth thinning to a hard line, Trace rose from the chair, crammed his hands into his pockets and stared at the plush carpet beneath his feet for long moments. When he spoke, his voice was flat, remote. "I was arrested when I was sixteen."

Borell picked up a pencil and began to make notes on a pad. "What was the charge?"

"Robbery."

The pencil stilled. "We're not talking kids stealing candy, are we?"

"No. When my parents died, I took my anger out on the world. I was a real hellion. Running with a wild bunch, daring anyone to knock the chip off my shoulder and ready for all comers. Nearly drove my grandparents crazy." Trace looked past Nathan into the wedge of light between the drapes. "Matt was in the navy. He came home on leave and..." A sad smile curved the corners of his mouth. "...set me straight." Several moments of silence passed before he focused his attention on Nathan and added, "I'm clean as a whistle after that incident, but I do have a record."

"Well . . ." The lawyer sighed. "I don't think a judge will make us pay for a rebellious youth, considering the trauma of your parents' death. But I'm much more concerned with convincing the judge of your current ability to provide Danny with a stable, healthy environment."

Until now Carly had been silent, practically sitting on her hands to keep from jumping to Trace's defense. "Nobody in the world could love Danny as much as Trace," she said quietly. "And as one of Danny's nurses, I've seen, first-hand, how much Danny loves Trace."

"I'm sure you're right, Ms. McShane. Unfortunately, when it comes to a child's welfare, the courts are less concerned about love than they are about the kind of stable home two parents can provide." He looked directly at Trace. "You want it straight?"

Trace nodded.

"Deirdre and Walker make a good case. They appear to have a solid marriage, financial independence and good educations, and they are directly related to the child's parents."

"So am I."

"You, on the other hand," Nathan went on as if Trace hadn't spoken, "although you have a steady, substantial income from your business, don't possess the kind of money Andrews does. You live a bachelor life-style, and, let's face it, Trace, your relationships with women have been fleeting at best." With a weak smile directed at Carly, he quickly added, "Present company excepted, of course."

"So, you're saying because my bank account's not six figures, I'm single and not living in a mansion, that I may lose Danny?"

"No. But we're talking about stability, Trace. We have to show that you are reliable."

"Or prove they aren't. Did you know Deirdre drinks? And Walker's affairs are too numerous to count. Just how damn *stable* does that sound?" Trace crammed both hands into his pockets. "I want to hire a private investigator."

"A welfare case worker will investigate the Andrews, and you, as well. A report will be filed with the court and copies sent to both attorneys."

"How much weight does this report carry?"

"Quite a lot."

"And how long before we can expect it?"

"Probably six to eight weeks."

"So I have to wait around for the opinion of some old-maid social worker who Andrews is probably already trying to buy off."

"Be careful, Trace. The judge could decide *neither* of you is guardianship quality, and then Danny would become a ward of the state again."

"Again?" Carly asked, puzzled.

"Danny's adopted," Trace said. Frustration laced his words.

Nathan turned to Carly. "Matt and Jennifer worked unsuccessfully with adoption agencies for years, and then a doctor friend of theirs helped them acquire Danny."

"Oh" was all Carly could think to respond.

Trace leaned across the massive teakwood desk, hands braced wide on its smooth, glossy top. "I don't give a damn where Danny came from. What matters is where he's going. So I screwed up when I was a teenager. That doesn't mean I can't give Danny everything he needs."

"Hey." Whether as protection against Trace's anger or as a symbol of surrender, Nathan Borell leaned back in his chair, holding both hands in the air. "I'm on your side, remember?"

"So long as it's the winning side," Trace said coolly. The commitment he had made days earlier on a frozen mountaintop was branded across his mind.

Carly watched Trace's fierce expression, felt the heat of his anger and knew beyond a shadow of a doubt that anyone who tried to take Danny would be in for the fight of their life.

By the time they left the office fifteen minutes later, Trace had calmed outwardly, but though he tried to pretend otherwise, Carly knew he was worried. The return trip from Seattle to Union City was made in total silence. She searched for the right words to reassure him, but they all rang trite and hollow beside the possibility that he might be separated from Danny.

"Thanks for coming with me," he said when they were inside the Fitzpatrick house.

"I'm afraid I wasn't much help."

Carly had deposited her coat in the vestibule closet and started upstairs to her room when his hand on her arm stopped her. "You were wonderful."

As before, the impulse to touch him was too powerful to deny. Her soft slender hand covered his.

"You *will* win," she whispered.

Trace was having an impulse or two of his own, and he couldn't resist the urge to brush aside a wisp of wind-tousled blond hair. "You should get some sleep."

"I suppose so." She sighed, pleasantly surprised at his touch and loath to break the connection.

The kitchen door burst open, and Fitz, followed by a fresh-faced girl in tight jeans, a bulky sweater and an apron, made her undeniable presence known.

"About time you two got home. Bridget, dear, don't forget to call the newspaper and tell them that pimple-faced little runt of a delivery boy is *still* throwing the paper smack-dab in the middle of the hedge. You know the number at Annabelle's. The bridge game should be over by two, unless she serves tuna again, in which case I'll be home early. The dolphins, you know." She bobbed her chin for emphasis. "They get tangled up in the tuna nets. Won't eat the stuff."

Fitz yanked her coat from the spot beside Carly's, slipped it on, then turned to address them. "It's going to rain, so don't track mud across my clean floor when you take Carly out for dinner, which I'm sure you intended to do without my prompting. No meals served on Saturday nights. Besides..." With a flourish befitting Gloria Swanson in *Sunset Boulevard,* she tossed a scarf around her wrinkled neck. "I have a date." Messages and edicts delivered, Fitz opened the front door and disappeared.

Bridget waved a doubled-up fist at the door her grandmother had just closed. "She's going to drive... me...bonkers!" She flung her hands heavenward in surrender, then stomped off to the kitchen.

Trace and Carly burst out laughing.

"We're living in the middle of a sitcom," Trace said, trying to catch his breath.

Carly wiped tears from her eyes. "More like the Three Stooges, minus one."

Laughter finally subsiding, Trace looked at Carly. "Someone needs to write a book about those women."

"No one would believe it was nonfiction."

The way no one would believe he was standing here laughing, feeling better than he had in weeks, months? Seeing her incredibly warm smile and that one enticing dimple, Trace knew it had been longer than he cared to admit.

When was the last time he had stopped to notice a woman's dimple? Or to state unequivocally that her skin looked velvet soft? Hers did. Soft enough to sweetly cushion the brush of a man's whiskered cheek. And when, in the overworked, hysterical schedule of the last three months, had he taken time to recognize that apricot-tinted lips—the upper curved just enough to fire a man's imagination, the lower full enough to fulfill a man's fantasies—were his favorite? He had been extremely cautious where women were concerned, and for the life of him, he couldn't figure out why this petite bundle of sunshine had slipped right through his best defenses.

"You don't have to surrender, you know."

Was she reading his mind now? "Surrender?"

"To Fitz's manipulations."

"Oh."

"And I'll speak to her about her rather obvious attempt at matchmaking," Carly promised. "She means well."

He shrugged. "No harm done."

She smiled. "Right, no harm done." There was absolutely no reason for her to remain standing at the foot of the stairs, close enough to see flecks of gold dancing in his eyes. There was absolutely no reason to wish she could remain this close—even closer. But she did.

"Well," she finally sighed, knowing the longer she stayed, the more she wanted to stay.

"What *will* you do for dinner?" He hadn't actually intended to voice the question. It had just jumped out. "I mean . . . since you don't have to go to the hospital . . ."

"I do . . . I mean, I will . . . but not to work. To see Danny."

"Oh . . . good. That's good. Me, too."

"Going to see Danny?"

"Uh huh."

"We could go…" For some reason Carly wasn't ready to examine, she hesitated to use the word *together*. "At the same time."

"Yeah. We could."

A long, silent pause followed, until Carly finally added, "And you're certainly welcome to share whatever I can concoct out of Fitz's kitchen." Was it her imagination, or had the foyer become stuffy? The old house suddenly seemed much smaller, more…intimate. "I mean, we both want to visit Danny, and we both need to eat. There's no reason for us to go out of our way to do those thing separately."

"No reason."

"Fine, then."

"Fine," he echoed.

Carly took a deep breath and a step up the stairs. The mood was broken.

"Thanks again for going with me to the lawyer's office," Trace said again.

"You're welcome."

"See you later."

"Later." Carly turned, hurried up the stairs and into her room.

She undressed, slipped into an old, well-worn sleep shirt and settled on the sofa bed. This is silly, Carly told herself. Visiting Danny and sharing a potluck meal doesn't mean a single, solitary…thing. Except perhaps that she was trying too hard to tell herself it didn't mean anything. Or that the refreshing nap she needed stood little or no chance of happening while thoughts of spending time with Trace paraded around in her head.

"This is silly," Carly said out loud, but not an ounce more convincingly. She spent a lot of time in the company of men—doctors, orderlies. Trace Holden was just another man. A nice man. A handsome man. But just another man. Carly fluffed the pillow beneath her restless head.

And it wasn't as if she was uncomfortable around handsome men. Take Linc, for instance. He was devilishly handsome, and she had never felt uncomfortable around him or stumbled over her words as she had done with Trace a few moments earlier. And it wasn't as if she had sworn off men in general, though God knew, after the nightmare Ken had put her through, she had considered doing just that. Now, though, her thoughts of Ken were of a man more deserving of her pity than her hatred.

But it hadn't always been so. Some of her memories of her marriage, at least the early ones, were happy. But within weeks of their wedding day, Ken had begun to show signs of moodiness. Carly had tried to be supportive, gladly sharing Ken's eagerness to have a child as soon as possible.

When his moodiness became depression and his behavior changed so drastically and cruelly, Carly had taken part of the blame, certain she had failed her husband in some way. As the days and weeks progressed, so did Ken's depression and the deterioration of their marriage, but her determination to shore up the sagging relationship had remained steadfast until Ken's behavior turned violent. After he attempted to strangle her, barely a month before Brian was born, Carly was forced to admit that the relationship was beyond redemption. Frightened for herself and her child, she left Ken and filed for divorce.

Only months afterward, when she was called from Dallas to identify Ken's body in a Seattle morgue, had she learned that a malignant brain tumor had driven him to the brink of madness. Had caused him to abduct his own son.

After torturous months of guilt and recriminations, Carly had realized that Ken's problems, both mental and physical, had started long before their marriage. A diseased brain, and not the gentle, caring man she had first known, had been responsible for taking Brian from her. She forgave Ken. The one person she couldn't forgive was herself. As a nurse, she should have recognized Ken's symptoms, or at least realized the possibility of a physical cause for his unbalanced conduct. But she hadn't.

Carly catnapped for the next three hours, until a nagging sense of things left undone and pure old-fashioned guilt drove her off the couch. Since Danny and Trace had tumbled from the sky and into her life, she had neglected her usual weekly routine of phone calls to the Dallas police and various child-finding connections she had established over the months. *How could you forget something so important?* she asked herself. *How could you forget about hope?*

If she were honest with herself, Carly had to admit that since coming to Seattle and virtually starting over, she had begun to feel an increasing need to move on with her life. But moving on equaled leaving behind. Leaving behind people, memories. And how could she ever leave behind a single memory of Brian? How could she leave hope behind? The word gnawed at her conscience, a conscience she tended to ignore more often of late because it reminded her that she had spent her hope, like her money, and now both were almost gone.

Carly spent the next hour and a half assuaging her guilt and running up her long-distance bill. And the result was the same as it had been since the trail had gone cold in Seattle four months earlier.

Nothing. No word. No clue. Nothing.

Calling upon the strength she never questioned for fear it would evaporate, Carly dragged herself to the shower. While hot water soothed her tense muscles, she treated herself to the familiar self-pity-is-too-expensive pep talk. As she dressed in a casual rose-pink wool skirt and pale pink blouse, her thoughts turned to Danny and the few precious minutes she would spend with him. He was a tangible reminder that hope springs from even the most hopeless situation. And hope was the center of her life.

"Did you see that pile of books and toys beside his bed? The kid's made out like a bandit," Trace said as they returned to the apartment after an hour-long visit with Danny. "Every nurse is eating out of the palm of his hand." He hung up their coats and followed Carly into the kitchen.

"Guilty as charged," she admitted, perusing the skimpy contents of the refrigerator. She found sufficient ingredients for ham-and-cheese sandwiches to accompany a container of Fitz's leftover corn chowder. Trace made a pot of coffee and set the table, and within minutes they sat down to enjoy their plain but hearty meal.

"I'm afraid life with me will be a letdown after all the attention Danny's been getting."

"He'll be fine once he settles in."

"I hope so. That's why I'm leaving for Seattle in the morning."

"Seattle?" Involuntarily, her fingers tightened around her cup.

"I want to check in with my partner before Danny leaves the hospital. Should take most of tomorrow. In fact, I'll probably spend the night."

"Oh." Relief trickled through Carly, but she knew she was only postponing the inevitable. Sooner or later, probably sooner, the Holden men would exit her life for good. She picked up the dirty dishes and carried them to the sink. "So, you'll try to find a place for you and Danny in Seattle?"

"That's the plan."

She heard an implied "but," and a drop of hope splashed her heart.

"The more I think about making permanent decisions, the less I think about living in Seattle."

"But your business?"

"A half-hour commute to and from one of the bedroom communities isn't intolerable," he said as they turned out the kitchen light and walked into the parlor. "Besides, I'm not sure yet...."

"Not sure about what?"

"A week ago, I was a flier with part interest in a business. Now I've got a part-time business and a child to raise."

"You're going to quit flying?"

He shook his head. "Flying is as natural to me as breathing. Giving it up would be giving up a part of me." Then, with a glint of steely determination in his eyes, Trace added, "But if that's what it takes to keep Danny, then there's no choice. He comes first. Hopefully, I can find a way to keep Danny *and* fly."

Carly turned at the foot of the stairs to discover they were standing close. Intimately close.

"I'm sure you'll work it out." Why hadn't she ever noticed that tiny scar above his left eyebrow? Was the faint, quarter-inch mark the result of some childhood accident? Had anyone been there to kiss it and made it better, and, if not, was it too late to make amends?

"Thanks. And thanks for dinner, too."

"Soup and sandwiches doesn't exactly qualify as dinner."

"It does if you're hungry."

She smiled.

He smiled.

And seconds of silence stretched into long minutes.

"Well—" they said in unison.

"Good night, Trace."

"Night."

She took two steps up the stairs.

"Carly?" She turned back. "I'm going to be out of here early. Will you give Danny something for me?"

"Of course. What?"

He took two steps up the stairs.

"This." His head dipped, and, ever so lightly, ever so tenderly, his lips brushed hers.

He drew away and stared at her lips. Then, slowly, giving her time to turn away, he lowered his mouth to hers again. If he had intended the kiss as an expression of gratitude, such intentions flew out the window the instant he felt her mouth beneath his. The kiss was sweetly warm, sunshine-through-clouds warm, and soft as a sleeping baby's sigh. It was new, fresh-from-the-heart new, and yet as old as man and woman's first kiss. Carly sighed, sending her moist, uneven breath mingling with his.

Her arms slipped around his neck.

His arms pulled her closer, settling her intimately against his body. His hard body.

Then sugar turned to spice as he twisted his mouth against hers, gently insisting she open to him. She did.

Lips—warm, soft and innocently inviting—parted, and forgotten intentions were replaced by remembered need. He needed to touch her, be touched by her. He needed to physically establish and verify the connection he had felt to her from the moment he had opened his eyes and thought she was an angel. But he had never expected the need to be so strong. Their tongues touched and spoke the language of longing—longing to be stroked, caressed, loved. Totally. Completely.

Carly's initial shock gave way to a delicious tingling and a flutter in the pit of her stomach she hadn't experienced in so long it was frightening. Sweet. His kiss was as sweet as Grand Marnier and just as intoxicating.

Trace deepened the kiss, knowing he shouldn't, knowing his need was hammering at the boundary of reasonable control. But need punctured a hole in reason, and desire rushed in, pulling him, drowning him, washing him away from sanity. Control was nothing. Need was everything.

Carly moaned as he ground his mouth into hers, then gave a groan of sweet satisfaction and the greedy demand for more. She wanted more. Oh, so much more.

His hand crept up her ribs until it met the soft undercurve of her breast. It stilled; then his thumb began a tantalizing sweeping motion. Stroking. Arcing across the soft fullness of her flesh until her nipples tingled and bloomed against the soft fabric of her blouse and other sensitive parts of her body throbbed with a pleasant ache.

He tilted his head first to one side, then the other, trying to get closer, wanting more of her. His tongue plunged deep, retreated, then plunged again. Carly's body flushed shades of hot, hotter and too hot. She pulled her mouth from his, and they both gasped for air.

Breathlessly, they stared, both pleasure-stunned. Neither seemed to quite understand the high-potency moment.

Without another word, not even goodbye, Trace turned and walked across the foyer and out the back door, locking it behind him.

Carly stared at the closed door. How had that happened? she wondered, touching a finger to her slightly swollen lips. *Try inevitability,* a small voice answered. *Try to rationalize it any way you choose, just don't deny you enjoyed his kiss.* She had enjoyed it. Very much. Too much. *Careful, Carly. You may be in danger of breaking your own rules of no involvement.* Danger was the operative word. Because in the span of one simple yet complicated kiss, she had realized that Trace Holden was the kind of man she could fall in love with.

On the short walk to the carriage house Trace asked himself just what the hell he thought he was doing, but got no answer. Then he asked himself what he wanted to do, and the answer was simple. And complex.

Inside a Tudor mansion in an exclusive section of Seattle, Walker Andrews knew exactly what he wanted to do. The problem was how to accomplish his goal. The custody suit for the Holden brat was in motion, but moving much too slowly to satisfy him. He had spent the better part of his day reassuring a couple of his backers who were becoming impatient to go forward with the takeover. If he didn't have complete control of the company soon, he might lose his chance, and that was something he had to prevent at all costs.

What he needed was an insurance policy, an ace-in-the-hole. Something powerful enough—or intimidating enough—to guarantee success.

Chapter 5

Carly couldn't forget their kiss.

In fact, she thought about little else all the following day. A day without seeing Trace. A day in which she visited Danny twice before her shift, not because he needed her, but because *she* needed the distraction.

As she rounded the end of the corridor and headed toward the pediatric ward a full two hours before it was time for her to report for duty, she told herself for what seemed like the hundredth time that she was making much too much of a simple, friendly kiss. No big deal, right?

Then why did she keep remembering the delicious feel of his mouth on hers? And why, for a heart-pounding second, had she longed for him to... *Oh, for heaven's sake, Carly. Stop this!*

What she couldn't stop was the languid warmth that swept through her body whenever she thought about the kiss she kept telling herself not to think about. Tender warmth. A warmth she hadn't realized she had missed until last night.

As she stepped into the ward, Carly was thankful that her first glimpse of Danny helped her to shelve her disturbing and tenacious thoughts about the kiss.

Gazing down into Danny's smiling face, Carly couldn't imagine why anyone in her right mind would ever have given him up. Whoever Danny's biological parents were, they were missing a special, precious child.

But then, Ken hadn't been in *his* right mind when he gave Brian away. As she had every day since identifying her ex-husband's body in a Seattle morgue, Carly offered a silent prayer that in Ken's last days of sanity he had left their son with someone who would care for and love him. That daily prayer kept her sane, kept her hanging on to a hope few thought realistic.

"Hello, Sunshine," she said, bending over Danny's crib. He extended his chubby little arms, and it was all the invitation Carly needed. As usual, she couldn't resist the urge to pick him up and cuddle him. Holding his warm little body next to hers was both ecstasy and agony. Ecstasy because he smelled so baby sweet and felt so wonderful in her arms. Agony because he wasn't hers, and deep down in her heart she was ashamed because she couldn't help but wish he was.

Carly's conflict was the chief reason she had tried so hard to keep a loving distance from the children she had worked with since Brian's disappearance. But with Danny, keeping her distance was a lost cause. Being with him, feeding him, playing with him, was the bright spot in her day. She was so enthralled with Danny that she didn't even hear Linc's approach.

"How was your weekend?" he asked, walking up behind them.

"Fine. And yours?" Carly laughed softly as Danny patted her cheek.

"Boring. Do anything . . . special?"

"No." Carly returned Danny to the crib, making a fuss of straightening his blanket. *Not unless you count being kissed.*

"You're a terrible liar, Carly McShane."

Carly's head snapped up.

"You and Trace Holden have been thicker than thieves since he checked out of the hospital. And people," Linc's eyebrow arched mischievously, "being people, will talk. Half the staff is busy speculating about you and the dashing pilot, while the other half is busy manufacturing more speculation."

"Don't they have anything better to occupy their tiny little minds?" Carly asked, becoming more irritated by the minute.

"Naw. Been a slow week on the soaps. Besides, there's an inside source."

One look at Linc's know-it-all grin told her the identity of the "source." "I might have known. Fitz, right?"

"Well, did you?" he persisted.

"Did I what?"

"Go out with him."

"We had dinner—"

"Sounds like a date to me," he teased.

"It wasn't a date. He wanted to thank me for taking care of Danny."

"They make cards for precisely that reason, you know."

"Don't you think you're carrying the big-brother routine to extremes? It's really no one's business, but—"

"Whoa." Linc tilted his head and studied her for several seconds. "What *is* going on here?"

"Nothing."

"Hey—" his teasing expression sobered "—lighten up."

Carly looked her friend in the eye. "Can't a single woman and a single man share a meal together without everybody marching them down the aisle or to the nearest motel?"

"Sure. But *this*—" his finger tapped the tip of her nose "—single woman hasn't had a date since she came to town."

"It wasn't a date!"

"Then I give up." Linc shrugged in mock exasperation. "What the hell was it?"

Carly's gaze darted away. "I don't know."

"Ah, at last. An honest answer."

Carly saw the "gotcha!" gleam in her friend's eye. "You're a pest, Lincoln Garrison," she said, her beautiful face finally relaxing into a smile.

"Not exactly an endearment, but it'll do." Then, more seriously, he said, "I've been worried you were getting too attached to Danny, but maybe I've been worrying about the wrong Holden."

"Don't be absurd. Trace and I are friends."

"Uh-huh. Does he know about Brian?"

Carly's eyes widened, but she didn't answer.

"Thought so," Linc said when she didn't respond.

"Why should he? I . . . we barely know each other."

"Uh-huh, I see."

"Will you stop saying uh-huh?"

Linc shrugged. "I thought you might be hesitating for fear Trace would think your only interest in him was because of Danny."

"But nothing could be further from the..." Caught with her own words, Carly glared at Linc. "You did that on purpose."

"Moi?" He failed to hide an annoyingly triumphant grin.

Carly frowned, realizing just how attached to Trace she had become in such an incredibly short time. And how, until this moment, she hadn't questioned that attachment any more than she had questioned her feelings for Danny. Truthfully, the word attachment was a euphemism for attraction, and she knew it. *So, you're attracted. It's not the end of the world.* Quite the contrary, Carly thought.

At the touch of Linc's hand, she gazed into eyes that were now dark with concern. "By your own admission, you're not sure what's 'going on' between you and Trace. You're working too hard, and I think you're much more involved than you realize. You're a care-giver, Carly. It's only natural that you would be drawn to Danny *and* to Trace. They're lost sheep, and you're a sucker for strays."

"Is that so bad?"

"Be careful, Blue Eyes. I'd hate to see you hurt."

She was accustomed to Linc voicing his friendly advice and normally didn't object. But this time the brotherly concern came dangerously close to hitting a nerve. One she wasn't ready to acknowledge to herself, much less her best friend.

"Thanks." Her smile conveyed a great deal more bravery than she felt.

"Well," he said, not wanting to belabor the point, "what say we get to work before they can us both?"

Linc left the hospital shortly after they made evening rounds, and Carly was grateful he hadn't resurrected the uncomfortable topic. She had almost succeeded in putting Linc's overly cautious attitude from her thoughts when something happened that brought his warning back with startling clarity.

Around midnight she peeked in on Danny to discover he was restless and fretful. She checked the cast for any signs of irritation and found none. When she touched her hand to his brow, the heat she felt indicated that he might have a fever, but when she checked, his temperature was normal. Still, he was restless and obviously uncomfortable. Carly pulled his chart and noticed that Linc had made a minor change in medication that could account for Danny's unrest. And she noticed something else.

She had never looked at the sheet containing personal data with anything other than a professional eye. Why, at this moment, standing in the semidark ward, she decided to read it, Carly couldn't say. Later, when she reviewed the information, she would tell herself it was because her mind had been functioning on a much too personal level all day and that attitude had spilled over into her job. Later she would convince herself that her reaction had been entirely emotional and born of fatigue.

According to the form, Danny Holden's birthday was September seventeenth, the same day as the plane crash.

The same day as Brian's birthday.

Coincidence, she insisted, grasping for a rational explanation. But her hold slipped when she saw that Danny Holden's blood type was O-positive. The same as hers.

The same as Brian's.

Carly's mouth went dry, and her heartbeat vaulted to triphammer speed. Joy, fear, happiness and disbelief jumbled together, tangling in her heartstrings and clouding her mind. For one tortured, desperate moment, fantasy battled reality and almost won while she linked Danny and Brian together in her mind and thought . . .

You're exhausted, Carly. Your poor, tired brain is playing tricks on you. Danny Holden couldn't possibly be your son!

She sucked in a lungful of air, trying to clear her head. *You must be losing what little mind you have left, Carly McShane. Linc is right. You're working too hard.* But her hand trembled as she replaced the chart.

So Danny and Brian shared the same birthday. Undoubtedly so did thousands of other little boys, she reasoned. So they shared the same blood type. So did half the

English-speaking world. As she struggled to put facts and logic into perspective, Linc's words came back, as well. *They're lost sheep, and you're a sucker for strays.*

Possibly, Carly thought. Probably. But she couldn't resist a last wisp of hope curling through her mind, drawing her back to the chart for one more look. Brian had a birthmark, three tiny raspberry-colored splotches forming a perfect triangle midway up his left thigh. Would the emergency-room nurse have noticed a mark on Danny Holden's injured left leg? Or would she have thought such a blemish a result of the crash? She grasped the chart, then hesitated for a heartbeat before looking at the page.

There was no indication on the chart of any unusual discoloration or blotch.

And Danny's cast completely encased his little body from toes to hips, so she couldn't look for herself, even if she wanted to. And she didn't want to. Not really. Because deep in her heart she knew the result would be one more rung down on her shaky ladder of hope.

Not until she was walking home, with the fragrance of fir and early-morning dew sweetening every breath, was Carly finally able to put the incident into proper perspective.

Regardless of how she justified her feelings, since sharing so much time with Danny, she had less time to think about Brian. The admission was a hot blade scoring her heart. Unfortunately, facing the truth didn't alter the hard facts that did little to alleviate her guilt. After nine long months of searching for her son, emotionally and financially, Carly was at an all-time low.

From the moment Brian had been taken, every ounce of her energy and every cent in her bank account had gone into the search. She moved from her moderate two-bedroom Dallas apartment to an efficiency apartment, then finally to a rent-by-the-week rooming house. Each one was less expensive, but in the same neighborhood, so she could maintain her phone number. She had left those same seven digits with countless agencies, public and private. The same seven numbers she prayed someone would dial to tell her that her baby was alive and coming home. But months passed, money dwindled.

Her trip to Seattle four months ago had taken the last of her savings and almost the last of her hope. Carly had known her one-way-ticket decision to leave Dallas was risky. Now she had no choice but to remain in Union City until she could save enough money to continue the search. Although there were agencies offering help, the searching parents far outnumbered the dollars. So, for the time being anyway, she would simply have to deal with her guilt as best she could. And, for the time being, she would do whatever she could to help Danny.

What about Trace?

Carly couldn't deny that there had been some truth to Linc's assessment of the situation.

How much?

Too much.

She missed Trace. In light of Linc's comments, it was a costly admission that did not sit well after today's introspection. Still, it was the truth. But Carly had learned long ago that the truth, in all its simplistic beauty, could be the most complex of heartbreakers.

The minute Carly walked into the boardinghouse, Bridget and Fitz called to her from the kitchen. Dressed for class, books in hand and an anxious expression on her lovely face, Bridget was leaning against the counter as if braced for bad news. Fitz, musing over a cup of tea, appeared to be waiting for the same news.

"The feds were here for Trace," Fitz blurted when Carly was three feet into the kitchen.

"What?"

"Gran," Bridget cautioned. "They weren't *feds*."

"Don't know what else you'd call them. Dark suits, white shirts and narrow minds. I don't care what part they're from, all those government people look alike to me."

"Two Federal Aviation...whatever you call them, showed up right after you left for work yesterday evening," Bridget explained. "They wanted to know where Trace was and when he'd be back." She reached behind her and produced a plain white piece of paper. "They left a card."

"Did you tell them Trace was in Seattle?" Carly asked, realizing the men's visit undoubtedly had something to do with the crash of the Holden jet.

"Told them I didn't know for sure." Fitz's tone clearly proclaimed her loyalty to Trace.

"Gran's convinced they're going to haul Trace off to jail or some deep dark dungeon," said her granddaughter.

"Don't you mock me, Bridget Katherine. I tell you, that young man is in serious trouble."

"How do you know, Fitz?" In the relatively short duration of their friendship, Carly had learned to value the older woman's intuitive nature.

"Every instinct I've got tells me they weren't just mildly interested in his whereabouts. I've got a feeling they *want* Trace."

"Who wants me?"

All three women turned to find the subject of their discussion standing in the kitchen doorway.

Whether from surprise or joy, Carly's heart skipped a beat. He looked gorgeous in a hunter-green and camel-colored ski sweater.

"Uh...uh..." Bridget shoved the business card into Carly's hand, clearly anxious not to be the one to deliver bad news. "Guess I better go to class. See ya." She almost stumbled over her own feet in her hasty exit.

Fitz quickly rose from her chair. "Yeah, uh, that sounds like a good idea. Help yourselves to coffee," she said, making good her own escape.

"Care to explain the mass exodus?" Trace asked when they were alone. Only they weren't really alone, because the memory of last night's kiss was a vibrant, compelling promise in the room.

Trace couldn't help remembering the way she had moaned into his mouth, the way her breast had seemed to swell when he stroked her tender flesh. Had she ached as he had for the kiss to go on, and on, and...?

God, yes, he ached. Then and now. Just looking at her soft, full lips drove him to the hard edge of arousal. He wanted to touch her. He needed to touch her.

Carly couldn't stop staring at him. At his mouth. She vividly remembered feeling velvet roughness as his tongue plunged into her mouth, greedy for another taste. She remembered the heated touch of his hand on her breast, his thumb stroking, stroking, inches from her nipple. Delicious inches. Aching inches.

"Carly?" Trace swallowed hard.

"What? Oh, yes. They, uh..." She handed him the card. Trace glanced at it.

Carly's gaze followed his hand as it stuffed the card into the pocket of his jeans. Tight jeans. "Uh, Fitz said—"

"They caught up with me in Seattle." Trace cleared his throat. He walked to the cupboard, removed a cup and poured himself some coffee. When he faced her again, for the first time Carly noticed how tired he looked. Lying-awake-for-hours-worrying tired. And why did the phrase *caught up with me* suddenly have an ominous ring?

"What's wrong?"

He took a swig from the mug, studying her over the rim as if trying to decide if he should tell her and how much. "It appears," he said at last, "that a *concerned* citizen called the local FAA office insinuating that there are some unanswered questions involving the crash."

"I don't understand. They've already questioned—"

"Carly..." Trace was surprised at the calmness in his voice, given the fact he had been up half the night trying to deal with his rage. "The complainants were Deirdre and Walker Andrews. They suggested I might have deliberately... Well, let's just say they pointed out that this wouldn't be the first time money was a motive for murder."

Carly's gasp was almost completely drowned out by the whack of his half-empty cup hitting the counter. Coffee sloshed over the rim and onto the tiled surface.

How, Carly thought, could they be so cruel? How could they, or anyone, even think for one second that Trace would intentionally... "That's ridiculous," she blurted out, drawing herself up to her full five feet, five inches.

"Thanks for the vote of confidence. Mind calling the FAA and sharing your opinion?"

"The idea that you could, or *would,* sabotage that plane for money is . . . is . . ." Hands doubled into fists testified to her frustration and anger. "Ridiculous," she stated. A defiant toss of her head flipped her bangs down onto her forehead.

"Walker and Deirdre—"

"Are obviously desperate," Carly declared. She walked across the kitchen to stand in front of him. "You are *not* capable of such violence."

The certainly in her voice, the spark of determination in her eyes, did more for his confidence than a thousand public vindications. "You haven't known me long, Carly. How can you be so sure?" Unable to resist the urge to touch her, he gently pushed the wayward bangs from her face.

For a long moment Carly simply stared at him. "Because," she said finally, honestly, "My heart tells me so."

"And do you always trust your heart?"

"Not always." *But this time.*

His expression—something akin to pain softened by the need to have someone believe in him—stilled, and at the end of a long sigh he said a simple but heartfelt, "Thanks."

"What are . . . you going to do?" She caught herself a second before saying *we.*

"Fortunately the investigation has already turned up substantial evidence of mechanical malfunction. Enough to pretty well eliminate pilot error."

"So you've been cleared."

"Unofficially."

"Then—"

"Don't you see, Carly? Deirdre and Walker will use this during the custody hearing to try to influence the judge."

"But it's not true."

"I know that, and you . . . Well, you believe me, but I'm afraid even a whisper of suspicion will work in their favor."

"What does Mr. Borell say?"

"I don't know." A muscle twitched in his jaw.

"But surely you've spoken—"

"No, damn it!" The retelling of his predicament had reignited his anger like a doused pilot light, slowly hissing gas.

Trace whirled around, presenting her with his broad back and powerful shoulders. His hands gripped the edge of the countertop, frustration evident in the corded muscles of his neck. "I spent all of yesterday reorganizing my life so I could be the kind of parent Matt wanted for Danny. Then *this* . . . crap surfaces, and that fool Borell is out of town!"

His anguish was a palpable presence in the room as he turned to face her. The fingers of one hand replowed the existing furrows in his coffee-brown hair while the other hand sought the security of a pocket.

He's scared right down to his toes, Carly thought. So scared he wants to lash out at anyone within striking distance—at the world. But the truly awful part is that he knows it wouldn't help. "When will Borell be back?"

He studied the toes of his boots. "Late this afternoon."

She touched his shoulder, and when he looked up, Carly wanted to cry at the pain she saw in his eyes.

"I can't lose him, Carly," Trace whispered.

"You won't." But even as she spoke, she knew she was denying a real possibility.

"You don't understand. I . . . promised Matt."

The simple statement said all there was to say, as far as Trace was concerned. He had made a promise, and he intended to keep it. Pure and simple. Black and white. No room to negotiate. "No matter what Borell or anybody else says, I won't give Danny up."

In Carly's mind, even measured amounts of time with a child you loved were better than no time at all. She sought for a way to make him see that if the worst happened he could still be a part of Danny's life. "Trace, even if—God forbid—Deirdre and Walker should win in court—"

"No!" The word rolled from the depths of his soul as he straightened his body to a hard-line stance. Both hands raked his hair, then dropped to bracket his hips. "A week ago I was a brother and a doting uncle, and then my whole world went haywire. At first I thought it was just a nightmare and I would wake and find everything was the same as before. Well, it's a nightmare, all right. One you *can't* wake up from. One minute Matt and Jenny were happy and alive, the next minute they were gone. But Danny is still here. Sweet. Smiling. Only wanting to be loved.

"In the beginning," Trace said softly, "Danny needed me. Now I . . . I need Danny." He bent his head. "I don't know if I can make you understand how often I think about him when I'm not with him. How much I miss—"

"The way he smiles when he wakes up." Carly finished his thought.

"Yes." Trace turned to face her, but she wasn't looking at him.

"Or that funny, happy little sound he makes when he first sees you in the mornings. Or . . ." Memories of Brian came rushing back, and she fought the gathering tears. "The way he smells of baby lotion and pure, wonderful sweetness. And when you hold him, the world seems so . . . right, so good and worthwhile, and you have a worthwhile place in it."

The battle lost, tears spilled from beneath her lashes to trickle down her pale cheeks. Her voice broke with the words, "You're wrong, Trace. It's not hard for me to understand at all."

"Carly," he whispered, moved by the depth of her emotions. "I—I didn't realize how much you'd come to care for Danny."

"I do care. And I know all the anguish you're going through at the possibility of living without him." Then, in a barely audible voice she said, "And I can describe in intimate detail the lonely nights and endless days of pain to come if you lose him."

Trace suddenly remembered that Carly had said she knew what it was like to lose someone. Was it possible she had had a child of her own? She must have, Trace decided. *Oh, God, she must have lost a child!* How else could she *know* what he was going through? The haunted look in Carly's eyes, the way she wrapped her arms about her slender waist as if trying to hold herself together, substantiated his suspicion. Watching her, Trace realized she was talking not about him, but about herself.

"Sometimes you wake in the middle of the night and listen...listen," she whispered, "for the sound of his breathing. Even when you know he's gone. And sometimes your arms just...ache because there's no warm, wiggly little boy to hold. Nights are the worst. They're so long. And you feel so...empty. So very empty...." Her voice trailed off, and her eyes closed.

Chapter 6

When she opened them, she was in Trace's arms.

The decision to walk across the floor and take her in his arms hadn't been a conscious one. He couldn't even remember taking the first step. All he knew was that his desire to comfort her surpassed all else.

"Don't cry," he whispered against her temple, helpless in the wake of her tears.

"H-he was s-so little, Trace."

"Your son?" Holding her close, he stroked her hair.

"Y-yes. My s-son, Brian."

At the mention of his name, memories, good and bad, threatened to overwhelm her. With her cheek nestled against Trace's chest and his heart beating a strong, secure rhythm beneath her ear, for the first time in months Carly felt she could share those memories.

"When Brian was three months old my ex-husband, Ken, came to the apartment and begged to see him. Our divorce was ... difficult. Ken's behavior had gone from moody and belligerent to violent. But that day he—he seemed so much like the old Ken, the good Ken, that I . . . He pleaded for me to let him see Brian.''

Carly's fingers clutched the front of Trace's sweater, and she took a deep breath. ''Like a fool, I agreed. While I was heating Brian's formula, Ken . . . Ken took him. He kidnapped my baby.''

''Oh, Carly, Carly,'' Trace said in a rough voice. He hugged her trembling body to his. ''I'm so sorry.''

She lifted her head and looked into his eyes. ''I've looked everywhere, Trace. I've talked to the police, the FBI, anyone who would help. We searched and searched, but they'd vanished. The earth simply swallowed them up. It's been almost a year. So many leads that didn't pan out. So many false hopes. And always someone telling me the odds are against me ever finding Brian. But I-I won't give up looking, Trace. Not ever.''

''I know you won't.''

''And I'll find my son. N-no matter how long it takes. I promised myself if I ever found . . . when I find him, I'm going to make up for all the time we've lost. Nothing, *nothing,* could ever be as important as Brian. I *will* find him.''

''Of course you will.''

Tears glistening in her eyes, she took a deep, shuddering breath, rested her forehead on his chest and whispered, ''Of course I will.''

Trace held her until the river of tears ebbed. Held her until her body ceased to tremble. Held her until he was sure she didn't need to be held anymore.

When she finally pulled away, he reluctantly let her go.

''I'm . . . I'm sorry,'' Carly said, turning away, too embarrassed to meet his gaze. ''I didn't intend to fall apart like that.''

He turned her to face him. "Even brave people deserve to lean on someone once in a while."

"I'm not brave."

"Yes, you are." His fingertip captured a tear clinging desperately to one of her lashes. "You are the bravest person I've ever known. My troubles seem trivial compared to what you've been through."

"Oh, no, Trace." She hurried to assure him. "And you must never give an inch in your fight to win Danny. Never!"

"Believe me, if that thought ever crossed my mind, the last few minutes have driven it right out of my head." He brushed another tear from her cheek, surprised to discover his hand was shaking.

"And you'll win, Trace. I know you will."

"So do I. Now. Just like I know you'll find Brian."

"Yes. I-I have to keep believing that he's somewhere safe, hopefully with people who care about him. Love him."

"Not with your ex-husband?"

Carly shook her head. "Ken died four months ago. That's what brought me to Seattle. I was called to identify his body, but there were no clues to Brian's whereabouts."

"I see," he said, only because saying "I'm sorry" again seemed totally inadequate.

The quiet of the kitchen settled around them, cloaked them in the intimacy they had shared. Carly had never intended to burden Trace with her troubles, but if, in doing so, she had strengthened his resolve, it was worth all the resurrected pain.

"Ken died of a a brain tumor. He'd been sick for months, even before the divorce, but he wouldn't see a doctor. He didn't tell me. He didn't tell anyone. Then he—he lost touch with reality. After he became abusive, shortly before Brian was born, I filed for divorce." Carly sighed. "There was a nasty custody fight."

Emotional fatigue etched her delicate face, and Trace led her to a chair beside the kitchen table. He poured two fresh cups of coffee and set them down. "What about your family, Carly? Or your ex-husband's? Isn't there someone you can depend on for help?"

She took a sip of the steaming brew, then shook her head. "No. Ken's mother had a stroke the year before we married. She's confined to a nursing home in Dallas."

"Is that where you met and fell in love?"

Her gaze darted away. "It's where we met, yes. But I can't honestly say I fell in love with Ken so much as that I fell in love with the idea of marriage and security."

"And you feel guilty about that, don't you?"

The lack of censure in his voice was a balm to her bruised spirit. "Yes," Carly whispered. She swallowed hard. "Perhaps if I had loved him more, if we had been close the way married people are supposed to be close, I would have identified his symptoms as something other than a bad temper and moodiness."

"Carly, you can't blame yourself for not suspecting a brain tumor."

"I'm a nurse, Trace. I should have seen what was happening."

"He was your husband, not a patient."

"You don't understand, Trace. If I had just realized what was happening, I could have stopped it. I could have gotten him to a doctor. If..." The rush of words trickled away. Then she took a deep breath, her fingers clutching the cup like a lifeline. "Because I couldn't, or wouldn't, see what was right in front of my eyes, I lost the most important thing in my life—my son."

Carly pushed the mug of cooling coffee away as if it contained the hateful words and she wanted no more of the bitter contents.

Across the table, Trace saw fresh tears pool in her beautiful blue eyes and wanted more than anything to soothe her, to ease her pain. But how could mere words ever soothe the kind of trauma she had experienced?

He reached across the table and took both her hands in his. "You'll find him, Carly."

"Yes . . . yes. It just takes time. And patience. Sometimes I run way short on that commodity."

"I doubt that very much."

She tried to smile. "Patience is like money. When you've got it, you don't always need it. When you haven't . . . it's a necessity. The hardest part is the endless waiting. Waiting for leads. Waiting to see if they pan out. I've flown to five major cities in the last eight months, and each time I've come away empty-handed." *And more and more disillusioned,* she could have added, but didn't.

"And you've paid a high price," he said, thinking of the emotional cost of five disappointments. Of the sleepless nights and anxious days.

"Money doesn't count for much, except for paving the way to find Brian."

The mental picture of her sleeping in cheap motel rooms and eating take-out food while she waited to find out if her child was dead or alive was heart-wrenching.

"Isn't there a government agency that can help?"

"The National Center for Missing and Exploited Children does a wonderful job of disseminating descriptions and information to state law-enforcement people, but they can only do so much. Most of the searching is left up to parents and NPOs."

"NPOs?"

"Nonprofit organizations. Local groups of searching parents and concerned citizens. A lot of the leads come through a network of groups all across the country."

"And following these leads is expensive."

"Very. Thank God for my nursing degree. Whenever I reach the bottom of my bank account—like now—I work until I've got enough cash in case a lead turns up somewhere."

"How long has Brian been missing?"

"Over nine months."

A little quick addition told Trace that Carly's son would be about...

Danny's age.

He stared at her, recalling the incalculable hours she had spent caring for Danny. The innumerable smiles and endearments, the outpouring of love. Even though he didn't doubt her sincerity, now he wondered if Danny had been a substitute for the son she couldn't hold.

Almost as if she had read his mind, Carly said, "If you're thinking the only reason I devote so much time to Danny is because he reminds me of Brian, you're wrong. Yes, they're the same age. They even have similar coloring, but Danny is wonderfully unique and special. I would never demean him or myself by trying to make him a substitute." This time her mouth effortlessly curved into an unconscious smile. "He had the one qualification guaranteed to make me fall head over heels in love with him—he needed me."

Need. The word reverberated inside Trace's head like notes struck on a kettle drum. One word out of millions, but it demanded personalization. One word that went straight to your gut, to your heart.

"I..." He cleared his throat. "We were lucky you were around."

They lapsed into silence, gazing into each other's eyes.

Carly was the first to speak. "Well...I should go upstairs." She pulled her hands from his and instantly missed their warmth. "Will I see you at the hospital later?"

"Absolutely."

She walked to the door, then stopped. She glanced back over her shoulder. "Trace?"

"Yes."

"Thanks for... well, for lending me your shoulder."

"Anytime." She looked as fragile as a snowflake, and he fought the urge to take her in his arms again. He settled instead for a simple, "Sleep tight, Carly."

A short time later, as she courted sleep, Carly remembered the way Trace had held her and how being in his arms felt like the most natural thing in the world. And how in that brief second when she opened her eyes and realized she was surrounded by his strength, Trace Holden had become very precious to her. He possessed an irresistible tenderness and an endearing vulnerability. No matter how gruff a front he presented to the world, he cared. Genuinely cared. Regardless of the triteness of the expression, he would make some woman a wonderful husband. Some very lucky woman.

Some honest woman, her conscience insisted. *Which leaves you out, doesn't it?*

She hadn't been honest with Trace about substituting Danny for Brian. But how could she express her nagging suspicion that Danny and Brian might be one and the same without sounding demented?

Seated at the oak breakfast table in the carriage house, Trace sipped strong, hot coffee, his thoughts on Carly. Good Lord, how she had suffered! How she must still be suffering, not knowing where her son was, or even if he was alive. Trace thought about Danny. Though newly formed, the bond they shared was powerful, but it couldn't begin to compare with the bond Carly shared with her infant son. Looking back, now he understood why he had felt an instant connection to Carly McShane.

She was on a first-name basis with pain. And only someone so intimately acquainted with pain could have empathized so completely with his loss. Could have touched him
when he thought there was nothing left in his soul but ice
and loneliness.

The ringing of the phone jarred Trace out of his thoughts,
and he hurried into the living room to answer it.

"Trace? Nathan Borell here. I got back into town early,
and my secretary gave me your message. Is there a problem?"

"Maybe. Deirdre and Walker contacted the FAA, trying
to sell the idea that I might have had something to do with
the plane crash."

"I see," Borell said. "Well, your information doesn't
come as a surprise, but fortunately for our case, the FAA
has a great deal of evidence to substantiate the theory of
mechanical failure. So it appears the Andrews' mudslinging efforts will be ineffective."

"But will this mudslinging damage my case?"

"Not severely. But, let's be honest, it won't enhance your
image one bit."

"No way to prove Deirdre and Walker aren't the pillars
of the community they make themselves out to be? What
about a private detective?"

"I've told you, Trace. That sort of thing might swing the
judgment in your favor, or it might backfire on you. And if
you get into a who-fired-the-first-shot situation, a judge
may decide *none* of you are suitable parents, in which case
Danny could become a ward of the state."

Trace's frustrated sigh richocheted off the telephone receiver.

"Otherwise, how are you holding up?" Borell asked.

"Fine."

"I'm glad to hear it. And how is Ms. McShane?"

"She's fine."

"A lovely, intelligent young woman. I was quite impressed. If the relationship is serious, I must say you've chosen wisely."

"No..." Trace said, his thoughts still on Borell's statement about Danny's becoming a ward of the state. "I mean, yes. She's very beautiful."

"A shame the two of you aren't already married. It would certainly improve your chances of winning the custody—"

"What?" A hundred images—Danny in a strange home, Danny frightened and alone, Danny gazing into unfamiliar faces—had paraded through Trace's mind, and he hadn't paid much attention to his attorney's last comment. "What did you say, Nathan?"

"I said... Well, never mind. It's really none of my business, anyway. I'll call you as soon as the case is placed on the court docket. Until then, think positive."

"Yeah. Fine. Thanks." Trace hung up the phone, unable to erase the disturbing images.

Borell had already told him it could be weeks or even months before the case went to court. Months! How could he live for months with the threat of losing Danny hanging over his head? He had to *do* something. Hadn't Matt taught him that success depended on action, not reaction. Automatically, Trace's gaze went to the neat white envelope lying on the coffee table. Matt's letter. He hadn't been able to bring himself to read it until now. Carefully, almost reverently, he opened the envelope, removed the note and started to read.

Trace,
If you're reading this, inevitability showed up sooner than I expected, and you're probably scared right down to your flight boots about the responsibility of being a

parent. Don't be. Just love each other and do the best
you can.

I'm sorry you and I didn't have an opportunity to
discuss this beforehand, but believe me, there was never
any question in our minds about who should raise
Danny if we couldn't. We know you'll keep us alive in
his heart and help him grow to be a fine man.

I counted on you and me sharing our lives until we
were in rocking chairs playing with our grandchildren.
Now I'm asking you to do that for both of us. I love
you.

                                                    Matt

Beneath Matt's signature Jenny had penned a postscript.

Don't stop looking for that good woman. And don't
worry, I know when you find her, she'll love Danny as
much as you do. I love you, too.

                                                    Jenny

His hands trembling, Trace read the letter again, then
gently folded it and returned it to the envelope. He wouldn't
let Matt down. No matter what he had to do, he would never
give Danny up. And if Nathan Borell couldn't offer anything better than "think positive," then maybe it was time
to find another lawyer.

Recalling the attorney's too pat phrase brought other
words to mind.

*A shame the two of you aren't already married. It would
certainly improve your chances of winning....*

An idea so bizarre that Trace's first instinct was to sum-
marily dismiss it out of hand began to take shape in his
mind. An idea too simple to apply to such a complex and
complicated set of problems. Yet the idea took root and
flourished.

Marry Carly.

Wouldn't work, Holden. Whatever makes you think she wouldn't laugh in your face?

Instinctively Trace knew Carly might be shocked, even angry, but she would never laugh. How would she react to such an off-the-wall idea? Hell, he thought, how would he react if he were in her shoes? *I'd think I'd lost my mind,* he decided.

Still, the idea persevered.

He rose from the table, poured himself another cup of coffee, then abandoned the drink a moment later. He began to pace the confines of the tiny kitchen, his mind reeling with what ifs. What if Borell's estimation of how much influence marriage could have on the judge's decision was wrong? What if Carly turned him down cold, without even giving him a chance to explain the obvious advantages in the situation? What if she actually thought he was totally insane and wouldn't have anything more to do with him...or Danny? What if...?

What if you just get a grip on reality, Holden? Trace stopped pacing long enough to cram his hands into his pants pockets, then resumed his pacing. *Forget it. Put the whole, loony idea right out of your head. There has got to be another way.*

What way? He sure as hell didn't have the megabucks to buy his way out. By virtue of his lack of experience he couldn't *prove* he was decent father material any more than he could...could...

Could get the ridiculously absurd idea of marrying Carly McShane out of his head. Followed closely by the thought that if he had to marry, Carly McShane headed the list of candidates.

Ridiculous or not, he had to make some decisions. Now. Trace went to the phone and punched out Nathan Borell's number.

* * *

Carly was dressing for work when a knock sounded at her door. Clothed only in a silky white full slip, she snatched up her ancient but cherished terry-cloth bathrobe and went to answer it.

"Who's there?"

"Trace."

From the other side of the wooden panel his voice sounded strained, uncomfortable. Carly unhooked the chain latch and opened the door. The tension in his voice was negligible compared to the grim set of his jaw and the intensity in his eyes.

"Can I come in?" His hands nervously searched for the security of his pockets. Without waiting for her reply, he stepped inside.

Fear knotted in the pit of her stomach as she closed the door and faced him. She gathered the robe tighter to her body, cinching the belt around her slim waist. "Is...is something wrong? Danny? Has something happened to Danny?"

"No." Trace rushed to calm her fears. "He's fine."

Relief whispered through her body. "Thank God."

"Carly." His eyes were bright, almost feverish, as they gazed into hers.

"Trace, what is it?"

"Are you still willing to help me keep Danny?"

"Of course I am. Whatever you need."

"Then, will you marry me?"

Chapter 7

"M-marry—"

"Marry me. And before you call the hospital and send for two big guys in white coats to haul me away, please give me a chance to explain."

Stunned, Carly watched him walk across the room and stop in front of the fireplace. For several moments he gazed at the toes of his boots, as if they might hold the secret of world peace. Finally he lifted his eyes to hers.

"I know my proposal came out of left field, but believe me, I am not stark raving mad, nor am I drunk."

When she started to speak, he held up a hand to silence her.

"No, wait. I've got to say this before I lose my nerve. When I'm finished you can ask all the questions you want or just tell me to get the hell out." Trace said a quick prayer, took a deep breath and plunged into his hastily rehearsed explanation.

"I'm..." He mentally edited out the word scared, for fear she would think his plan the work of a desperate man—which, of course, it was. "...concerned justice might be blind, or at the very least nearsighted. Then Borell called and said it was a shame you and I weren't already married, because it would increase my chances of winning the custody battle."

"Mr. Borell s-suggested we marry?" she asked incredulously, not at all certain Trace hadn't stumbled across Fitz's secret stash of sherry.

"Yes. No. He just..." Gazing at the confusion in Carly's clear blue eyes, Trace called himself several kinds of a fool for believing she would agree to his unorthodox plan. She deserved moonlight and roses, all the romantic frills. She deserved a man who would love and cherish her, a man who could satisfy all her needs, make all her dreams come true.

Now, hearing his idea spoken aloud, he suddenly realized that his first assessment had been correct—the idea was ludicrous.

"Carly, I...I was wrong. I *must* be stark raving mad."

"Trace, I don't understand—"

"Just forget everything I said." He slashed the air with his hand. "Bad idea. Ridiculous idea. What in the world ever made me think it would work in the first place?" he asked, more of himself than her.

"Trace?"

"And why, in my wildest dreams, did I think you would go along with my harebrained scheme? You don't just knock on someone's door and—"

"Trace?"

His head jerked up. "What?"

"Would you calm down and tell me what's going on?"

IT'S FUN! IT'S FREE!
AND IT COULD MAKE YOU A
MILLIONAIRE

If you've ever played scratch-off lottery tickets, you should be familiar with how our games work. On each of the first four tickets (numbered 1 to 4 in the upper right) there are Pink Metallic Strips to scratch off.

Using a coin, do just that—carefully scratch the PINK strips to reveal how much each ticket could be worth if it is a winning ticket. Tickets could be worth from $10.00 to $1,000,000.00 in lifetime money.

Note, also, that each of your 4 tickets has a unique sweepstakes Lucky Number…and that's 4 chances for a **BIG WIN!**

FREE BOOKS!

At the same time you play your tickets for big prizes, you are invited to play ticket #5 for the chance to get one or more free book(s) from Silhouette. We give away free book(s) to introduce readers to the benefits of the Silhouette Reader Service™.

Accepting the free book(s) places you under no obligation to buy anything! You may keep your free book(s) and return the accompanying statement marked "cancel." But if we don't hear from you, then every month we'll deliver 4 of the newest Silhouette Intimate Moments® novels right to your door. You'll pay the low subscribers-only price of $2.74* each—a savings of 21¢ apiece off the cover price! And there's *no* charge for shipping and handling! You may cancel at any time.

Of course, you may play "THE BIG WIN" without requesting any free book(s) by scratching tickets #1 through #4 only. But remember, that first shipment of one or more books is FREE!

PLUS A FREE GIFT!

One more thing, when you accept the free book(s) on ticket #5 you are also entitled to play ticket #6, which is GOOD FOR A GREAT GIFT! Like the book(s), this gift is totally free and yours to keep as thanks for giving our Reader Service a try!

So scratch off the PINK STRIPS on all your BIG WIN tickets and send for everything today! You've got nothing to lose and everything to gain!

Here are your BIG WIN Game Tickets, worth from $10.00 to $1,000,000.00 each. Scratch off the PINK METALLIC STRIP on each of your Sweepstakes tickets to see what you could win and mail your entry right away. **(SEE OFFICIAL RULES IN BACK OF BOOK FOR DETAILS!)**

This could be your lucky day – GOOD LUCK!

TICKET 1
Scratch PINK METALLIC STRIP to reveal potential value of this ticket if it is a winning ticket. Return all game tickets intact.

LUCKY NUMBER

10 494402

TICKET 2
Scratch PINK METALLIC STRIP to reveal potential value of this ticket if it is a winning ticket. Return all game tickets intact.

LUCKY NUMBER

3A 491245

TICKET 3
Scratch PINK METALLIC STRIP to reveal potential value of this ticket if it is a winning ticket. Return all game tickets intact.

LUCKY NUMBER

9W 502596

TICKET 4
Scratch PINK METALLIC STRIP to reveal potential value of this ticket if it is a winning ticket. Return all game tickets intact.

LUCKY NUMBER

5V 493383

TICKET 5
FREE BOOKS
We're giving away brand new books to selected individuals. Scratch PINK METALLIC STRIP for number of free books you will receive.

AUTHORIZATION CODE

130107-742

TICKET 6
FREE GIFT
We have an outstanding added gift for you if you are accepting our free books. Scratch PINK METALLIC STRIP to reveal gift.

AUTHORIZATION CODE

130107-742

YES! Enter my Lucky Numbers in THE BIG WIN Sweepstakes and when winners are selected, tell me if I've won any prize. If PINK METALLIC STRIP is scratched off on ticket #5, I will also receive one or more FREE Silhouette Intimate Moments® novels along with the FREE GIFT on ticket #6, as explained on the opposite page.

(U-SIL-IM-03/91) 240 CIS ACGY

NAME _____

ADDRESS _____ APT. _____

CITY _____ STATE _____ ZIP _____

Offer limited to one per household and not valid to current Silhouette Intimate Moments® subscribers.
© 1991 HARLEQUIN ENTERPRISES LIMITED.

PRINTED IN U.S.A.

Carefully detach card along dotted lines and mail today! *Play* all your BIG WIN tickets and get everything you're entitled to—including FREE BOOKS and a FREE GIFT!

NO POSTAGE
NECESSARY
IF MAILED
IN THE
UNITED STATES

BUSINESS REPLY MAIL
FIRST CLASS MAIL   PERMIT NO. 717   BUFFALO, NY

POSTAGE WILL BE PAID BY ADDRESSEE

SILHOUETTE READER SERVICE
THE BIG WIN SWEEPSTAKES
3010 WALDEN AVE
PO BOX 1867
BUFFALO NY 14240-9952

"I, uh..." Embarrassed, he glanced away. "I had this bizarre idea that if we got married, it would influence the outcome of the custody suit. You know, two parents are better than one."

"Oh." For just a heartbeat Carly had thought, hoped...what? That he would profess undying love? A twinge of disappointment, keener than she would have thought possible, momentarily pricked her pride. A proposal of marriage was the last thing she expected from Trace, so why the heavyheartedness?

Because she couldn't deny that for just a heartbeat she *had* hoped for something more.

"I told you the idea was bizarre."

"Would it?"

"Would it what?"

"Help you keep Danny?"

"According to Borell, yes."

A string of questions swirled through Carly's head. Not the least of them was why she even *had* questions when reason insisted she was insane to contemplate getting involved in Trace's preposterous plan. Yet she couldn't resist knowing the scope of his plan.

"Wouldn't the Andrews think it strange if you got married out of the blue?"

The fact that she hadn't rejected his proposal out of hand sparked hope. "I'll tell them we really *have* known one another for a long time, and that the accident made us realize just how much we needed each other. Even Deirdre thought we were more than patient and nurse the day you met her."

How clever, Carly thought, before she remembered that the circumstances were less than admirable. She shook her head. "They'll never believe it's for real."

Trace captured her eyes with his. "We could make it believable," he said, remembering their one kiss and her un-

expectedly delicious response. "After all we . . . like each
other." The word "like" barely scratched the surface of his
feelings for Carly, but it was the only word he was prepared
to use. For now.

"Yes," she said, thinking just how much she liked him,
how good being with him felt.

"And we both love Danny."

"Yes." There was no denying she had loved Danny since
the moment he had been rolled into the emergency room.
And maybe even before? a small voice added.

"A lot of married couples start with less." Trace rolled his
broad shoulders in a slow shrug. "How difficult could it
be?"

Difficult enough to break her heart, she thought.

"We, uh, would need to stay together a reasonable time
after the custody suit."

"So we don't arouse Deirdre's and Walker's suspicions."

Trace nodded.

"How long?"

"Probably eight months to a year."

"Y-you'd be willing to live with someone you didn't love
for a whole year?"

Trace looked straight into her eyes. "I'd live with the devil
himself if it helped me keep Danny."

How many times had she entertained similar thoughts if
only such a deal would help her find Brian? Another question came to mind, one of how she should define the term
"living with." Was Trace talking about a real marriage?
And if he was? What then?

"What about . . . I mean . . . we'd actually be married?"

"Of course. Perfectly legal."

"No, I mean . . . *married*. Married as in—"

"Oh, uh, I see. You mean would we be... *living* together?"

"Yes."

"No. That is, we would be living together... but we wouldn't be... sharing a bed."

Her delicate mouth formed the word, Oh, but never gave it voice. Images of her fantasy about just such an experience flashed across her mind. Carly sent the thought packing.

"Carly, are you..." He winged a prayer heavenward. "Are you considering accepting?"

"I don't know."

"There's something else," he said hesitantly.

"What?"

"If... if you decided to..." Struggling for the right words and convinced she deserved something better, he mentally discarded phrases such as, "go through with it" and "agree to this arrangement" in favor of, "... marry me, you'll be able to continue your search for Brian without worrying about the expenses."

"I don't—"

"Please don't misinterpret what I'm about to say. It's just that I know finding Brian is your top priority. I'm not a wealthy man, but I can afford..." His voice trailed off, and he sighed in self-disgust. "I can't believe what I just said. This sounds like I'm offering to pay you in exchange for marrying me." His head dropped forward. "God, I'm sorry."

"I'm not insulted, Trace."

His head snapped up. "You're not?"

She should have been insulted—livid, in fact. But she wasn't. She had never doubted the sincerity of this second offer any more than she'd doubted the sincerity of his first. "But I can't take any money from you."

"And I can't expect you to put your search for Brian on hold for a year any more than I can sit idly by while Deirdre and Walker stack the deck against me. What's the difference between me giving money to one of your NPOs so you can use it and paying a private detective? What matters is using every resource to find your son.

"I know I'm asking a lot, and you have every right to turn me down and forget we ever met. But before you do..." In desperation Trace followed hard-to-resist logic with a surefire point-scorer guaranteed to tip the scales in his favor. "Remember that Danny needs you, and I... I need you, too."

She gazed into his eyes and saw the same fear and vulnerability she had seen the first time she looked into Danny's eyes. Finally she voiced her last question, not so much wanting an absolute answer as reassurance.

"Trace, are you sure this will work?"

"No, but I can't give up Danny." Then he looked her straight in the eye and played his trump card. "Any more than you can give up your search for Brian."

He scored a direct hit. Carly realized that no matter how outrageous Trace's scheme sounded, one thing was for real. His love for Danny.

"Trace, I—"

"Don't give me an answer now, Carly. Promise me you'll think about it."

"I don't know...."

"Promise?"

Carly nodded. "All right," she said softly, knowing she should be telling him no... and meaning it.

"Thank you." His shoulders sagged with relief. "Well, I... guess I'd better go. You'll be there in the morning, won't you?"

"Why?" His offer of marriage had so undone her that she couldn't even remember her schedule.

"I'm checking Danny out tomorrow, remember? Tonight is his last night in the hospital."

"Oh . . . yes," Carly whispered, her heart feeling as if it were being squeezed in a vise. After tomorrow she might never see Trace or Danny again.

Carly didn't remember Trace leaving her room. She didn't even remember walking to work. All she could think about was the fact that in less than twenty-four hours Trace and Danny would be out of her life, and she would be faced with the pain of loss yet again.

Unless she agreed to marry Trace Holden.

Once she was at work, Carly operated on the theory that idle hands were the devil's tools. She kept herself busy, kept her mind clear of thoughts of Trace and Danny, until a minor emergency shortly after midnight brought her face-to-face with a friendly warning in the person of Linc Garrison.

"Wasn't as bad as it looked when they brought him in," he said as they walked out of the emergency room. "Maybe next time that guy decides to wrap himself around a telephone pole, he'll think twice when he looks at that scar on his forehead."

"He was lucky," Carly agreed, her fingers massaging the taut muscles in her neck. "And he had a good doctor."

"Aw, shucks, ma'am. Tweren't nothin'," Linc drawled.

She smiled. "That's what I like in a man. Unaffected modesty."

"Is that Holden's secret for attracting beautiful, soft-hearted nurses?"

Her smile faded at the mention of Trace's name and the reminder of her dilemma.

"Hey," Linc said, watching her brows draw together. "Did I hit a nerve?"

"No."

"You're still a terrible liar, Carly. Now, come on." His arms dropped across her shoulders, and he guided her toward the coffee room. "Tell Uncle Lincoln all about it."

She stopped and looked directly at her friend. "What would Uncle Lincoln think if I told him Trace Holden had asked me to marry him?"

To say Linc was shocked would have qualified as the understatement of the decade. The stunned expression on his face didn't fade for a full ten seconds.

"I'd think you've obviously lost your cotton-pickin' mind."

Carly sighed. "You're probably right."

They were standing just outside the staff lounge door. Linc grabbed her arm and pulled her inside. "You're damn right, I'm right. What the hell is going on?"

"Nothing."

"You call a marriage proposal from a man you've known less than two weeks *nothing?* Pardon me if my middle-class, middle-American upbringing has reared its head, but don't you think that's just a tad off-the-wall?"

"Maybe."

"You're not considering *accepting,* are you?"

"No. I don't think so."

"You don't think—" Fingers beneath her chin tilted her head until Linc could look into her eyes. "Mind starting at the beginning, because I got lost somewhere between 'you're probably right' and 'I don't think so.'"

Over not one but two cups of a hot, thick liquid that could only loosely be described as coffee, Carly related the details of Trace's plan.

"I see" was all Linc said when she had finished.

"Lord, I'm glad somebody does, because I'm so confused I don't know if I'm coming or going."

"Want my opinion?"

"Yes," she said honestly.

"I think marrying Holden would be a big mistake. You don't get married to win custody suits or to have enough money to fly all over the country following leads on Brian."

"The money isn't important—"

"Then why the hell are you even considering saying yes?"

"Who says I am?"

"I do."

"Well, you're wrong. I mean you're right ... about making a mistake." She studied her half-empty mug. "If it wasn't for my attachment to Danny, I would have told him no on the spot."

"Don't use a helpless child to get out of facing the truth."

Carly's head snapped up. "What are you talking about?"

"I'm talking about you not being willing to get on with your life, no matter who it's with. Or, more importantly, who it's *not* with. I'm against this union for a lot of reasons, Carly, but I'm not worried, because you'll never marry again until you can accept one simple fact."

"And that is?"

"You may never find your son. Ever."

Linc's words slashed through her heart, ripping open old wounds, carving new ones.

The fingers of his right hand closed over hers. "Carly, you're a strong woman, but sometimes strength can work against you. I'm not telling you to give up all hope, and I'm certainly not telling you to stop searching. But you live every day in your own little world of guilt, blindly telling yourself that you'll find him today, or tomorrow, or the next day. And with God's help, you might. *Might,* Carly.

"You've exhausted every source, spent every dime and consistently refused to see that you can't put your own life on hold indefinitely. And that's why I know you won't marry Trace Holden or anybody else. Because you're not ready to move on."

Carly stared at him as though he were a stranger. How could he think she would ever stop searching for her baby? *My God, doesn't he know I would give my life to find Brian? How can he be so cruel?* But hadn't she had similar thoughts lately? Hadn't she begun to realize that her life *had* to go on without Brian?

The pain in her eyes was almost Linc's undoing. He had never intended to say so much, but once he had started, the words and feelings rushed out like a flooded river overflowing is banks. And if the truth were known, there was a splash of jealousy in the tumbling waters of his emotions. Trace Holden had accomplished something Linc had been unable to do in all his months of friendship with Carly. Trace's proposal had, however briefly, caused Carly to think about the future. Her future.

"I know I've hurt you, and I'm sorry, but this is something that needed to be said. As painful as it may be, you need closure on that part of your life."

"H-how do I close off a part of my life, Linc?" she asked, her eyes clouding with tears.

"All I know is that in spite of the pain, life goes on. Our only choice is how we live it—with or without love," he said sadly. "You know, there's one other factor in this pseudo-marriage you haven't mentioned."

"What?"

"Trace. You obviously care about him, or you wouldn't be giving his proposal a second thought." When she didn't respond, Linc pressed her for an answer. "Carly? You haven't fallen in love with Trace, have you?"

"I . . . I . . ,"

A nurse stuck her head through the door and announced that another doctor was on the telephone for Linc. The summons effectively ended their conversation.

The rest of Carly's shift was mercifully busy, leaving her little time to dwell on Linc's comments. The only thing she couldn't put out of her mind was saying goodbye to Danny.

Purposefully waiting until the last possible moment, she slipped into the pediatric ward and made her way to his crib. A part of her prayed that he would be awake so she could savor one last heart-melting little smile. Another part prayed that he would be sleeping and leave her the coward's way out.

He was sound asleep. Carly bent over the side of the crib and gave his soft cheek a parting kiss. Five minutes later she stepped out into a gray, rainy morning. As she glanced skyward, tugging up the hood of her raincoat, it was difficult to tell whether the moisture on her face was rain or tears. She knew she was breaking her promise to Trace to be with him when he checked Danny out, but she couldn't bear it. She had to leave.

As Carly walked the three blocks to Fitz's boarding-house, Linc's words, no longer overshadowed by work, played again and again in her mind. At first she denied their validity, deliberately confusing herself to forestall any point of view other than the one she clung to so tenaciously, so righteously. But slowly—and against her will—his words began to stand out from her self-imposed bewilderment with startling clarity.

Sometimes strength can work against you. But willpower had always been her ally. How else could she have survived these long months since Brian's disappearance?

You're not ready to move on. Was she? A few days ago she had been ready to believe Danny might even be Brian.

Even now, she admitted clinging to an infinitesimal tatter of that dashed hope.

Linc had been right about one thing. She had blindly refused to even consider the odds against finding Brian because that might mean giving up. How could she move on, if it meant leaving Brian behind? Linc was right about something else, too. Life does go on.

Had he also been right when he'd asked, *You haven't fallen in love with Trace, have you?* Had she? She ached for his touch. Longed for his kiss. Was that love? He was strong. In his arms she felt safe, secure, less lonely. But she had learned from her marriage that security wasn't a thing or a person, but rather an inner peace. Peaceful was hardly the word she would use to describe her relationship with Trace, yet she couldn't deny the fact that in his arms she felt a sense of belonging, a joy, a rightness, she'd never known. Was that love?

Questions only brought more questions. Why did so many of life's decisions require trade-offs? Because there really is no such thing as a free ride, she answered herself. Because you have to give in order to get. Because life is a series of compromises. Clichéd though the answers might be, Carly had to decide if she had the guts to look forward instead of back.

Halfway home, Carly changed her mind and turned around. She needed to see Trace, needed to ask him one final question.

He was in the pediatric ward. A nurse's aide Carly didn't recognize was dressing Danny in preparation for leaving. When Carly entered, Trace glanced up, a guarded expression on his face.

"Hi."

"Good morning." She deliberately kept her eyes off Danny, but the sound of his happy jabbering tore her heart in two. "Trace, I . . . I need to talk to you."

"Sure." He gave the aide a smile, then turned and followed Carly out into the hall.

"I—I've been thinking about . . . everything, and I—"

At that moment Danny's terrified scream halted all conversation. Both Carly and Trace raced back into the ward.

Danny was hanging over the side of the crib. He was upside down, partially supported by the young and very frightened nurse's aide. His foot, half covered by the cast, was wedged between the rails of the crib. Danny was yelling while the girl tried to calm and extricate him at the same time.

Trace grabbed Danny's head and shoulders and lifted him enough to relieve the downward pull of his stout little body.

"I don't know how it happened," the aide said, on the verge of tears herself. "I was lifting him out of bed, and he twisted in my arms and lunged forward. The next thing I knew, he was caught."

"Hold him still," Carly ordered, her own initial panic-induced rush of adrenaline subsiding. Her fingers worked to free the trapped foot. "Just a bit more.... There. He's out!"

"Oh, thank you. Thank you," the young woman said, reaching for Danny. "I'm so sorry."

But Danny was in no mood for substitutes. Frightened, he wanted immediate and certain comfort. He wanted Carly. Fat teardrops glistening on plump cheeks, he reached out for her.

Carly's heart melted like ice cream in the summer heat. She picked him up. "Shh, shh. Don't cry, sweetheart."

Chubby little arms wrapped around her neck, and he buried his face against her shoulder.

"Is he all right?" Trace asked, stroking the back of Danny's head.

"I think so, but we should get him to X ray just to be sure." She turned to the aide. "Call Dr. Garrison."

"Right away." Shaken and remorseful, the girl hurried from the room.

Trace released a long sigh. "I was so scared. For a minute I thought . . . Lord, I was so scared, I don't know what I thought." Danny had stopped crying, and Trace patted his back as if to reassure himself the child was indeed unharmed. Carly noticed that his hands were trembling.

"Me, too." Danny still clung to her, and Carly thought there was no sweeter burden in the world.

"What's going on here?" Linc asked as he entered the ward several minutes later.

"I think we've had a near miss." Carly described the incident, and after Linc agreed that X rays were in order, they trooped downstairs to the laboratory. Danny refused to be pried out of Carly's arms, so she carried him. After a questionable moment or two she was finally able to hand him over to a technician.

Trace paced while Danny was being X-rayed. "What if he's reinjured his leg?"

"Trace . . ."

"What if they have to do more surgery?"

"Trace . . ."

"What?"

"I really don't think there was any serious damage."

"Honestly?"

"Honestly." She managed a smile, as much for her own benefit as his. There *was* a chance that his questions were valid. If the fall had twisted the cast even slightly, the need for additional surgery would be more than a possibility, it would be a probability.

Displaying more trust than Carly thought she deserved, Trace sat down beside her. He reached over and took her hand.

They waited. Trace squeezed her hand reassuringly. Still they waited. Carly couldn't help but remember the hours she had spent waiting for word about her son. There was no greater torment than waiting for news that a loved one was all right.

And oh, how she loved Danny. The instant his little arms had encircled her neck, nothing could have been more certain in her mind. Just as nothing could be more certain than the fact that sitting beside Trace, holding his hand, was the right thing to do, the right place to be.

"Carly."

She looked into Trace's eyes.

"I'm glad you're here. When I realized you'd left the hospital without waiting for me, I thought . . ."

"I came back."

"Why?"

"I wanted to ask you—"

The side door of the lab opened, and Linc walked out carrying the new X rays, followed closely by the gurney bearing a much happier Danny than the one who had gone in.

Trace and Carly shot off the waiting room bench.

"No new damage," Linc said, smiling. "We'll keep him overnight just to be sure the leg doesn't give us any swelling problems, but basically, he's right as rain."

Trace pulled Carly to him in a jubilant hug. "Thanks, doc."

"Thank you, Linc."

Linc looked from Trace to Carly, saw the way Trace's arm remained long after the hug ended, then replied, "No sweat.

They'll take him back to pediatrics, and you can see him later.''

"Hey, partner," Trace said bending over the by-now-smiling youngster.

Danny responded by repeatedly chattering a newly mastered nonword that sounded like "uh-oh."

As an aide wheeled Danny away down the hall toward the elevator, Trace turned to Carly. "You said you came back to ask me something."

Carly looked at Trace, and whatever question she had intended to ask vanished in the wake of a simple truth. No matter how ironclad a lease Danny held on her heart, Trace was the sole proprietor.

"How...how soon did you want to get married?" she asked, and silently prayed she hadn't just asked for more hurt than she could handle.

Chapter 8

"Carly McShane, if you don't stand still I'm going to draw blood with this needle," Fitz warned, her nimble fingers whipstitching a row of beads back into place along the neckline of Carly's "wedding dress."

The borrowed crepe suit in a soft blue just a shade lighter than Carly's eyes could have come right out of a stylish 1940s romantic movie—and might have, given Fitz's fondness for costumes of that era. Regardless of its origin, the outfit, with its elegant styling and crystal beads at the neck and on the sleeves, looked designer-chic on Carly's slender frame.

"There." Fitz gave the restored beadwork a final pat. "Good as new and looking like a million bucks. I wore a suit just like this one to a USO dance one New Year's Eve in Portland. Let's see, that must have been 1942, no, it was '43, because—"

"Uh, listen, Gran," Bridget interrupted, fearing another one of her grandmother's lengthy reminiscences. "Are you sure Judge Randolph will be here on time? You know how he is—"

"Martin Randolph will be late to his own funeral, but not to this wedding. Besides, I threatened to cancel our regular Wednesday night get-together if he was even a minute late."

Over Fitz's head, the young girl rolled her eyes and mouthed, "Get-together?"

Hands on hips, Fitz turned to her granddaughter. "Shame on you, Bridget. Now you've gone and made me lose the gist of my story."

Bridget grinned innocently. "Sorry, Gran, but I really do think you should check on the good judge."

"Oh, all right. Carly probably doesn't want to hear an old—" Fitz cleared her throat. "A mature woman talking about the past, when the future is so bright and shiny and just a kiss away."

Carly smiled and hoped Fitz's perceptive eyes didn't notice how plastic the smile actually was. Or how much her hands were trembling. Nerves that had already been strained at the weight of her decision to enter this unorthodox marriage were now almost completely frazzled. She clasped her hands together to still their shaking. "You've been wonderful. Both of you. How you've managed to pull the wedding together in only two days, I don't know. I can't thank you enough for offering your home." She glanced down at her beautiful outfit. "Your clothes . . . everything."

"Nonsense, Carly, dear. I wouldn't dream of letting you get married in a sterile old mayor's office."

"City hall, Gran," Bridget corrected. "The same place you go to get a license. Don't you think—"

"And just how is it, my darling granddaughter, that *you* know so much about city halls and marriage licenses?"

"Oh my God," Carly said, hoping to forestall what was sure to be at least a three-rounder between the other two.

"What?" Fitz and Bridget asked in unison.

"I...I...uh." Carly closed her eyes. "I feel a little light-headed."

"Get a fan," Fitz ordered.

"Get some water."

"No, no! Get a damp cloth."

"Get Trace."

"*No!*" Carly's eyes flew open. Good Lord, she was nervous enough already. The last thing she needed at this moment was Trace. "I'm fine. Really," she rushed to assure them.

Fitz laid a wrinkled hand across Carly's brow. "Not a degree of fever." Withdrawing her hand, she stepped back, gave her friend a visual once-over and promptly pronounced her diagnosis. "Wedding-day jitters."

"You're probably right."

"C'mon, Gran. We should get out of here and give Carly a few minutes of privacy."

"Of course. You run along, dear, and I'll be down in a moment." When Bridget had hugged Carly and departed, Fitz turned to the bride-to-be. As if by magic she produced a handkerchief from the sleeve of her dress and handed it to Carly. "You must have this."

Seeing the delicately embroidered *F* in one corner of the lace-trimmed square of fine linen, Carly realized the handkerchief was undoubtedly an heirloom.

"I carried it on my wedding day," Fitz said softly.

"I can't possibly accept such a treasure," Carly protested.

"You can if I say so."

"But, Fitz, you should save this for Bridget—"

"Poppycock." She waved a hand in dismissal. "If it isn't neon and geometric, Bridget thinks it's hopelessly outdated."

"I don't know what to say," Carly whispered, her eyes bright with tears.

"Ohh." Fitz stamped her size-four shoe. "I absolutely, positively, promised myself I wouldn't cry until they played the 'Wedding March,' and look at me." She retrieved the handkerchief, dabbed at her eyes, then handed it back to Carly. "Oh, well, what's a wedding without a few happy tears?"

"Yes." Carly glanced away, afraid Fitz's sharp-eyed gaze would detect that her tears held more than a touch of sadness.

"Be happy, Carly, dear. You're a lucky woman."

"Y-yes, I will." Carly couldn't tell her that luck had very little to do with her marriage to Trace.

"Good Lord have mercy," Fitz said suddenly. "What are we doing standing here when that gorgeous hunk is waiting downstairs with a ring and a judge? At least," she frowned, "Martin had *better* be down in my parlor by now or he'll have hell to pay from me." So stated, she gave the cluster of red curls atop her head a reassuring pat and walked out the door.

Carly turned to retrieve her bouquet of miniature ivory roses and fresh baby's breath. Her gaze fell on Bridget and Fitz's wedding gift. She lifted the exquisite nightgown from its nest of tissue paper. The creation of black silk and lace slithered from Carly's fingers. She grabbed a wisp of smooth fabric and caught the bodice. The rest of the garment tumbled to the floor. What there was of the lacy bodice hung precariously to her fingers by one thin strap. Until this moment she had given little thought to the actuality of living *and* sleeping in the same house as Trace.

Carly remembered Fitz's comment. "Every woman needs to wear such a nightgown, my dear." Fitz had walked to the door, turned and winked. "So she can experience the pleasure of having her lover take it off."

Carly gazed at the gown dangling from her hand. Her trembling hand. *I could never… It wouldn't be… What would Trace think…?* But try as she might, she couldn't shake the image called up by Fitz's parting words. *…the pleasure of having her lover take it off.* But Trace wasn't her lover. And he would never see her in this stunning nightgown.

Then why did an image of a man's hand— Trace's hand— slowly, tantalizingly pushing a thin black silk strap from her bare shoulder cause her skin to flush and her heart to beat faster? And why did her back arch in response as she pictured those same hands gliding softly down to cup her breasts, kneading them with the motion of his fingers, reshaping the nipples…?

Carly jerked herself mentally upright. These flights of fantasy had to stop. Her marriage to Trace was based on… *On what? Trust?* Yes. *On mutual respect?* Unquestionably. *And now we come to the sixty-four-thousand-dollar question: What about love?*

Carly knew Trace didn't love her, but facing the reality didn't make it any easier to live with. *And what happens when this mutually trusting "arrangement" comes to an end?* She tried not to think about the day when she would have to give up Trace and Danny. But once again, reality refused to permit escape.

Her first marriage had been based on fantasy, at least on her part. The fantasy of happily ever after. The dream of security. And the marriage had been a mistake. Well, Carly had learned from her mistake. She was going into this marriage with her eyes wide open. And her heart? *Okay, maybe I'll get hurt. But life is full of hurts. I can't retreat. I must go on.*

Moments later, clutching her wedding bouquet, Carly paused at the doorway to the small parlor. The prerecorded strains of the "Wedding March" filled the air. On the left side of the room stood Linc and Bridget. In the center, in front of the fireplace Fitz and Trace's business partner, Archie, flanked the judge. And on the right stood Trace.

He turned as she entered the room. Carly's breath caught in her throat, and she licked her lips. He was so gorgeous that her knees went weak. Dressed in a navy blue suit, an ivory shirt and a tie, dark blue with ivory pinstripes, Trace Holden was, quite simply, the handsomest man Carly had ever seen.

He moved toward her, took her hand and tucked it into the crook of his arm, and together they stood in front of the judge.

The ceremony was informal and brief. So brief, in fact, that Carly felt she'd scarcely taken a deep breath between the time Judge Randolph said, "Do you, Trace Winslow Holden, take this woman..." and his short personal addition to the regular civil ceremony.

"Will you face each other and repeat after me, in unison, 'I will cherish you for all my life and beyond. For now and forever. All that I have and all that I am is yours.'"

When they finished, Carly's throat ached with the need to cry. Then the judge smiled and said, "You may kiss your bride now, son."

She turned to Trace, not knowing what to expect. A noncommittal peck? A thank-you-very-much smooch? She got neither. To Carly's surprise and supreme delight he lowered his mouth to hers without hesitation. His lips were parted, warm and gentle as he touched her mouth in a tender kiss. Her own lips parted in response, and for a heartbeat she felt the urge to lean into the kiss.

The moment Trace lifted his mouth from hers, they were pulled apart by the well-wishers. The judge pumped Trace's hand warmly, while Fitz proceeded to kiss everybody in the room. Carly heard a cork pop, and a second later someone put a glass of champagne in her hand.

"To Trace and Carly." Judge Randolph raised his glass, and everyone joined in. "May they be blessed with a life filled with happiness and love." The clinking of glasses was followed by happy smiles and best wishes all around.

"Do I get to kiss the bride?"

"Linc," Carly said, turning to embrace him. "I'm so glad you came. The day wouldn't have been complete if you hadn't."

He shrugged off her appreciation. "What the hell, I may not agree with this madness, but I'll be damned if I can miss my best friend's wedding, no matter what the circumstances."

Carly lightly rested her hand on the lapel of his suit jacket and looked into his eyes. "Thanks. That means more to me than I can say."

"You know I only want you to be happy, don't you?"

"I know."

He stared at her for a moment, then smiled. "So, how about that kiss?"

Trace turned away from shaking the judge's hand for the third time to see another man kissing his wife.

It was only a congratulatory kiss, he reminded himself. A long-standing *meaningless* custom. Carly and Linc worked together. They were friends. Good friends. Trace reminded himself that he had no claim on her, at least, not in the way everyone thought. But if that were true, why did he feel such a sweeping wave of possessiveness as he watched their bodies press together? And why did the sight of Linc Garrison's hand caressing the small of Carly's narrow back suddenly make him want to rush across the room and pull them apart? She was *his* wife and no man...

Jolted by the unexpected hot stab of jealousy, Trace quickly downed his champagne. *Don't look and it won't bother you,* his saner self recommended even as he walked toward them. His eyes never left the embracing couple.

Linc disengaged himself and held out his hand. "Congratulations, Trace." He glanced down at Carly, then back at Trace. "Take good care of her or you'll have me to answer to." Without waiting for a response, he joined the others.

Trace's hands sought and found the familiar security of his pockets. "I wish you had asked me before you told Linc about our...marriage."

She glanced up in surprise. "Linc's my oldest friend in Union City. Besides, he pretty much drew his own conclusions about our wedding."

"And he doesn't approve, does he?"

Carly glanced away. "No."

At that moment, Fitz and Archie walked up, arm in arm. "Carly, dear, why didn't you tell me Trace's business partner was such a handsome devil?" The elderly man beside her grinned shyly.

"Better be careful, Fitz," Trace said, gazing over her head at Linc's broad back. "Arch is quite a ladies' man."

Archie blushed scarlet to the roots of his gray hair, but said nothing.

"Don't you think it's about time you two—" Fitz made walking motions with her fingers "—slipped quietly away to some cozy hotel room?"

Carly's head snapped up. "Well, we..." Trace's gaze caught hers, then slid away. "That is—"

"We've decided to wait until Danny is out of his cast before we take a honeymoon," Trace said, as if they had discussed the subject like a normal couple. "We get to bring him home from the hospital tomorrow, so we'll be spending the night in the carriage house."

"What did I tell you?" Fitz whispered to the man at her side. Archie smiled and nodded.

"I think perhaps we should go by the hospital and tuck Danny in." For all eyes and to Carly's astonishment, Trace lifted her hand to his lips and placed a soft kiss in her palm. "Don't you, Angel?" He drew her to him and slipped his arm around her waist.

"Yes." Carly smiled, uncertain how to deal with his unexpected display of affection. She felt less than honest standing next to Trace portraying the picture of happy newlyweds, yet she could hardly pull away without raising eyebrows.

Trace turned to Fitz. "Carly and I want you to know how much we appreciate everything you've done for us. We're extremely grateful." He smiled down into his wife's face, keeping her locked in a loose embrace.

A tear trickled down Fitz's cheek, and she hugged each of them in turn. "I'm so happy." She turned to Archie. "Aren't you happy?"

He nodded, grinning from ear to ear, then shook Trace's hand.

"We're just so happy," Fitz reiterated around a series of sniffles.

Everyone raised their glasses, except Bridget, who had mysteriously disappeared. After one more toast Trace guided Carly toward the door and, with a last handshake from the judge and a hug from Bridget, who suddenly reappeared, they were gone.

"I hope you didn't mind my little white lie," Trace said as they walked toward the carriage house.

"Lie?"

"It's already past Danny's bedtime, but I figured Fitz would have us all crying in our champagne if we stayed much longer."

"Oh, no it's...fine." What now? Carly wondered. Do we play Monopoly or curl up with a good book? What *do* you do on your wedding night when you're not actually married?

"We need to talk," Trace said when they reached the carriage house. He opened the door, reached inside and flicked the light switch. A split second later, Carly's feet left the floor as he swung her up in his arms and stepped inside.

"In case they're watching from the main house." Slowly he relaxed his arm beneath her knees until her feet were again on solid ground. When he turned back to close the door, Carly took a deep steadying breath and tried to calm the pounding of her heart. She hadn't expected him to carry her across the threshold. But the solid warmth of his chest set her pulse racing and her nerves jangling.

If she had been surprised by Trace's action, she was stunned by her first glimpse of the living room. There were flowers and streamers and balloons...everywhere!

"Good Lord," Carly breathed.

Trace walked up behind her. "She must have used a whole tank of helium." A loose balloon drifted past, and Trace batted it toward the ceiling.

"And emptied a florist shop." Neither questioned for a moment that the perpetrator was anyone other than their outrageous, but lovable landlady. "Look at this!" Carly exclaimed, walking through the living room to the kitchen. More flowers. More balloons, this time of shiny Mylar with the words Bride and Groom stenciled in white and decorated with red hearts. Despite the charade she and Trace were playing, Carly was deeply touched by Fitz's overwhelming display of love.

"She outdid herself."

"If this is any indication, what must the rest of the house...?" They looked at each other and, as if by telepathy, turned and headed for the master bedroom.

"I'm almost afraid to see what's inside," Trace said when they reached the room. He pushed open the door.

Carly wasn't sure what she had expected, but after what they had already seen, anything was possible. As frivolous and fun as the front of the house had been, the bedroom was both romantic and sensual.

Candles flickered from a multitude of locations, casting a soft golden glow over the entire room. A bottle of champagne sat chilling beside a basket of fruit tied with an enormous ribbon. The atmosphere was mellow, inviting...and utterly seductive.

Trace glanced at Carly. "This accounts for Bridget's disappearing act."

Staring at the king-size bed, comforter turned back, both pillows sprinkled with rose petals, Carly said softly, "She'd be heartbroken if she knew her efforts were wasted."

"That's what we need to talk about." He closed the door to the bedroom.

"About Bridget and Fitz?" Carly asked, following him into the living room.

"No. About everyone thinking we're married."

"We are."

"Technically, but it's important that the rest of the world thinks we're a normal, happily married couple. All Deirdre and Walker need is a suspicion that this marriage is less than it appears and all of this really will have been wasted effort."

"I see." So, Carly thought, that was the reason he had kissed her hand and held her to his side—playacting to substantiate the charade.

"I didn't actually discuss this aspect of the arrangement originally, and if you're uncomfortable—"

"No."

"No?"

"I'm not. I mean, I understand that we have to look and act like a normal married couple."

"A newly married couple. In love."

"Y-yes."

"Than you won't object if I occasionally kiss you or touch you . . . in public, of course."

"Of course. I don't mind if you don't."

"I don't mind. I mean, what man in his right mind would? You're a beautiful, compassionate woman—"

"I am?"

"You are."

"Oh."

"Any man would be lucky to have you for a wife." When they realized how incongruous his statement sounded, they both laughed.

"Well," Carly said as the laughter subsided, "I guess I'd better get to bed . . . to sleep."

"Yeah."

"Are you an early riser or a sleepyhead?"

"Middle-of-the-road."

Her fingers absently worried the stems of her bouquet. The fragrant cluster of roses and ribbons trembled. Trembled. A good word to describe what her insides were doing. "What does middle-of-the-bed—*road* mean?"

"It means I get up early unless I have a good reason to stay in bed." *Like making love.* Trace cut off the thought just short of adding, "to you."

"Oh." She turned to leave.

"Carly?"

"Yes."

"I uh . . . that is . . . you don't have to go with me to bring Danny home in the morning if you don't want to. I mean, I know it's not often you have the opportunity to sleep late and—"

"I want to go."

"You do?"

"Very much."

He smiled. "Thanks. I, uh, hoped we could go together, then I remembered an errand I have to run beforehand."

"No problem. I'll just meet you in Danny's room."

"Thanks."

There seemed nothing left to say, yet each was reluctant to say a final good-night.

"It was a nice ceremony, don't you think?"

"Lovely. Everything was . . . lovely."

"Fitz and Bridget really went all out."

"They were fantastic. I never could have pulled a wedding together in two days. Everything was just . . . great."

"Yeah, great," Trace said, his hands finding the familiar security of his pockets. "Especially you. I don't even want to think about what might have happened if you hadn't agreed to help me."

Carly stared at him, suddenly wishing she hadn't committed herself to doing what was probably the most foolish thing she had ever done in her life—yet simultaneously happy she had. And all the time she was battling a guilty conscience for not telling Trace that deep in her secret heart she harbored the pitiful hope that Danny might be her son. She should tell him, should admit that, no matter how unreasonable, hope *had* played a part in her decision to marry him.

But when she opened her mouth to speak, the only words that came out were, "You're welcome."

"Good night, Carly."

"Good night, Trace."

Behind her closed bedroom door, Carly leaned against the cool wood and called herself the worst of cowards. And fools, she added moments later as she crawled into the wide bed. King size bed. Lovers-in-a-tangle-size bed. Her fingers glided over the satiny smoothness of the percale pillowcase. What would it be like to wake up next to Trace, to see his handsome face across a pillow the first thing every morning?

Foolishness, Carly warned herself. *Daydreams, fantasies. You have to face reality.* Ah, yes, reality. Reality was lying alone in a bed that was intended to be shared. Reality was wishing for the touch of a man who didn't love you. A couple of great endorsements for reality. Still, Carly couldn't stop thinking about Trace. *What's he doing? Is he as restless as I am?*

Only a wall separated them. Sheetrock, plaster and paint. Mere inches, solid though they might be. But not solid enough to inhibit her imagination. This was her wedding night, no matter how unorthodox. She was entitled to use a little imagination. Like picturing Trace stretched along the full length of the bed, a sheet tangled loosely around his torso. His naked torso. A patch of dark brown hair curled enticingly across his chest, narrowing into a thin line that arrowed downward. Over his flat abdomen. Dipped below his navel and disappeared beneath cotton sheets.

Every inch a woman, Trace thought. He was married to an incredibly sexy woman. Innocently sexy. Was that possible? Could a woman be innocent and sexy at the same time? Carly could. Mouth-watering sweetness and breath-stealing sensuality all packaged in a body designed to set a man's blood afire. And she was in the room right next door.

What's she doing? Is she thinking about me? About us? Together? In that big, wide bed? Good thing he didn't have to answer the same questions, Trace thought, shifting his legs in deference to the throbbing ache in his groin. If the million-dollar question was, "Trace Holden, where would you most like to be at this very moment?" he could give a shockingly expensive answer.

If the next question was, "Trace Holden, how are you going to live with a beautiful, sweet, sexy, caring woman and keep your hands off her?" he was cold busted.

The plan he had first thought so brilliant was losing luster—fast. She was his wife, but she didn't love him. They were married, but he couldn't, shouldn't, touch her....

...Touch him. In her fantasies Carly could touch him to her heart's content. Stroke him. Kiss him...

She licked her lips and buried her face in the pillow.

Not a bad endorsement for fantasy, Carly thought, but she would much rather have the real thing.

Carly woke at first light, thinking about Trace. And Danny. In a few short hours Danny would be out of the hospital and they would become a "family," albeit short-term. And even though she knew the situation was temporary, she couldn't help but wonder what it would be like if the arrangement was permanent. What would a real marriage to Trace be like? *Passionate.* What would it be like to be Danny's mother for real? *Wonderful.* For Carly, a loving marriage and motherhood were more than wonderful. They were the stuff wishes and dreams were made of. While a nagging voice warned if wishes were horses, beggars could ride, she ignored caution, her heart filling with hope. Today was too special to drape with doubts and dark thoughts. Today she was happier than she had been in a long time, and she wanted to demonstrate that happiness, to relish it, if only for a while. She wanted to celebrate. Celebration, Carly thought, a delightful idea forming in her mind.

Trace had expected to find Carly and Danny packed and ready to go when he arrived at the pediatric ward. What he found instead was a party. Balloons, some he recognized as recent decorations from the ceiling of the carriage house and other obviously new and bearing the inflated message Happy Birthday, were tied to every child's bed. A medley of children's songs drifted from a nearby cassette player, and nurses were serving a breakfast of pancakes with party favors on the side. Carly and Danny were smack-dab in the middle of the gaiety.

"We're having a party." She smiled up at Trace.

"So I see. Who's the lucky kid?"

"Danny."

"Danny?"

At the stunned looked on Trace's face, Carly wondered if her impulse had been a mistake. "I, uh, discovered his birthday was the day he was admitted and I thought... Well..." She shrugged. "Why not? And the other kids certainly didn't complain about being included." When he didn't respond she rushed to add, "If you're upset because I didn't ask you—"

"No. I'm not upset." He gazed into her smiling face and for one heart-stopping moment fought a powerful urge to take her in his arms and kiss her. He had completely forgotten Danny's birthday, but Carly had not only gone to the trouble to find out the date, but to make up for his lapse of memory, as well. "I'm ashamed that you had to make up for my mistake."

She took his hand. "Trace, you've lost part of your family, and now you're struggling to hold on to what's left.

Don't blame yourself for Danny's birthday getting lost in the shuffle. Besides," she said honestly, "every little boy deserves a birthday party."

His fingers entwined with hers. "Thanks," he whispered. If ever the title of Angel applied to an earthly being, it applied to Carly.

By noon they had cleaned up after the party, checked Danny out of the hospital and gotten him settled in at the carriage house. Trace had been busy during the two days before the wedding, because Danny's bedroom had been completely furnished, including the double bed for himself. The final touch had been his errand that morning to pick up a lamp, complete with nightlight, for Danny's room. Now, at least to all outward appearance, they were a happy family.

Even though the conditions were slightly cramped, Trace had decided he liked the slower pace of small-town life and that commuting to his business was preferable to living in Seattle. As far as Carly was concerned, the carriage house was a palace compared to the tiny room she had left in Dallas. Trace, on the other hand, was used to the wide-open sky and virtually no boundaries.

When he decided the kitchen wasn't big enough to turn around in, she promptly labeled it compact. When he complained that the soles of his boots became scorched when he propped his feet on the coffee table because the furniture was too close to the fireplace, she called the living room cozy. By the end of the day they both agreed that their best common meeting ground was Danny.

Trace was determined to fulfill the promise he had made to Matt on that snowy mountaintop weeks ago. He intended to be active in every part of Danny's life, down to the smallest detail. All he lacked was experience.

"What's that?" Observing from the doorway to the bathroom that connected their bedrooms, he pointed to a hand towel wrapped around the faucet of the tub.

Holding the wiggly toddler upright in order to prevent the plastic-wrapped cast from getting soaked, Carly shrugged. "My foster mother used to do that when I was a kid. It helps protect a child's head if he accidentally hits the faucet."

"Foster mother?"

She glanced up him. "I grew up in three different foster homes." Danny squealed in delight, splashing in the sudsy water that barely rose two inches in the tub. Carly took advantage of his happy disposition and washed his face and ears.

"I'm sorry, I didn't know."

"It's all right. I had it better than a lot of other kids."

"Any idea who your real parents were?"

"Nope." She lifted Danny out of the tub, stripped the plastic covering from the cast and quickly wrapped the dripping wet youngster in a fluffy towel. "My mother, who didn't want me, left me with an aunt who didn't want me, who decided I was the state's problem and not hers."

Trace stepped inside the bathroom. Stooping until his face was almost level with hers, he said, "No wonder you agreed to marry me."

Her eyes snapped up. He reached out and removed a smidgen of suds from her water-splashed cheek. "Family means as much to you as it does to me."

His hands felt wonderfully warm against her cool, damp skin, and his face was so close she could see flecks of gold in his sherry-colored eyes. "It means everything," she whispered.

They stared at each other, more comfortable with the shared intimacy than either would have thought possible, or cared to admit. Gazing at her, Trace couldn't imagine how anyone could look into those honest, innocent blue eyes and deny her anything, much less abandon her. He silently cursed the mother who had deliberately forfeited the joy of this woman seated cross-legged on a tile floor caring for someone else's child.

Finally pulling her gaze from his, Carly said a little breathlessly, "I'd better get him diapered and dressed."

"I'll do it," Trace offered, scooping Danny into his arms as he rose. By the time Carly collected herself and joined them, Trace had Danny dressed and ready for bed. They each kissed him good-night, then moved quietly out of the room.

"I, uh, I'll just clean up the bathroom, then go to bed," Carly said when they stood in the hall.

"I can handle that." Trace slid his hands into his back pockets. "Besides, I'm not sleepy."

"I don't mind."

"But I do. It's been a long day, and you're used to a different schedule. Go on to bed."

"If you're sure."

He nodded.

"Well, then . . . good night."

"G'night. And Carly . . ."

She paused at the door to her bedroom and glanced back over her shoulder.

"Sweet dreams."

Chapter 9

Carly buried her head deeper in her pillow and inhaled the lingering fragrance of roses as early-morning sunshine peeked through the window of her new bedroom. The first thing she saw on opening her eyes was the beautiful gold band Trace had placed on her finger only two days ago. Yesterday she hadn't taken the time, hadn't allowed herself the time, to actually consider the fact that she was now Trace's wife.

Glancing around the lovely, high-ceilinged bedroom, she thought, it would have been a perfect room for a honeymoon. She couldn't help but remember the uncomfortable moments on their wedding night when they had discovered Fitz and Bridget's wonderfully romantic treatment of the room. Too bad it had been wasted. Carly sighed, resisting the urge to snuggle beneath the comforter's delicious warmth. She stretched, then reluctantly abandoned the bed. Her bare feet had barely touched the floor when she heard

Danny cry. Heedless of the fact that she was still in her nightgown, she rushed into the other room.

With a smiling Danny in his arms, Trace turned when he heard her come into the room. His own fledgling smile faded when he saw Carly standing a few feet away. His gaze dropped from her blue eyes to her nearly bare shoulders to her softly rounded breasts. Lace-covered breasts. Barely covered. Finally to her very short and incredibly sexy nightgown.

Carly wasn't the only one who had responded to Danny's cry without considering their clothes. Trace was clad in nothing but the morning sunshine and a pair of briefs, and the sight of his beautifully muscular body took her breath away.

His chest was wide, strong, impressive, with a dark furring of hair—not too much, just enough—and it tapered to a narrow waist and flat stomach, where a thin line of dark hair disappeared into... Talk about fantasies come to life! She hadn't expected him to be so... The only word she could find on such short, startled notice was *beautiful*. Every inch a beautiful, virile, healthy male.

"Oh, I, uh..." She glanced down at the short pink nightie that barely covered the tops of her thighs.

"Good morning." *She's beautiful. Sleep-mussed and absolutely gorgeous. And her skin... Satin and cream, kissed with dew.* Trace had to force himself not to touch her.

"M-morning." She didn't know whether to turn and run, try to cover herself or act as nonchalant as possible. Nonchalance won, but only as the least embarrassing choice. Having made that decision, she was faced with another, much more difficult choice. How did she look at Trace when she talked to him, yet not *look* at him? How did she keep her gaze from straying to his almost naked body? Carly decided his shoulders would be safe. His broad shoulders.

Broad, smooth, well-muscled shoulders and powerful arms that looked as if they could hold a petite woman.... Her gaze darted to Danny.

"Did we wake you?" Trace asked.

Carly licked dry lips. "No. I... No, I was already awake."

"Oh." He watched her tongue disappear into her oh-so-softly-sexy mouth and felt as if he had received a good swift kick to the gut.

Fitz's wedding night decorating frenzy had extended to the baby's room, and several balloons still bobbed on the ceiling. Danny gleefully squirmed in Trace's arms, reaching for the ribbon attached to one of the balloons. His gaze trained on Carly, Trace seemed not to notice.

"He's probably hungry," Carly said.

"What?"

"He probably wants his breakfast."

Danny chose that moment to make a grab for the ribbon that was floating enticingly close. He almost tumbled out of Trace's arms, but Trace caught him as he lunged forward. The motion jerked the balloon downward and out of the child's grasp. It danced across the room, and Danny burst into tears.

"Oh, don't cry, sweetheart." Carly dashed forward, rose up on tiptoe and reached for the balloon. It evaded her grasp as if it were playing some whimsical game of tag.

"Here, let me." Still holding Danny, Trace came up behind her, stretching his considerably taller frame along her much shorter one.

Carly almost jumped at the touch of hair-roughened skin brushing against her bare legs. His body, the lingering scent of a woodsy fragrance she now identified as uniquely Trace, his totally male *presence*, surrounded her. Body heat—his to hers, hers to his—vaporized into a sensual steam.

"Got it," they said together, both grabbing the ribbon, their bodies only inches apart. Carly's heel touched the floor, and Trace was still directly behind her. Close behind her. Her satin-covered bottom bumped squarely into his cotton-clad front.

"Sorry."

"Excuse me."

She turned, then backed away slowly. "Uh, well...I guess you, uh, have everything under control. So, I'll...you know, go see about breakfast," she stammered, and without a backward glance, left the room.

Trace groaned. Danny mimicked the sound unsuccessfully. "Danny boy," Trace said, touching his forehead to his nephew's, "when you're older, we're gonna have a nice long talk about how best-laid plans land you between a rock and a hard place. A real hard place."

A short time later, a much more composed Trace carried Danny into the kitchen, the rescued balloon loosely attached to a chubby little wrist.

"Something smells wonderful," he said, placing the boy in his high chair and snapping the tray in place.

"Pancakes and link sausages okay with you?"

Trace rubbed his stomach and smiled. "Fine with me. How about you, sport?" he asked Danny, who whooped with joy as his new play toy danced in the air. Trace looked back at Carly. "Can he eat stuff like pancakes?"

"Probably, but I'm making him some oatmeal."

Watching her move around the kitchen, Trace decided that Carly McShane was every bit as efficient with an apron around her waist as she was in nurses' whites. *Holden. Carly Holden,* he reminded himself and promptly decided he liked the sound of it.

Within minutes, Carly set hot pancakes, sizzling sausages, butter, syrup and a pot of coffee on the table.

"Delicious," Trace declared after his first bite.

"Thanks." She smiled with the kind of pleasure that came not from the praise itself but because of the one who offered it.

"By the way, I've made some preliminary inquiries about day-care centers for Danny, but I'd appreciate it if you were with me when I interview them."

"Me?" she asked, scooping another bite of oatmeal into Danny's waiting mouth.

"Of course." He put down his fork and looked at her. "Unless you don't want to go."

"Well, I . . ."

"Carly, I want us to look and act like a real family. I think it's important—"

"Yes, I know. For the custody suit."

He had been about to say he felt it was important for them to spend some time alone, to get to know each other better. Trace sighed. Their arrangement would never work unless they could get past the awkwardness of living together. They might not be lovers, but they could be friends. *Friends? Is that what you want from Carly? Friendship?*

"And for us."

The spoonful of oatmeal she was aiming at Danny's mouth almost missed its target. "We'll never be able to pull this off unless you and I are comfortable with each other. Maybe if we went through the motions of being a normal married couple, we could increase our comfort level, so to speak."

"What do you mean?"

"I mean we should do things together. Go out."

"Out? You mean like a . . . date?" Surprisingly, Carly managed to spoon another bite of oatmeal into Danny.

Trace grinned. "Sounds a little backward, doesn't it?"

She couldn't help but return his smile. "A little."

During the last few tension-filled days he had almost forgotten how wonderful her angelic smile made him feel. Gazing at her now, he wondered how he could ever have forgotten that her smile lit up a room and lightened his heart. "I've missed your smile," he said without thinking.

"My smile?"

"Yeah. Your smile is practically the first thing I remember from when I woke up in the hospital. Warm, sweet . . . just like now."

"I only have one dimple," she said by way of apology, unable to pull her gaze from his face.

"That makes you unique."

"Or lopsided."

"Uh-uh. Definitely unique. I've thought so from the first."

"You have?"

"Uh-huh."

They stared at each other. The atmosphere in the tiny kitchen suddenly constricted intimately. The air was hot, as thick as slow-moving molasses.

Trace wanted to hold her. Wanted to make certain life never dealt her another crushing blow, to guarantee that she would never have cause for anything other than sweet smiles.

And he wanted to kiss her.

The realization was startling, its intensity even more so. He wanted to fit his mouth to hers and tell her in ways he could never find words to express how precious she had become.

Carly could have sworn there was something wrong with her heart. It beat wildly in her chest. The thumping grew louder by the second until it became a banging. . . .

His neglected breakfast clasped between his hands, Danny repeatedly banged the bowl of oatmeal on the plastic tray of his high chair, demanding attention. The noise snapped Carly and Trace out of their mutual trance.

"Oh, no," Carly said, turning to the child, who had obviously decided to feed himself. Wads of oatmeal decorated his hair, face and clothes.

Trace cleared his throat. "Looks like our boy here needs a lesson in table manners," he said, helping her release the plastic tray.

"You're a mess." Carly grinned. Danny laughed out loud and kicked his legs. "This calls for a major cleanup effort."

"With a garden hose," Trace threw in as the two headed in the direction of the bathroom.

"Good as new," Carly said when she returned to the kitchen ten minutes later. "And in his playpen in the living room." She noticed that the breakfast dishes had been rinsed and stacked in the sink, and the countertops had been wiped clean. "You didn't have to do all of..." A sweep of her hand indicated the results of his efforts. "...this."

"Believe me, of the two jobs, I got off light."

"Thanks."

Trace dragged his gaze from her inviting mouth. "Uh, Carly, I was thinking that perhaps you might like to have some of your friends over, since you have some time off. We could maybe have them come for dinner." He had no idea where such a thought had come from, but once voiced, it wasn't totally unappealing.

Carly could have hugged him for the suggestion. During the entire time she had been cleaning up Danny's mealtime mishap, she had been berating herself for taking a whole week off from the hospital. What in heaven's name would she and Trace do—alone together—for days? "I think that's a wonderful idea. Maybe Linc and one of the nurses—"

"Linc?" The idea that their first guest would be Linc Garrison hadn't entered Trace's mind.

"You like him, don't you?" Unreasonably, she half hoped Trace would say no. As soon as she had suggested Linc, she wanted to take it back. Linc was the only other person who knew she and Trace were man and wife in name only. Part of her was relieved she wouldn't have to pretend. Another part wished she could.

"Sure." At least, he had liked the man before he saw him kissing Carly with something other than brotherly affection.

"I'll call him and set it up for tomorrow night, if that's okay with you."

"What? Oh, yeah. Fine," Trace said, trying to erase the mental picture of Linc's hands on his wife's slender back.

Great, Carly thought, wondering how she had single-handedly made an uncomfortable situation more uncomfortable. Now I can be a nervous wreck in front of three people instead of one.

"You're a nervous wreck," Bridget said the following night, watching Carly rearrange a tray of hors d'oeuvres for the second time.

"Give her a break. It's her first dinner party," Fitz advised, sneaking a taste of the cheese dip.

"You'll do great," the younger Fitzpatrick announced. "Everything's under control. Danny is bathed and ready for bed. The steaks are marinating. Salad's in the fridge. Dessert is cooling, your gorgeous hunk of a husband is due back any second with the wine, and Dr. Garrison and his date should be here in a few minutes."

"I'll bet your gorgeous hunk was thrilled." Fitz plopped a tortilla chip in her mouth.

"He didn't seem to mind," Carly responded, searching through the cabinets for cloth napkins.

"Extremely...tolerant if you ask me."

"He passes right by the liquor store on his way home."

"Yes, sir, very trusting."

"What?" Carly asked, standing on her toes in order to reach a wooden salad set.

"Well, it's none of my business if you married one of those liberated men."

Carly glanced around at her landlady. "What *are* you talking about?"

"I'm talking about Trace's attitude toward Linc."

"Linc?" Carly frowned. "How did he get into this conversation?"

"He's been in it from the beginning—"

Bridget held up both her hands. "Hold it, Gran. What does Dr. Garrison have to do with Trace buying wine?"

"Absolutely nothing."

Carly and Bridget exchanged looks. As usual, trying to follow the elder Fitzpatrick's train of thought was like trying to follow the plot in a bowl of alphabet soup.

Fitz looked at them as if they didn't understand plain English. "Don't you think a man is broad-minded when he invites his wife's ex-boyfriend to dinner?"

"Linc was never my boyfriend," Carly stated flatly.

"Only because you wouldn't give him half a chance."

"I still don't understand," Bridget interjected, but she was ignored.

"It wasn't like that. Linc and I have been friends from the beginning."

"Tell it to your liberated husband."

"Tell him what?"

"Now it's beginning to make sense," Bridget said, a wide grin splitting her face.

"Exactly," Fitz said to her granddaughter.

"Trace is jealous," the young woman announced with a shrug and all the satisfaction only a hopeless romantic could generate.

"Jealous?" Carly's voice cracked. "That's absurd."

"Not if you had seen the take-your-hands-off-my-wife-or-I'll-kill-you look he gave the good doctor while he was kissing you the night of your wedding."

As bizarre as it sounded, Carly didn't doubt Fitz's powers of observation. If it happened in her house, Fitz knew about it. Still, her relationship with Trace was... She searched for an appropriate word and, finding none, settled on platonic. Why would he care if an old friend gave her a kiss of congratulations? The answer was simple. Because of appearances. The expression Fitz had seen on Trace's face might have been one of anger, but not for the reason Fitz supposed.

Unable to explain the real reason for Trace's behavior, Carly had no choice but to allow the others to hang on to their assumption.

"Oh, I think that's so sweet," Bridget crooned. "I'd just die to have two guys fighting over me."

"In my nightmares," Fitz retorted.

"They aren't fighting," Carly insisted. "I think you're way off base on this one, Fitz. Besides, Trace has no reason to be jealous of Linc." That much, at least, was the truth.

"Carly, dear," Fitz said, sneaking a last carrot stick, then nudging Bridget out the door, "You may know what makes a hospital night shift run smoothly, but you don't have the faintest idea what makes a man tick. Take it from me. Your husband does battle with the green-eyed monster every time Linc—or probably any other man, for that matter—so much as glances your way. Love makes people a little crazy that way."

Later in the evening, Carly pondered the older woman's words and questioned her own judgment when she noticed that Linc was paying more attention to her than his date. Trace noticed it, too.

Linc's companion, a statuesque nurse's aide named Tanya, obviously considered herself outrageously lucky to be out with the handsome doctor, because she rarely left his side all evening. But that didn't prevent Linc from focusing more than a fair amount of attention on Carly, most in the form of repeating stories and experiences only the two of them shared. As the evening wore on, Carly's patience with her friend grew thin.

"Did you know you've married a trivia buff, Holden?" Linc asked.

"Really."

"Ab-so-tively. Hey, Carly, remember that time we played Trivia Challenge and skunked ol' what's-his-name...?" He snapped his fingers. "That smart-mouthed intern—"

"Franklin," Carly tossed over her shoulder as she walked into the kitchen, wishing Linc would shut up.

"Yeah, Franklin and some girl with the sexiest, most incredibly—" he stretched the word out "—long legs." He glanced at Tanya. "Present company excepted," he said just as Carly returned carrying a serving tray topped with four plates of chocolate cake and a carafe of hot coffee.

"Ah." Linc glanced up. "'She walks in beauty, like the night....' You play any games, Trace?"

That does it, Carly decided. Whatever Linc was up to, and she suspected it was some kind of test to see if Trace was keeping to his part of the arrangement, he could go peddle his double entendres somewhere else.

"Would anyone like coffee and dessert?"

"None for me, thanks." Linc grinned. "I'm driving. One bite and I'd never pass the chocolate Breathalyser. Hey, did you bake that, Carly?"

"Yes."

"Is there anything the woman can't do?" he asked Trace.

"Apparently not."

Carly's eyes snapped up, her first bite of cake suddenly dry in her mouth. Though Trace had said very little during the evening, his body language spoke volumes. Tense volumes. Angry volumes.

Irritated with Linc and unsure of Trace's brooding quiet, Carly decided it was time to call it a night, but Tanya beat her to it.

"Sugar," Tanya crooned. "I think it's time we left."

Linc blinked slowly. "Why?"

She ran her hand over the front of his shirt, toying with a button. "Because."

"Uh-oh. You know what the look means, don't you, Holden?"

When Carly saw Trace's fist clench and unclench, she decided it was time to take matters into her own hands. "It means, doctor, that you've had a pleasant evening and now it's time for you to go."

"Nice to see you, Linc. Here's your hat. What's your hurry?" the doctor said in an overexaggeratedly nasal voice. He looked from Carly to Trace and back to Carly again. "Oh, well. C'mon, Tanya, let's go to my place and play Trivia Challenge."

"I don't know any trivia," she replied as they rose from the sofa.

"Then we'll just play challenge." They giggled.

Carly cringed. She could have sworn she actually saw a muscle jump in Trace's jaw.

"Linc was less than charming tonight," she said later as she collected the empty glasses and carried them to the kitchen. "I apologize. I don't know what got into him."

"I do," Trace said, barely three steps behind her. "The man is jealous."

"Jealous?" Carly flipped open the dishwasher and began removing the dishes she'd washed earlier. "That's ridiculous." Strange, she thought, that that word should come up twice in one day. And she couldn't see either occasion as valid.

"Is it? He practically followed you around like a puppy all night, making a fool of himself over everything you did. 'You're a marvel, Carly,'" Trace mimicked Linc's earlier words. "'Florence Nightingale, blushing bride, gourmet cook—every man's dream woman.'"

"You object to a man paying me compliments?"

"No." *Yes, damn it, but I don't have the right.* "I just don't like the way he went about it." Trace picked up a stack of clean plates and set them in the cabinet so hard that Carly was afraid they wouldn't survive the impact.

"Oh?" Unaware that Trace's temper had reached its limit, she didn't retreat from the brewing confrontation.

Dragging his hands to his jean-clad hips, he looked her straight in the eye. "What do you mean, 'oh'? You deserve something better than that—" he waved a hand in the direction of the front door "—drivel."

"I thought some of his compliments were rather sweet."

"You would."

"And I suppose you could do better?"

"In my sleep."

"And just what sort of *drivel* would you use?"

"For one thing, I wouldn't just tell you that you were beautiful. It's corny and boring. I'd mention that your hair was soft, silky and smelled like morning sunshine on a perfect spring day. And that your skin was soft enough to make every man within a hundred miles crave to touch it.''

With each word his voice softened and his anger dissolved into something much more volatile, much more dangerous. "I would...make sure you knew every day how desirable you are. How you've got the kind of sweetness a man looks for all his life and fears he'll never find. How every time..."

Involuntarily her lips parted.

"...I'm in the same room with you, I want..." His voice trailed off, and he swallowed hard.

Just walk away. You've said too much. And for God's sake, don't touch her. Trace stared into her wide blue eyes and felt himself drowning, felt himself being pulled under by some force he couldn't name and couldn't deny. His hands closed around her upper arms and pulled her to him. He had to kiss her.

He was going to kiss her. The realization sent Carly's heart plummeting against her chest. A wild heartbeat later, his lips touched her.

She half expected the kiss to be as hard as his anger and was half disappointed it wasn't. Instead his mouth moved slowly, enticingly against hers in a seductive demand that was infinitely more powerful. And when his tongue teased the seam of her lips, Carly eagerly obeyed, opening her mouth, wantonly, wantingly.

Trace moaned into her mouth. She tasted of chocolate and a sweet, wild need. He deepened the kiss. His tongue met hers, curled against it, then plunged deep, sending streamers of heat coiling through her body.

Somewhere in the back of his mind Trace tried to convince himself that the kiss was a result merely of male/female need and not the soul-to-soul kind. Need was costly.

Need was dangerous. But his mind couldn't deny what his body so blatantly demonstrated. He wanted Carly.

Somewhere in the back of her mind, Carly told herself that this had been bound to happen sooner or later, and that it meant nothing in the grand scheme of things. But she knew she was lying to herself. Knew the kiss meant more than it should. More than her heart could handle.

Worse yet was the realization that she had made an unforgivable and, she feared, irrevocable mistake and fallen desperately, hopelessly, head over heels in love with the man she had married.

Chapter 10

They both tried to pretend the kiss had never happened. And failed. Miserably. They settled into a kind of truce that neither knew how to end.

Carly returned to work, grateful that her time with Trace was limited to brief breakfasts and hastily shared dinners and only a few scattered compromising situations, like the afternoon when she walked in on him changing clothes.

Carly gasped when she heard the rasp of a zipper. His back to her, obviously unaware of her presence, Trace proceeded to tuck a freshly starched shirt inside his jeans. Mesmerized, Carly watched as strong hands—hands she remembered kneading her shoulders while his mouth did wickedly wonderful things—poked cotton shirttails into well-worn denim. The zipper rasped again in the otherwise quiet room, followed by the clink of a metal belt buckle.

After years of nursing, shirttails, belt buckles and brief glimpses of snowy white underwear were nothing new. What in the world had gotten into her, Carly wondered, acting like she had never been in the same room with a man while he dressed? Staring like a high school freshman at her first sneak peak inside the boys' locker room? But try as she might, she couldn't forget the incident any more than she could forget the morning she had come home from work and tiptoed into Danny's room while Trace was showering.

Bent over the crib, she had whispered a soft "good morning" to the sleepy-eyed baby, so enthralled with Danny's smile that she hadn't heard the running water stop. A second later the bathroom door swung open, and a shaft of light streaked across the floor. Steam billowed into the bedroom. Unwilling to dash for escape for fear of discovery, Carly retreated into a corner. Once again, Trace seemed unaware he was being watched.

And Carly was definitely watching. Standing in the darkened room, free to look her fill, she stared. And admired. Admired the way the towel, knotted just below his navel, hugged his trim hips and thighs. And the way the muscles in his shoulders—gorgeous shoulders—literally rippled as he towel-dried his hair. Or the way he checked his shadowy beard in the mirror, his long fingers tilting his chin toward the light. His water-darkened head moved from side to side, and Carly held her breath for fear of discovery. He whipped the towel from his hips, turned to replace it on the rack... and presented Carly with a heart-stopping view of his sleek, bare body from shoulder to heel.

Sleek was the operative word. Man sleek. Carly held her breath. No words, no expression, regardless of how superlative, could adequately describe the sheer male beauty she beheld. Only through force of will was she able to command her feet to move, to carry her out of the room before he turned back and saw her watching him. Had he done so, there could have been no mistaking the look in her eyes for anything other than sheer, unadulterated desire.

Back in her room, her heart drumming in her ears, Carly thanked her lucky stars for a narrow escape. Eyes closed, she couldn't get the picture of Trace out of her mind. Trace, bare and beautiful. Trace, in all his male glory. Only now imagination overrode reality, and in her fantasy he whisked the towel from his body and turned to face her.

She stepped from the shadows.

He came toward her. Slowly. Provocatively. Boldly. And reached for the buttons on her white uniform. First one. Then another. And another. Until the shirtwaist-style dress was open enough for her to step free. She shed the dress and what was under it along with her inhibitions. At last they were flesh to flesh. Desire to desire. Male to female. Hardness to softness . . .

Fantasies, Carly finally decided, were neither friend or foe. She simply gave up fighting them where Trace was concerned.

But reality, evidenced in two separate incidents a week apart, convinced her that their "arrangement" was wreaking havoc on hers, Trace's *and* Danny's life.

On the third Saturday of their marriage, Carly made a round of calls to Dallas and several child finding agencies when she came home from the hospital. As usual, the results were negative. Depressed, she decided to take a nap, so she could spend the rest of her day with Danny. She woke to the unnatural sound of quiet. Why was the house so still? Danny was usually awake at this time of day and in an active play mode. She listened, but still no sound. Where was Trace? Perhaps they had gone for a walk, or out to run an errand. She slipped out of bed, threw on her robe and wandered into the living room.

Trace was sound asleep on the couch, one leg hanging over the sofa's edge, the other on the cushions, one arm flung over the back, the other wrapped around . . . Danny!

Wide awake and playing with a pencil he had obviously taken from his dozing uncle.

"Danny!"

Trace woke with a start, instinctively tightening his hold on his couch mate. "What?"

"Trace, you fell asleep." The censure in her voice brought him instantly alert.

"Is he all right?"

Danny gurgled, his newest attempt at communication.

"No thanks to you."

If Trace had had any doubts as to her temper, the horrified expression on her face dismissed them.

"Do you have any idea what could have happened while you were getting your beauty sleep?"

"I—"

"For your information, this baby may not be able to walk, but he can sure as hell crawl. Even with his cast. He could have crawled into the kitchen and pulled open a drawer, or into the bathroom and found Lord knows what kind of dangerous things. Or he could have gone—" her face went deathly white "—outside!"

In the space of a heartbeat her voice went from screech to broken whisper. Tears filled her eyes. "He's so little, and there are so many terrible things.... You wouldn't *ever* be able to forgive yourself if anything..."

With Danny locked securely between his forearm and his chest, Trace shot off the sofa and took her in his arms. "God, Carly, I'm sorry. We were playing and...I had no idea I was so tired. That's no excuse, but I... Angel, I'm so...so sorry." His lips brushed her temple in sweet apology.

The danger past, Carly relaxed, desperate anger seeping from her body. "I-I over r-reacted." She nestled her head on his shoulder and knew the first peace she had felt in a week. "It's just that I know what can happen and—"

"Don't," he begged. "Don't, Angel. I was thoughtless, and it will never, *never* happen again."

At the insistent pat of a small hand on her damp cheek, Carly opened her eyes and looked up at the third and seemingly least affected party in the drama. Danny, happily displaying his newly acquired teeth, leaned down, reaching for Carly to take him. She did so gladly, placing a somewhat wet kiss on his tousled blond head. Danny immediately reversed his decision, holding out his arms to Trace, clearly saying, "Da-da-da-da-da."

Carly's sniffles quickly became happy gasps. "Did you hear that?"

Now it was Trace's turn to fight tears. "Yeah. Think that means I'm forgiven?"

Carly's fingertips grazed Danny's cheek, then came to rest on the spot directly over Trace's heart. "I think that means you're a lucky man."

Gazing into her eyes, he suddenly realized the truth in her words. He *was* lucky. Lucky to be alive. Lucky to love Carly.

And he did love her.

Trace waited for a bolt of lightning or for the earth to move. It didn't. He waited to be overwhelmed by some mystical, magical spell of the sort chronicled by poets. Instead, what overwhelmed him was an intensely quiet moment of joy so sweet, so deep-in-his-soul perfect, that there were no words powerful or poetic enough to describe it. It was simply the most perfect, right moment in his life.

"Carly, I . . ."

"What?" she asked, gifting him with her angel's smile.

On the verge of declaring his feelings, Trace was suddenly uncertain. Not of himself, but of her. Was it possible that he could be the luckiest man in the world? Because he would be, if Carly loved him back. But he wasn't ready to flight-test his newly discovered emotions. Not yet.

"Thanks for caring enough to worry…about both of us."

"You're both very important to me."

"Are we?"

"Very," she said softly. So softly only her heart knew how much.

The following Saturday, Carly came home bone tired and hours late from no less than three emergencies that had extended her shift for what felt like forever. Her back ached, her feet hurt and her head was pounding as if it contained a platoon of jackhammer operators. Trace was bent over some business papers, and Danny was seated at the edge of the living room rug, stacking plastic blocks. Quietly, so as not to disturb Trace, she slid into an easy chair, closed her eyes and relaxed for the first time in hours.

Moments later she realized the muted sound of block hitting block had ceased. She looked around and discovered that Danny had managed to drag himself over to a small table. Atop the table was an antique chess set that had once belonged to Fitz's late husband.

"No!" Carly yelled, just as Danny grasped one of the chess pieces and crammed it into his mouth. Nerves frayed from fatigue and in the throes of easily activated parental fear mixed with anger, she dashed across the room, snatched the carved wooden knight from Danny's fingers, then spanked his hand. His pouting bottom lip quivered as his face crumpled and he gave way to a full-fledged wail.

"What the hell?" Trace was beside them in a flash.

"I—I…" Carly stared down at her offending hand as if it belonged to someone else. Some evil person.

Trace scooped the squalling child into his arms. "What happened? Did he fall or something?"

"I . . . I spanked him." She still couldn't believe she had actually struck the child she held so dear. "He had the chess piece and—"

"In his mouth?"

"Yes."

"Could he have swallowed it?"

"Probably."

"Then he needed to learn he couldn't have it," Trace said simply.

"But—"

"Don't worry about it, Carly. He'll survive. Look." Trace chucked Danny under the chin and received a grin for his trouble. "See, he's already forgotten all about it, haven't you, sport?"

Carly released a tortured breath. "I won't. How could I have done such a thing?"

"Such a thing," Trace said, placing a pacified Danny in his playpen, "is a natural reaction. Don't be so hard on yourself, Angel."

He came up behind her, pushed her hands aside and began to massage the tense muscles in her neck. Her head lolled back against his shoulder. "Hmmm, that feels wonderful." His hands kneaded her shoulders, upper arms and all the way down to her fingers. She loved the comforting feel of his strong, sure hands. And she loved the way he called her Angel, a name he used more and more frequently. More and more naturally.

"Bad day?"

"Night shift from hell."

He laughed, his breath tickling her ear. "You're wearing yourself out. A full shift at the hospital, then spending mornings with Danny and me. Not that we're complaining." *Especially me,* he thought. He treasured their mornings together, but he had noticed that Carly extended the time to the point of robbing herself of much-needed sleep. "But I'm afraid you're doing too much."

"Uh-uh," she murmured, reveling in the magic of his hands. Reveling in the delicious sensations that told her his magic had extended to other areas of her body. Secret places. Aching places.

"I'm going to take you to bed."

The exquisite lethargy dissolved into hard reality. Carly turned in his loose embrace and stared up at him. "What?"

"I'm marching you straight into the bedroom and personally tucking you in."

"Oh," she replied, slightly embarrassed by the note of disappointment in her voice. Did Trace hear it, too?

"Then . . ." he said as he made good on his promise and guided her toward the bedroom, "I'm going to take you on a nice long drive and feed you a nice, relaxing dinner."

"What about Danny?"

"I'll seduce Fitz or Bridget into baby-sitting."

Coming from his lips, the word "seduce" suddenly caused all her secret, aching places to tingle. "But—"

"No buts." He pushed open the bedroom door and ushered her inside. "I don't want to hear your sweet voice or see your smiling face for at least eight hours."

In almost exactly that amount of time Carly was awakened by a knock at her door. "Carly?"

She tossed back the covers and slid her legs over the edge of the bed. "Come in," she answered sleepily.

"Hey, lazybones, rise and—" Trace stopped dead in his tracks two steps over the threshold. The sight of Carly, blond bangs teasing her eyes, soft skin rose warm from sleep, and the well-remembered pink nightie riding at the top of her thighs, stopped his breath, as well. Lord, he thought, how much is a man supposed to take?

It took every last sliver of control he possessed not to walk across the room, push her back onto the wide bed and kiss her until they were both senseless. To take her in his arms and tell her how much he loved her. Wanted her. Again he hesitated. *You're a coward, Holden. Tell her.* He wanted to. Oh, Lord, how he wanted to. *And what if she doesn't feel the same way? What if friends is all you can ever be?* He didn't want her friendship. He wanted her. Loving him. Letting him love her. In all the ways that count for a man and a woman.

Trace remembered thinking once that she deserved moonlight and roses. All the romantic frills. And she was going to have them. He was going to give them to her. What did they say in historical romance novels? Woo. He was going to woo her. Beginning tonight.

"I, uh, wanted to wake you...." *Now and every morning.* "Uh, I thought I'd better wake you up."

"Hmm." She brushed her hange back. "Thanks."

Her voice sounded the way she looked, soft and warm and seductive.

"Are we..." He cleared his throat. "Do we still have a dinner date?"

Carly blinked, as if only now realizing that Trace was standing in her doorway. Glancing down at her bare legs, she quickly flipped a corner of the sheet across her lower body. The top half of her, however, was still exposed. How ridiculous would she look if she jerked the sheet up to her collarbone? *Outrageously ridiculous. Just stay calm. He's not here to claim his conjugal rights.* Although the idea did have its merits.

"Dinner. Uh, yes."

"Good." He tried not to look at the enticing swell of her breasts above the whisper of pink lace. "Well, uh, how long will it take you to get ready?"

"Not long." *How can I think with you standing there looking so...*

"Good."

Oh, yeah. Definitely good. "Can you wait half an hour?"

"Half an hour is perfect."

"Okay."

"Fine."

They stared at each other until it was obvious that one of them had to do something or they would both be in danger of taking root. Trace was the first to give in. "See you in a half hour." He wondered if Carly noticed that his hand shook as he closed the door.

They drove up the coast to a cozy, out-of-the-way inn that offered delicious seafood and a dance band Fitz would have killed to hear play Glenn Miller tunes. After a scrumptious meal, they drove back, content to carry the mellow mood home with them.

Neither of them mentioned the fact that Trace had been in her bedroom earlier. Or that she had been only partially clothed at the time. Or that, for a few moments, the atmosphere in the bedroom had become disturbingly intimate. Neither of them mentioned any of those things, but they thought about them—constantly.

At the carriage house, Trace thanked Bridget and overruled her objections at being paid for baby-sitting while Carly went to check on Danny. *Just like an ordinary married couple,* he thought, waiting for her. He was about to congratulate himself on achieving one of the original goals of the arrangement when he realized their relationship *looked* natural because it *felt* natural.

"Sleeping like a baby," Carly announced on her return.

Trace smiled, and she wondered if he knew how handsome he was when he smiled. How incredibly handsome. "I had a lovely evening, Trace."

"So did I. Feeling better?" He was feeling great. Nervous, but great.

"Absolutely. I didn't realize how tense I was until tonight."

"You give a lot to your job," he said, discarding his sports jacket and settling himself on the sofa. *Talk to her, Holden. Don't let her leave. Woo her, remember?*

"Yes. But it gives me a lot in return. I can't imagine not being a nurse."

Trace nodded. "That's how I feel about flying." He didn't want the evening to end. He didn't want her to go to bed and leave him alone. He had an overwhelming need to be part of her life in a way no one else could. A need to be close to her.

Carly had every intention of going straight to her room. But intentions, good or bad, don't always follow their original course. Perhaps it was the mellow, intimate mood that had pervaded the evening. Perhaps it was the husky sensuality in his voice that changed her mind. Whatever the reason, suddenly the idea of being alone in her room—no, the idea of being apart from Trace—was unacceptable. She walked to the sofa and sat beside him.

"Did you always want to be a pilot?" Strange, Carly thought. Their pasts had brought them together, in a way, yet they never discussed that part of their lives. She had spoken of Brian only briefly. And he had talked about his brother and the crash only in terms that related to Danny, not himself.

"Ever since my brother told me straighten up or he would personally kick my..." He looked at her and smiled, slowly, sadly. "Since Matt made me clean up my act."

Carly remembered him telling her about the trouble during his teens when they were in the lawyer's office. "When you were a teenager?"

"Yeah. When our folks died I went . . . crazy. Wild and crazy. I found a new group of friends. Misfits, like myself, who just didn't give a damn. Got busted a couple of times. You know, driving while intoxicated, drunk and disorderly, but the charges were dropped. Then some of my friends decided to rob a convenience store. I didn't actually participate, but I was hauled in along with everybody else. My grandparents did their best, but I was too much for them." He hung his head. "I gave them a lot of grief."

"But that's all you had."

His gaze lifted to hers.

"Grief must have been the strongest, most powerful thing in your life. You were trying desperately to isolate yourself from the pain of losing the two people you loved most, and at the same time you were angry at them for leaving you."

"Everything changed when Matt came home from the navy." He turned to face her. "He talked to me, Carly. Nobody had really talked to me about what I felt, what I wanted."

"You mean after your parents died."

"Even before then." He ran his fingers through his hair. "Don't get me wrong. My mother and father were great. But I always felt . . . separate from them. Not alienated, just separate. They loved Matt and me, and they were proud of us, but they shared something that was uniquely theirs. So strong and so deep that everyone else was excluded." He sighed. "Matt was the only one who really *talked* to me."

"What about his wife?"

"Jenny was—" a grin, warm and wide split his face "—sensational. If Matt wasn't around for me to talk to,

Jenny was. I wish you could have met them," he said, his voice soft with remembering.

"So do I."

He leaned back until his head rested on the back of the sofa. "Tell me about Brian."

The out-of-the-blue request took her by surprise. "W-why do you want to know about Brian?"

"Because I just told you more about my past than I've told anyone. Because it's your turn." *Because I don't want you to walk into that bedroom without me.* "And..." He took a deep breath then admitted the truth. "Because I need to know what's important to you."

"My son is important to me." *And so are you. And Danny. More important than I ever realized could be possible.*

"Does it bother you to talk about him?"

"No. As a matter of fact, it helps," she said, absently fingering the hemline of her soft knit dress. "Somewhere along the line I got the idea that the more people who knew about him, the better chance I had of getting him back."

"Makes sense."

"I only wish it also made progress. There hasn't been one single new lead since Ken died."

"Nothing?"

"Not even a whisper."

"You stay in constant contact with the authorities in Dallas?"

"Of course. The police did everything they could when Ken first kidnapped Brian, but after time passed..." She shrugged hopelessly. "Brian is only one of hundreds of kids just like him in the Dallas metroplex and thousands nationwide."

"But the FBI is involved, aren't they?"

"Yes. And no. All the information concerning Brian's case has been entered into the FBI's National Crime Information computer in Washington, D.C."

"And they're searching."

"No. They don't actively search for missing children. Sad to say, but in this country a stolen car has a better chance of being returned than a stolen child."

Although her voice was devoid of bitterness, Trace clearly sensed her anger and frustration. "But if the FBI isn't looking and the local authorities only have limited time and resources to devote to the case, then who the bloody hell is out there looking for all those kids?"

Taking a deep, calming breath, Trace suddenly realized his own anger and frustration were but pale shades of the blackness Carly had lived with for a year. He was mad. Mad that her child—that any child—could be snatched from his loved ones without having it deemed a national emergency.

The touch of her hand on his surprised them both. Trace glanced down and discovered that her fingers were covering hands doubled into fists. She hadn't made a conscious decision to touch him, it had just...happened. And now that it had, she was glad. Touching him seemed right.

"There *is* help, but it's not always easy to find," she said, understanding the surge of emotion evident in his face and body language. "Unfortunately, not all states have clearing houses that offer information, so it's difficult to bring all of the limited resources to bear at one time. That's why less than five percent of missing children are ever found."

Trace was stunned. "That's..." Words like absurd, asinine, not to mention several very colorful expletives that came to mind, seemed totally inadequate to express his indignation.

"I know," Carly said. "If you start to think about it in terms of numbers and percentages, you'll go crazy. So I don't."

"God, I had no idea it was so complicated."

"Sometimes. Others times it's as simple as someone recognizing a child from a photograph on a milk carton or one of the fliers that get sent through the mail. Or an officer stopping an ordinary traffic violator, only to discover the computer shows an outstanding warrant for kidnapping or a custody violation."

"Is that how you found out your ex-husband was in Seattle?"

She shook her head. "The King County coroner's office found identification on Ken's body. The Seattle police turned up the warrant for his arrest and called the Dallas police, and they notified me. Of course I flew out immediately, but there was no sign of Brian."

Trace stared at her, awed in the face of the courage this delicate woman beside him evidenced on a daily basis. The hand beneath hers relaxed. His fingers meshed with hers. "Calling you the bravest person I know was a gross understatement on my part."

"God doesn't give any of us faith or courage in extra quantities, just enough for one day at a time." Carly sighed, her eyes misty with regret and hope. "Some days I have to scrape and dig for every last ounce. Some days when the phone rings I'm terrified, wondering if it might be good news or bad. Because no matter how hard I pray or how often I tell myself not to give up, there's always the possibility that Brian might be . . . that it'll be too late. . . ."

Trace's heart broke along with her voice. Gently, he pulled her into his arms.

Any thoughts of protest died on the winds of Carly's need. She needed him to hold her. Touch her. Love her.

Trace held her to him, lightly caressing her shoulder. She felt so good in his arms. Who was he kidding? She felt better than good. She felt right. So right that comforting took a left turn toward desire. *Easy, Holden. You may be married to the warm bundle of femininity in your arms, but don't let that go to your head.*

His head wasn't the problem. His body, on the other hand, was reacting to her femininity in a totally masculine way. What kind of a jerk pours his guts out to a woman, then tries to make a move on her? he asked himself. *Does the name Trace Holden ring a bell?* What he was thinking—that she fit next to his body perfectly, and that the words "perfect fit" sparked all sorts of sensual images—was bad enough. But what he was feeling, or, more accurately, wanting to feel—like his hands caressing her warm, bare skin, touching her without the restrictions of clothes or time—was dangerous. He should send her to bed. Alone.

Carly lifted her head and looked into his eyes.

Trace stopped thinking, concentrated on feeling and threw "should" out the window.

He kissed her the way he wanted to. The way he had been dying to kiss her for weeks.

Hot.

Hard.

Deep.

His tongue took possession of her mouth. Staked an irrefutable claim, boldly declared sole ownership. Her mouth belonged to him, and he took full advantage. His tongue plunged again and again. Sweeter, deeper with each erotic stroke.

Carly wanted the kiss to go on forever. Her hands splayed across his chest, she leaned closer, closer. Wanting more, more. And he was eager to accommodate, eager to please, eager to arouse. Her body responded unconditionally, uncontrollably. And while his tongue did wicked, wonderful things to her mouth, his hands caressed, courted her body, each touch an invitation.

Suddenly fighting for the control he was perilously close to losing, Trace dragged his mouth from hers. "Carly, Carly," he whispered against that mouth. "Stop me before I can't stop myself."

"Trace?" she breathed, dazed by this kiss, by her own response.

His finger against the softly swollen mouth he had just kissed and longed to kiss again silenced her. "You're not sure what's happening."

She nodded slowly. His finger coasted over her still-wet lips; then his hand slipped around to loosely cage her neck. "Neither am I. A little scary, isn't it?"

She nodded again.

"But good?"

"Yes " She finally found her voice.

"Very good?"

"Yes."

"I think so, too." His thumbs gently caressed the skin just behind her ears. She closed her eyes and luxuriated in his touch. "Carly?"

"Yes?" she whispered.

"Has it been a long time since you've... I mean, has there been anyone in your life since—"

She opened her eyes. "No."

He was delighted and worried. Delighted to learn there had been no one else, and worried because it meant his promise to woo her might take longer than he had anticipated. Gently he rested his forehead against hers. "I think we should...call it a night." His breath was moist and fragrant against her cheek.

"Y-you're probably right." What was right was the feel of his lips on hers and her body next to his. And while a part of her wanted his mouth again and again and again, until there was no beginning or end, another part instinctively knew this was not the right moment for them.

He rose from the sofa and pulled her up along with him, but he didn't release her immediately. He didn't kiss her again; he simply held her close, their bodies pressed together, locked in a gentle embrace. After what seemed like hours Carly reluctantly stepped out of his arms. Equally reluctantly, he let her go.

Chapter 11

Their married life was a series of compromises. Trace craved World War II air-combat movies, while Carly adored classic love stories. They compromised by buying a VCR and their own copy of *Top Gun*. Carly enjoyed a good book by a sunny window. Trace was exhilarated by all-day hikes in the mountains. They compromised by spending Sunday afternoons in the park with Danny. Trace loved flying and Carly was feet-on-the-ground certain she was terrified of anything higher than the second floor. They compromised with a hot-air balloon ride. And they learned to laugh with, and at, each other in a hundred delightful ways. Husband-and-wife ways. Ways that said they trusted and cared.

As far as their physical relationship was concerned, that, too, was a compromise. By tacit agreement they did their best to ignore, or at least avoid, the ever-present sensual undercurrent. Compromises being what they are, success was limited.

Trace vowed not to allow passion to overrule better judgment in his plan to win Carly. She promised herself not to allow her traitorous body to become the instrument of a broken heart. And her body was unpardonably traitorous. As surely as night followed day, desire sprang anew each time their bodies accidentally touched, and Carly knew a broken heart was just a matter of time. And her heart would break. It would shatter beyond repair if she allowed him to make love to her knowing he didn't love her. As the holiday and the first month of their marriage drew near, Carly wondered if she would survive to the end of their "arrangement."

Thanksgiving Day was unexpectedly sunny. Carly, Trace and Danny had been invited to the main house for a traditional Fitzpatrick, honest-to-God, Norman Rockwell-painting-imitation, Thanksgiving feast. A couple of Fitz's bridge buddies joined them, and Bridget brought along a young German exchange student. Linc came alone.

For a few tense moments Carly was afraid that Trace and Linc might be uncomfortable in each other's company. But Trace snuffed any such fear when he met Linc in the hall and shook his hand warmly, welcomingly. Carly watched as a silent understanding passed between two of the three most important men in her life, and her eyes misted with happy tears.

The day was all Fitz had promised and more. They laughed and ate. They regaled each other with stories of past holidays and ate some more. They were, for a short time, a big, robust, happy family giving thanks for all of life's joys. Carly thrilled to the warmth and joy of a table heaped with food and a house filled with warmth and laughter. If contentment had a fragrance, it was the aroma of butter-basted turkey and hot rolls. *This is what happiness feels like,* Carly thought. She wanted to hug the day to her and never let go.

Hours and incalculable football games later, a weary, but wonderfully contented threesome made their way back to the carriage house. Late-afternoon sunshine slanted through the trees, scattering patterns of light across their path. Danny, his little tummy still bulging from mashed potatoes and pumpkin pie, slept soundly in Trace's arms.

"I may never eat again." Carly sighed as she hung her lightweight jacket in the vestibule. Trace nodded in agreement and wordlessly took Danny off to bed.

Carly collapsed onto the sofa, closed her eyes and wiggled into cushiony comfort.

"Move over," Trace ordered moments later.

"Did you remember to tuck his teddy bear in with him?" she asked lazily.

"Two stuffed bodies properly tucked," he reported as he settled beside her and closed his eyes.

"In his fuzzy blanket?"

"Done." His hand found hers, and their fingers interlocked.

"Night-light on?"

"Hmm."

"Did you—"

"Yes, Mother. I did everything I'm supposed to. Just like you taught me." He turned his head and opened one eye. "Worrywart."

"Killjoy. Don't you know we nurses get our kicks worrying about people we love?" The word just slipped out, and Carly held her breath, waiting to see if Trace noticed, if he would ask, *What people? How many? What are their names?* Trace and Danny, she supplied silently. When he made no comment, relief whispered through her body.

Both eyes now open, fingers still entwined, he raised her hand to his lips and kissed each knuckle, the back of her hand, her wrist. "In case I haven't mentioned it, you're doing a marvelous job with Danny. And impressing me right out of my socks while you're at it."

She opened slumberous eyes and glanced at his boots. "Liar."

He laughed, his breath warm and moist against her skin. "I'm serious. You have a full-time demanding career and still manage good quality time with him."

"You help."

"Yeah, sure. I do a couple of loads of laundry, occasionally shop for groceries. Big deal. You do most of the work."

She turned her head and looked at him as if he couldn't possibly be serious. "You're great with Danny. You dress him, feed him, cart him to and from the day-care center. All while I'm snoozing away."

"A woman's got to have her beauty rest." He nibbled on the pad of her thumb. "Not that you need it."

The day had been too warmly wonderful, too hand-in-hand intimate. Too... seductive in the most subtle of ways. All the talk of holidays, family and mothers was too much. Now, sated and sequestered, only a heartbeat apart, intimacy once again settled around them like soft summer rain settles to the earth.

"You're good for my ego."

She had never been this close, this free to touch his face. Or this eager. Lightly, hesitantly, Carly touched his cheek and stroked his surprisingly soft stubble with the back of her hand. Back and forth, back and forth. She couldn't get enough of the bristly texture against her skin. Her fingers skimmed over his cheekbone, traced his brow, then impatiently submerged in the thick mahogany waves of his hair. Gently she massaged his scalp. Her hands surfaced, slipped to the back of his neck and repeated the massage.

A sound that was half sigh, half moan escaped Trace's parted lips.

Her investigative finger coasted over the sensitive outer rim of his ear. Along his jaw. Over. Up. Down. Until her fingertip touched his lower lip. Skimmed across its fullness. Then slipped inside.

Trace sucked in his breath, as a white-hot heat filled his sex.

Immediately she withdrew her finger and would have ceased touching him altogether if he hadn't captured her wrist.

"You know what you're doing, Carly?"

"Touching you."

He swallowed hard. "You know what you're doing . . . to me?"

"My touching . . . bothers you?"

He brought her hand to his lips, and his greedy tongue licked her index finger. Carly's blood pell-melled through her veins in a wild rush. Her heart double-timed, and the juncture between her thighs grew hot, moist and sweetly swollen.

"Does that bother *you?*"

"Yes," she admitted breathlessly, shamelessly.

His hand released her wrist to glide up her arm to her neck. His thumb worried the smooth line of her jaw, and with just the slightest pressure, he tilted her head backward.

"A lot?" His mouth delivered moist kisses to her earlobe. Her throat.

"Yes. Oh, yes." She lolled her head back, arching her neck in delicious submission.

"You taste—" he nibbled at her ear "—so . . . good." When his seductive tongue probed her lips, then penetrated, Carly's body liquified into molten desire. "Sweet . . ." He nipped at her bottom lip. "God, Carly, you're sweet." The last syllable was lost in another to-die-for kiss.

His tongue teased, swirling over and around hers. Coaxing. Demanding. Mating. Again and again. Finally, gasping for air, his mouth abandoned hers. But only briefly. Then, slowly, deliberately, his tongue flicked the corner of her mouth. Teased. Tormented. Then began a wanton track of kisses starting at her chin and moving downward. By the time he reached the sweet hollow at the base of her throat, the first two buttons of her blouse were undone. He pushed aside the fabric. His fingers slipped beneath the peek-a-boo lace trim of her bra to smooth, warm flesh.

Heat burst inside Carly, enough heat to rival a thousand suns. His fingertip found and caressed one rosy nipple until it pearled into hardness. "Oh . . . oh, Trace. Trace."

"That's it, Angel. Let it happen. Let us happen." In less than half a heartbeat the tip of his rapier tongue skimmed up her neck and back into her mouth. Her waiting, wanting, wet mouth. Moaning, she sucked his tongue deep inside. Desire sang through her body. Every passion-laden nerve ending jangled . . . jangled . . .

The jangling of the telephone finally penetrated the sensual fog surrounding them. "Damn!" Trace swore. Two seconds later it stopped. Trace's mouth was halfway to hers when it started again.

"We'd better answer it," Carly murmured.

Reluctantly Trace disentangled himself from their heated embrace, stamped across the room and snatched the receiver from its cradle.

"Hello?" he snarled. "Yes, she is. Just a moment." He placed his hand over the receiver and said in a calmer voice, "It's for you. A Detective Fowler from San Diego."

"Oh my God!" Carly shot off the sofa and raced across the room, heedless of her gaping blouse. But when she reached Trace, reached for the phone, she hesitated as though she was afraid to even touch the receiver. A cold, hard knot formed in the pit of her stomach.

"Carly? Is this guy someone you know? If he's not, then I'll—"

"No!" She grasped the phone but didn't immediately put it to her ear. "He's...he's..." *Oh, God, please, please don't let this be bad news.* "I've talked with him before. He handles missing-children cases..." Her voice trailed off as she lifted the receiver to speak into it.

Trace saw the wild mixture of fear and hope in her eyes. Saw her dig deep inside herself and draw a measure of courage. He reached for her hand, held it tightly. And prayed.

"H-hello, Detective Fowler?" Carly tried to swallow the lump in her throat. "Fine, thanks."

Trace watched as her tongue made a futile pass to moisten dry lips. Lips that, only moments ago, had been parted in passion. Lips he would give his life to see smile at the very moment.

"No. I...I haven't found him." Her gaze swung to Trace's.

I need you. Don't leave me, her blue eyes begged.

Never, his gaze assured her.

Trace couldn't hear the other end of the conversation, but he didn't have to. Tears, enough for a lifetime but not enough to wash away the pain, filled her eyes. Fear, the dark primeval, ugly fear he had come to know too well recently, twisted and clawed at his insides like a demon escaping from hell.

"Yes," Carly whispered to the caller. "I understand. No guarantees. I don't know. Can you hold on?" She held the receiver loosely caged in her hand. "Trace, I—"

"Tell him we'll be on the next plane out."

A single tear, then another and another, trickled down her cheeks. "There's no hurry."

Trace rescued the phone seconds before it slipped from her grasp.

Transfixed, Carly walked toward the fireplace, only vaguely aware of Trace introducing himself, agreeing to a meeting time. A time to view... Her mind shut down tight, refusing to finish the thought.

Trace walked up behind her but didn't touch her. He was afraid to touch her. Afraid his touch might destroy what little control she was fighting so bravely to retain. At the same time he couldn't *not* touch her. Nothing in his life, not even losing Matt and Jenny, had prepared him for the raw, naked, soul-ripping pain he had witnessed in her eyes. He wanted to comfort her, love her, wipe away the anguish, more than he wanted his next breath. He wanted, but couldn't have. He longed to tell her that he loved her, would always love her, but he was afraid she would perceive his declaration as pity.

Now was not the time to ask for love. It was the time to give it.

"Do... do you need to pack... or something?"

She shook her head.

"I told Fowler we could probably get a flight out in the morning." This was killing him. *But better me than someone less gentle, less caring.*

Her shoulders quivered ever so slightly, then went still and straightened. A fleeting memory of something Carly had once told him streaked across his mind. *God doesn't give any of us faith or courage in extra quantities, just enough for one day at a time.* She turned to face him.

God must have been working a double shift.

Somewhere, somehow, Carly had found the extra portion of courage she so desperately needed to face the ordeal ahead. Hope, faint as a distant star, shimmered in her eyes.

"They're . . . not sure. . . ."

"I know."

"I need to call the hospital. No, wait." She clasped her hands together. Trembling hands. Fragile, beautiful hands. "I'm off because of the holiday."

"Carly?"

"If I get an early flight and come back late—"

"We."

"What?"

"If *we* take an early flight. I'm going with you."

"But . . . but what about Danny?"

"I'm sure Fitz will be glad to watch him."

"What if she can't?"

"Then Bridget."

"What if—"

"Damn it, Carly. If I have to hire a nanny—ten nannies—and fly them to Union City myself, I'm . . . going . . . with you."

"T-Trace." His name was a broken plea. A fragmented entreaty. One he couldn't deny. He gathered her in his arms.

The dam broke, spilling tears and need, desperate need. Carly sobbed against his shoulder, then scooted closer and pressed her face into the warmth of his throat.

Trace held her for long minutes. Minutes that felt like days, weeks. What did it matter? He held her until she cried herself out, until her body went limp from exhaustion. Then he carried her unresisting form into the bedroom, one-handedly flipped back the covers and lowered her to the bed as if she were gossamer.

"Don't," she whispered when he started to leave. "I don't want to be . . . alone."

"You won't be." He brushed the forever-stubborn bangs from her eyes. "Try to sleep." *You're going to need all your strength. And all of mine.*

She sighed, snuggling closer. "Can't."

"Then rest, Angel. I'm not going anywhere."

"Rest," she murmured into his shirt, her moist breath finally sliding into the rhythm of sleep.

"Yes, my love. Rest."

Carly opened tear-swollen eyes to a day as bleak as her heart. Dismal. An insistent rain beat against her window. An insistent pain beat against her heart.

She was alone. Still muzzy from too little sleep and too many tears, she faintly remembered Trace carrying her into the bedroom; after that, everything faded to gray. Glancing at the sheets and the indented pillow, she laid her head where his had been and breathed the haunting woodsy scent she loved so. He *had* slept with her. More accurately, she had slept with him. In his arms. All night? Faint snatches of memory came tumbling back. At one point during the night she had whimpered and reached out for him, and instantly his arms had tightened around her. Later, when dream induced restlessness began, his hands had caressed gently. *He stayed with me,* she thought, reaching for the only joy she could claim. *All night.*

"Morning."

Carly looked up to see the object of her thoughts standing in her doorway. He had never looked so good or so welcome.

"Good morning."

"How do you feel?"

"Rested." *Then rest, Angel. . . . Yes, my love. Rest.* Had Trace said those words? Or had she dreamed them?

"I, uh, made some reservations."

Suddenly the events of last night rushed in like a spring flood. Carly's throat constricted, and she fought back tears. "What time do I— do we leave?"

"Eleven forty-two."

"What time is it now?"

"Seven-eighteen."

Hours and hours before she would know for sure. Long, tortured, endless hours before she would have to . . .

More tears threatened. "I need a shower," she said hastily, throwing back the covers.

"I just finished, but there's still plenty of hot water left. By the way, I've already taken Danny over to Fitz."

For the first time she noticed he was shirtless. And damp, his hair curling against his neck like a lover's caress. Another time she might have been uncomfortable with his half-dressed state, but not today. Today she needed him any way he came.

Heedless of his presence, she padded to the bathroom. "Thanks."

By the time Carly had showered, applied fresh make-up and dressed, she felt better. Still shaky, but better. However, nothing in her cosmetic bag of tricks could conceal the ravages of her emotional night.

"Coffee?" Still bare-chested, he handed her a steaming cup as she entered the kitchen.

"Thanks."

"Hungry?" Carly glanced at the barely touched bowl of cereal on the counter and realized his appetite was no better than hers. She shook her head. "You should eat something," he said, offering advice he had obviously ignored.

"Trace, are you sure you want to—"

"Yes."

"But it may not be . . ."

"Easy? No, it isn't easy. That's why I'll be there with you."

Carly lifted her eyes to his. To a shadow of not-too-distant pain. *Isn't easy.* Present tense. He had already been through the horror she was facing.

"Oh, Trace, I can't ask you to do this. Not after what you've already been through."

The heartrending tenderness of his warm gaze didn't ease her conscience a whit. "You're not asking." He quoted her own words. "I'm volunteering." *My heart. My soul. Everything I am.*

"But—"

"I'm going." He took her hand, leaned over and kissed her gently on the mouth. "And that's final."

He was on the verge of a return trip to her lips when the phone rang. Carly almost jumped out of her skin.

Trace squeezed her hand. "I'll get it."

Carly waited, nerves frayed to the breaking point.

"Hello? Oh, Detective Fowler."

Carly swung around, eyes wide.

"Yes, as a matter of fact we're holding tickets for the eleven—are you sure? You're absolutely certain?" A smile broke across Trace's face. "No mistake? I mean, you won't call back later and—yes. Yes! Of course I'll tell her. And thank you, Detective, thank you!"

Carly was almost afraid to ask, afraid to hope.

"It wasn't Brian," Trace said as if he couldn't believe such wonderful news. "It wasn't Brian!" He scooped Carly into his arms and swung her around crazily. She threw her arms around his neck and hung on for dear life.

"Are you sure? Oh, God, please don't let this be a dream," she breathed, afraid to believe.

"Yes."

"There's no mistake?"

"No. No. No! Fowler said they turned up a positive identification. A new piece of evidence proved conclusively that it couldn't possibly be Brian!"

"Oh, Trace. It's too good to be true."

"Detective Fowler said to tell you he was extremely sorry for putting you through hell, but until the lab results came in sometime in the wee hours this morning, they still thought there was a possibility you'd have to make the trip." His grin went almost from ear to ear. "But you don't."

He kissed her hard on the mouth. "Oh, God, I'm so glad." He kissed her forehead. Rocked her in his arms. "So glad."

Tears coursed down Carly's face. Tears of relief. Tears of happiness. Tears of pure unadulterated joy. At the same time her heart cried for the grieving loved ones who were not so lucky. She said a quick and heartfelt prayer for God's peace and grace.

Trace swung her around again. "Let's celebrate."

"Celebrate?" She swiped at her tear-stained face.

"Yeah. I'm so damn happy, I feel like it's Christmas already. That's it. Let's go Christmas shopping."

"On the day after Thanksgiving? Have you lost your mind?"

"Why? Are the stores closed?"

Carly clapped a hand over her mouth to keep from laughing. "Not hardly," she said against her fingers. Totally astonished that she had gone from heartache to rapture in such a short time, she stared at Trace.

Breathing hard from the excitement, he dragged a hand to his hip and stared back. "What?"

"I feel . . . good."

He tweaked her nose. "You feel great!"

"I feel so good, I should feel guilty. Only a few moments ago I came so close to . . ."

Trace hauled her into his arms again. His hands roamed her back, caressing, soothing. "Don't think about it anymore."

"I'm so glad you were here. Always before, I've . . . been alone."

Her gave her a quick squeeze, then drew back and looked into her eyes. "You won't ever have to go through *anything* like this by yourself again." His lips brushed hers. "Ever," he said against her mouth. "I'll always be with you. Always."

Carly's head was spinning from so much joy and happiness, her heart filled with so much new hope, that she almost didn't hear him. Had he said always?

Trace cupped her face in his hands. "Ah, Carly, Carly. Do you have any idea how precious you are? How much I need you?"

"No," she murmured.

"Until you came into my life, I was afraid to need. And now I'm afraid to lose. Afraid to lose you. We started out together for all the wrong reasons and wound up so right. I love you, Carly. And if you don't love me back, I can wait. Just give us a chance."

She couldn't believe her ears. Trace loved her!

He lifted her hand from his face and kissed the center of her palm. "Carly McShane Holden, I . . . love . . . you," he said slowly. Clearly. Forever-after clearly. Till-death-do-us-part clearly.

Trace waited.

"This wasn't supposed to happen," Carly whispered, her moment of joy cut short by the fact that she knew she hadn't been completely truthful. She didn't deserve his love.

"Well, it did."

She wanted to tell him how much she loved him, but at the same time she wondered if he would even want to hear the words once he knew the truth. "Trace, I—"

"All I want is a chance to make our marriage real, Carly. A chance to be happy."

Was there a chance for happiness so long as she kept her secret suspicions? Her heart's desire, at least one of them, was within reach. Trace loved her. But did she dare accept that love under false pretenses? Her head said be careful. Her heart said go for it.

He deserved to be happy. "You deserve—"

"You. That's all I want, and I'll take you any way I can get you, because we're right together. I know it. I feel it."

"Yes," she said unable to resist the truth, unable to resist her own emotions. *Please, Lord, let me be doing the right thing,* Carly prayed. The one honesty she could afford was showing him how much she loved him.

"Will you do something for me?" she asked after long, torturous minutes.

His heart sank. "Anything." *Anything but stop loving you. Anything but stop hoping you'll love me.*

"Wait right here?"

Trace stared at her, his heart breaking. "Carly—"

"Just five minutes. Promise?"

He nodded, and she turned and fled the room.

Trace raked both hands through his hair. What the hell had he done, scaring her to death with his declaration of love? Was she trying to let him down easy? If she didn't love him, why didn't she just say so and he could take his battered pride—

"Trace."

He whipped around. His breath hit the back of his throat, then left his body in a slow hiss.

Carly stood in the bedroom doorway, framed by pale morning light. He couldn't see her face, but he didn't need to. Wearing nothing but the love shining in her eyes and the sexiest black nightgown he'd ever seen, she held out her hand.

"Come here," she said softly, seductively.

When he stepped toward her, Trace knew her heart answered his.

Even though it was broad daylight, candles flickered from a dozen locations around the bedroom. The covers of the king-size bed had been turned back. And rose petals were strewn across both pillows.

"There's no champagne," she said apologetically.

"I—It's . . . Why?" he finally managed.

"Because I love you," she said, compelled to tell the truth no matter what the consequences. "I love you."

Chapter 12

He was supposed to do something. Like move toward her. Like take her in his arms...something! But he couldn't move, couldn't find the right words to express the joy welling up from his soul. He could only stare at the beautiful woman who had just spoken the three most important words in this lifetime or the next.

"Why...?" he finally managed to say. "Why...?"

"Do I love you?"

"Why did you wait so long to tell me?"

"Because I..." Her heart ached to tell him everything, but she couldn't. "I thought you only wanted me."

"I do." He came toward her. "I want you every way a man can want a woman. In his bed. In his life. In his heart."

"Yes. I want you like that."

"Do you, Angel?" His knuckle grazed her cheek.

"Yes," she breathed, turning her head so that her lips brushed against his fingertips.

"And I—" his hand slid to the back of her head and urged her closer "—want—" his lips touched hers, tenderly, tentatively "—you." Then he fastened his mouth to hers in a deep, demanding kiss that left no doubt as to just how much he wanted her.

She stepped into the circle of his embrace, slipped her arms over his bare shoulders and around his neck.

The instant their bodies touched, Trace crushed her to him. His mouth slanted across hers, hungrily. His hands cupped her sweetly rounded buttocks, and he ground himself into her. She returned the kiss with equal hunger, her body straining against his, eager for him, eager for more of what he could give her.

Trace forced himself to gentle the scorching kiss for fear neither of them would last past the next second. But, sweet heaven, she tasted so good! Felt so good! Her full breasts were flattened against his naked chest, and the only barrier between her hot flesh and his was a mere whisper of black lace. Without completely breaking contact, he eased her away so that only the tips of her lace-covered breasts teased his bare skin. His tongue played naughty games along the curve of her lips, and he rubbed his chest back and forth, tormenting her until her nipples tightened and she moaned.

"Trace, Trace…" His name dissolved into another moan.

"Look at you," he said, continuing the exquisite torture. "Just look at you," he whispered, glancing down. "Look at how you respond. I love that. Your nipples feel so… Carly, you're driving me crazy." He kissed her again, his restless tongue seeking, finding, mating. This time, when his mouth finally left hers, his lips traced a trail of hot kisses to her soft, warm shoulder.

Slowly, deliberately, he eased a finger beneath one narrow strap and pushed it over her creamy skin. The strap glided down, black lace sliding in its wake, revealing the top of one rose-scented breast. He stepped back just far enough to trace a path along the strap, over lace as dark as his desire. He didn't removed the remaining strap. Instead he toyed with the satiny ribbon of fabric, gliding his finger over the smooth edge so his skin touched cool satin and desire-warm skin at the same time.

Carly's breath fragmented in her chest, and a lazy heat spread through her body from the spot where he touched her to the spot where she wanted him to touch her. The spot where she needed to be touched, filled, claimed as his. Her lips parted in anticipation of another mind-stealing kiss.

But he didn't kiss her. Instead, his hand still on her shoulder, he walked slowly around her. Denim slid around silk, desire rubbed desire, until he stood directly behind her. For heart-stopping seconds she waited for him to touch her, to bring their bodies back into burning contact. Finally he pushed the remaining strap down. Black lace shimmered over her satiny breasts, skimmed her smooth, flat tummy to cascade to the floor. She stepped from the silken folds, casting the garment aside. And waited.

He reestablished contact in one, quick, sure motion and brought her body flush with his, hair-roughened bare chest to smooth bare back. Faded denim to warm, willing skin. One hand skimmed down and took possession of a breast; the other slipped farther down to gently cup her soft woman's heat and destroy her very sanity.

He pressed himself to her, holding her body captive between his hand and his body's hard arousal. "Feel me. Feel how much I want you." His mouth took liberties with the nape of her neck, and he rotated his hips against her buttocks at the same time that his fingers investigated her moist femininity. Carly thought she would die from the pleasure. "Feel how much you want me."

She raised her arm around his neck and tried to bring him closer.

"Not yet," he whispered.

"Trace," she begged.

His hand kneaded the tender flesh of her breast, while his thumb moved over and around her tight nipple, gently pulling, reshaping, until the pleasure-pain stroking was almost more than she could bear. At the same time, she couldn't live without it. She whimpered, her hips moving in an ageless response.

"God, what a sweet sound." His tongue traced a hot trail across her shoulder. "Do it again." She complied as his finger delved deeper into her hot, slick center. "Again." She did. His fingers stroked her like lightning. "And again." He didn't need to ask anymore because she was incapable of doing anything but whimper, as she moved her hips to the sensual beat he commanded.

"That's it . . . yes . . . Oh, that's it, Angel. Move. Get closer." She tried, but it still wasn't close enough. "This is how I want you. This is how I'm going to take you. Hot, wet and deep. I'm going to fill you, love you, until we're both too weak to breathe."

"Yes, yes," Carly gasped, her body sheened with moisture as desire curled through her, swirling into the white-hot whirlpool of sensation he was creating within her. He stroked her to the point of madness. Sweet madness. Blessed madness.

Suddenly, as if he knew she was teetering on the edge of insanity, he released her. Carly's entire body went limp; the only thing preventing her from crumpling to the floor was Trace's arm around her waist as he guided her toward the bed.

Cool cotton caressed her back as he eased her onto the pillows. She heard the rustle of cloth over skin and knew he was now as naked as she was.

A second later her already-burning body became a million degrees hotter as he lowered his head and took one pebbled nipple in his warm wet mouth. Carly cried out her pleasure.

"Tell me what you want," he said.

"You."

"Before that. Do you want slow..." While he kissed her breast, his hand fanned across her belly, caressing. "Or fast..." His teeth nipped her hard nipple, and his hand again found her velvet heat.

"You" was all she could say. All she could feel was the inferno raging out of control in her body. All she wanted was for him to put out the fire, then rebuild it on the smoldering embers of the blaze.

"I want you slow." His fingers duplicated his words, making maddeningly slow strokes in, around her moist folds. "And I want you fast." His mouth joined the sensual assault, his tongue darting wickedly, repeatedly, between her parted lips.

Trace was dying by degrees, but he wouldn't have it any other way. She was soft, liquid fire in his hands. He was hard in her mouth, the way he wanted to be in her body, would be in her body. He buried his tongue deep inside the honeyed velvet of her mouth, exactly the way he wanted to bury himself deep inside her woman's body. He longed to stroke the walls of her silken heat the way his tongue was stroking the walls of her mouth.

Carly writhed as she felt the flames lick higher, higher. She welcomed the blaze. She sought it out, stepped into the white-hot center and allowed it to consume her body. "No...more..." she begged, digging her heels into the mattress. "Please, Trace," she cried as he parted her thighs.

Now! she wanted to scream. *Take me now.* Instead, she took him.

One, sweet, hot, hard inch at a time. Until he was so deep in her body she couldn't breathe. She tried to tell him how good he felt. How right and perfect. Tried to tell him this was the way, God, nature and her heart knew it was supposed to be, but she couldn't talk, so she let her body speak for her.

Carly closed her eyes and arched her hips into his, and together they began the dance of love, moving in the slow, sweet rhythms of love in the give-and-take, soft-and-hard world of lovers-only ecstasy.

"You're...ah, Angel...yes, oh, yes...like that, just like that," he said, his body sliding into hers. Over and over he entered her. Over and over she took him. Over and over until there was no beginning, no ending. Until the spiraling heat threatened to burn up the day, the night, the world, with its intensity.

Then it did. And they were burned and reborn from the ashes in a mutual, shattering climax.

"Will you marry me?"

Carly glanced up at her husband. "Have you forgotten that we're already married?"

"No."

"Then why did you ask me to marry you . . . again?"

"Because the first time I didn't ask for myself. The first time was for all the wrong reasons, justified though they were. Now I want to ask you for all the right reasons."

"What reasons?" She knew she was tempting fate, but she didn't care. Tonight was a night for hearts' desires.

"Oh, like I love you and I want to spend the rest of my life with you." A grin tilted the corners of his mouth. "Like I want to make love to you every night until we wind up in the Guinness Book of World Records or die trying."

"I've always wanted to be a world record holder in something. Guess this is my chance, huh?"

"So . . . will you?"

She tilted her head and looked up into his marvelous eyes. "Yes, I'll marry you."

He kissed her. Not with the passion of the moments that had just passed, but with the seal of lifelong commitment known by lovers through the ages. "Now," Trace said against her mouth.

"Now?"

"Right now. Right here."

"We can't—"

"Oh, yes, we can," Trace assured her as he slipped out of bed and collected a handful of candles, then arranged them on the nightstand by the bed. "There," he said, slipping back into bed beside her.

"Trace, what on earth are you doing?"

"Getting married."

"We're naked!"

"Yeah." He grinned. "I noticed."

"Be serious. We can't—"

"Be still. This is serious stuff. We're getting married."

"We're already married, you lunatic."

"Ah, but tell me, Mrs. Holden, have you really *felt* married until today?"

"Yes," she said, the grin dissolving into one of the angelic smiles he loved so much. "As crazy as it sounds, in my heart I've felt married to you all along. In fact, I've felt connected to you in some inexplicable way since the night they brought you into the hospital."

"I thought you were an angel."

"And I thought you were a loner," she said, tunneling her fingers through the hair at his temples.

"I was. Until I met a certain petite nurse with an angel's smile and enough courage for a whole legion of heaven's winged saints."

"I told you before—"

"Yes." He placed a fingertip against her lips. "God doesn't give us extra amounts of faith and courage. But I think you're wrong, because He gave me you. And you're far beyond anything I ever dreamed."

"I love you," she whispered.

He lifted her left hand to his lips and kissed the gold band encircling her third finger.

"I, Trace, take thee, Carly, to be my lawfully wedded wife...."

"I, Carly, take thee, Trace, to be my lawfully wedded husband...."

Trace paused, as if trying to recall the rest of the vows. He smiled. "I will cherish you for all my life and beyond...."

"For now and forever. All that I have and all that I am..."

"Is yours," they finished together. She lifted his left hand to her lips and kissed the gold band encircling his third finger.

"I love you, Carly," he vowed as his mouth took hers in sweet affirmation.

Moments later his body took hers in an even sweeter transformation from spiritual to physical vows. They gave themselves over to commitments made with whispered sighs amid the rustle of sheets and clinging bodies, forever promises made to be forever kept.

But in her heart Carly knew it couldn't last. Her stay in paradise would end when Trace learned the truth.

Wearing a sappy grin and humming "Santa Claus Is Coming To Town," Carly shifted her wiggly burden from one hip to the other while searching her pockets for keys. Astride her waist, Danny ignored her efforts in favor of a babbling conversation with a nearby squirrel. "Eureka!" She jingled the keys in front of the distracted toddler.

"Say, listen, bud. This is Christmas Eve. All good little boys and girls are supposed to hang on their parents' every word so they make out like bandits tomorrow morning."

Danny clapped his chubby hands, then went back to conversing with the squirrel. Carly shrugged, then leaned over to insert the key into the lock. The door swung open while the key was still in her hand.

"About time you two got home." One hand hiked on his hip, Trace surveyed his wife and child with a critical eye. "Now I see why you're so late."

"What?"

Trace's fingertip rescued a smidgen of creamy substance from the corner of Carly's mouth. He licked his finger. "Banana nut," he announced.

"I don't have the vaguest idea what you're talking about," Carly said, as if wide-eyed innocence was the next best thing to sainthood.

"Watch it, lady. You wouldn't want Santa to find out you told a whopping fib on Christmas Eve, would you?"

Carly looked at Trace, then back at Danny. "Looks like we're busted."

Taking Danny from her arms, Trace gave her a burning look and said, "If you'd like to throw yourself on the judge, we could talk about a suspended sentence."

"Doesn't that go, 'throw yourself on the mercy of the court'?"

"Yeah, but I'm the judge, and I like my version better."

She returned his look, flame for flame. "I'll just bet you do."

"So," he said, standing as closely together as Danny sandwiched between them would allow, "have you been a good little girl this year?"

She grinned, more than willing to play the game. "Oh, yes, Santa. Very good."

"Then how would you like to climb on my lap and tell ole Santa what you'd like for him to put into your...stocking."

"Oh, Santa. You're so naughty."

"Yeah," he drawled. "And you're soooo...nice."

Danny's head bobbed in between them, interrupting what promised to be a curl-your-toes kiss.

"Later," Trace promised.

Later turned out to be a lot later. Danny required extra attention to unwind from the bustle of being jostled by last-minute shoppers and indulged with too much ice cream. Carly almost sang herself hoarse with lullabies before he finally fell asleep.

"Thank goodness," she said, plopping down alongside Trace, who was sitting cross-legged on the floor beside the brightly lit Christmas tree. The room smelled of fir boughs and holly and home.

"What are you doing?" The area surrounding him was littered with sheets of instructions that appeared to be written in every language but English and a collection of miscellaneous nuts, bolts and screws.

"Trying to put this damn..." He snatched up the multilingual instruction sheet. "Pee Wee Jungle Gym together, but I only have a masters degree in aeroscience. I may need some help."

"Sorry, you're on your own." She stretched out on her side, propped her weight on one elbow and watched him.

After several frustrating moments of trying to fit bracket A with joint B, he gave up.

"Don't worry," Carly said. "By tomorrow noon, he'll have enough toys to go into competition with every toy store in town. By the time Fitz, Bridget and Linc get through, there won't be room left in the house for us."

"You're probably right. So—" he shoved bolts and screws, metal and plastic, to one side "—what do you want to do now?"

"What are my choices?"

He whispered some borderline pornographic suggestions into her ear. She blushed profusely, but said, "I'll buy one of everything you're selling."

Trace angled his body alongside hers. "Where's your sales resistance, madam?"

"Funny." She stifled a yawn. "But since I married a certain scruffy-bearded jet jockey, I don't seem to have any resistance at all."

He saw the teasing glint in her eyes and knew she was anything but sleepy. "Really?"

"Absolutely." Her hand worked the top button of his shirt free, then slipped inside to warm, hair-dusted skin.

"You wouldn't be interested in some—" he gasped when her fingers found the tender nub she sought "—swampland in Arizona...?" She rolled the hardened peak between her thumb and index finger, then gently pulled. "Ah...Lord, woman."

Suddenly her eyes sparked with desire. "Make love to me," she whispered urgently.

Trace needed no further invitation. In seconds they were both free of their clothes.

They drew together without a word. He was hot, heavy and thick. She was slick and swollen with need. Their joining was wild, fierce, like a thunderstorm rolling across the mountains. Like waves crashing against a rocky shore. And when it was over, they lay still joined, their sweat-slick bodies glistening beneath the tree's twinkling lights. In the aftermath of such sweet ecstasy, they both knew they already possessed the greatest gift of all.

The following morning was a riot of noise and gaily colored paper. With each present Danny squealed with delight, sending tissue paper and ribbon flying until he reached his prize. Carly and Trace had exchanged their gifts in the privacy of their bedroom, and now the beautifully decorated tree was virtually naked, neglected.

"Uh, oh, we forgot one." Carly retrieved a small square box that had been wedged between two limbs at the very back of the tree.

"Last one, Dan, my man," she said, waving the box in the air.

"It's not for Danny."

"Oh." She glanced at the tag, then back at Trace. "It . . . it's for . . . Brian."

"Open it."

With trembling fingers she unwrapped the box. Unnoticed, white ribbon slid to the floor, followed by silver foil wrapping paper. Carly lifted the lid and peered inside. Nestled in silver tissue paper was a star-shaped brass plate mounted on a wooden plaque. As she removed it from the box, a note sailed to the floor. She picked it up and read it. The copy informed the reader that there were millions of unnamed stars in the galaxy and that their gift was one of those stars. There was an engraving on the plaque.

This is official notification that star number MK30285 is hereby given the name Brian Patrick McShane and shall be so listed from this day, December 25 . . .

"Now Brian has his very own star." Carly raised tear-filled eyes to her husband. "No matter where he is, that star will shine down on him, and he'll know there are people who love him."

She couldn't speak; tears clogged her throat.

"And there will be a gift for every birthday and Christmas until we find him," Trace vowed as Carly stepped into his waiting arms.

Chapter 13

This is not a good omen, Carly thought, glancing at the bedside clock. Scarcely a week ago she had switched to a day shift, and she still wasn't acclimated to the change. But of all days for her to run late, today was the worst. Today was the day of the preliminary custody hearing.

Hurriedly, she stepped into black leather pumps while, with nervous fingers, she attempted to anchor a gold hoop in her ear.

"Take it easy, Angel. You're going to be a nervous wreck by the time we get to the courthouse."

Trace was only too happy to soothe her fears, since it kept his mind off his own.

"Do I look all right? This suit isn't too severe, is it?"

"No. You look fine." Actually, she looked gorgeous, but he didn't think now was the time to shower her with compliments. "Ready?"

"Where's Danny?"

"In his bed. He was a little fussy—"

"What's wrong with him?"

"Nothing, probably, but—"

"Is he sick? If he's sick, I can't leave him. We'll just have to call Mr. Borell and—"

Trace grabbed her fluttering hands in his. "Angel. He feels slightly warm to me, but—" She jerked her hands free and was out of the bedroom before he could finish his sentence.

When he followed her into the baby's room seconds later, she already had a thermometer out. "I think he's got a fever."

Carly released a pent-up breath as she read the thermometer a few minutes later. "No fever."

"Okay, worrywart. *Now* will you calm down?"

"Yes." She managed one of her single-dimple smiles. "Guess I overreacted again. Sorry, occupational hazard."

He kissed her gently. "Wouldn't have you any other way."

Trace went to collect their coats, while Carly gave Bridget some last-minute instructions.

"If he cries or becomes too irritable, there's some liquid infant pain medication on his chest of drawers. Give him one dropper full. That should hold him until I get back."

"Don't worry, Carly. We'll be fine," Bridget assured her.

Trace was waiting for her at the door. She stopped, turned and said to Bridget, "Before I forget—when you leave today, will you take Fitz's antique chess set with you? Danny can't keep his hands off it. He's always carrying the chessmen around the house. As a matter of fact, I had to move it completely out of his reach yesterday. There's a piece missing, but I'm sure I'll find it the next time I use the vacuum cleaner."

"Sure. No problem. See ya later. And good luck," Bridget called out.

The courthouse was intimidating, formal and cold, despite the heavy use of rich paneled wood and ornately carved moldings. Carly wondered how many children had had their fate decided within these walls. And how many prospective parents had had their hearts broken.

The minute she saw the smug expressions on Deirdre and Walker Andrews' faces, the knot in her stomach doubled. *They think the case is already won* She could see it in the secret smile on Deirdre's thin mouth, in Walker's flinty gaze. What did they know? What damning piece of knowledge could they have? And whatever they had *must* be damning, or else they wouldn't be acting so cat-that-swallowed-the-canary pleasant.

"I understand best wishes are in order," Walker said to Trace, but he didn't offer a handshake.

"Oh, yes. Congratulations," Deirdre added, gracefully peeling taupe leather gloves from her slender hands.

"Thank you," Carly replied. Trace's only response was a hostile glare.

"A civil ceremony, we were told. In a...boardinghouse?" Deirdre painstakingly folded the gloves and slipped them into a perfectly matched handbag.

"Yes." Carly was determined to be polite, although at that moment she would have liked nothing better than to wipe the smile off Deirdre Andrews' flawlessly made-up face. "We wanted just our close friends there." The customary *and family* was conspicuous by its deletion.

"How is Danny?" Walker finally asked.

"He's happy," Trace said in a tense, clipped voice. The unspoken *right where he is* hung in the air like a near-to-bursting thundercloud.

"Uh, well..." Walker cleared his throat. "I see our lawyer has arrived. Trace," he said with a curt nod, then led his wife away.

"Blood-thirsty bastard," Trace snapped.

"I almost feel sorry for them."

He whipped around. "Sorry? Why in God's name would you feel sorry for those two?"

"Because they simply haven't got what it takes to be happy." She gazed up at him with all the love in her heart shining in her eyes. "They haven't even got each other."

Trace pulled her into his embrace. "Oh, Angel, what would I do without you?"

Her arms slid around his neck. I hope you never have to find out, Carly thought. *He's scared, too,* she thought, running her hands over his back. Beneath the raw silk sports coat, muscles bunched. She glanced over Trace's shoulder. "Here comes Mr. Borell."

"Good morning," Nathan said. "I've got a copy of the welfare worker's report, and I want us to go over it before we go into court."

Trace frowned. "Is there something there that will make our case look bad?"

"Not exactly."

"What the hell is that supposed to mean?"

"Trace . . ." Carly put her hand on his arm.

"Sorry," he said to Borell.

The other man smiled reassuringly. "Don't look so glum, Trace. The odds are still in our favor."

"Does that means the welfare worker recommended us as parents?"

"She didn't *not* recommend you, which is almost as good," Borell said, pulling a file from his briefcase.

"I don't mean to repeat myself, Nathan, but just what the hell *is* that supposed to mean?"

He motioned toward a hardwood bench. "Let's go over here and sit down, shall we?"

Trace didn't like the sound of the attorney's invitation. The knot in his stomach tightened.

They went and sat down. "Carly, your husband is deceased, is that right?" Borell said without preamble.

"Yes."

"And your son has been missing for almost a year?" After their marriage, Trace had informed Nathan of Carly's past and Brian's kidnapping. Why was he going over old ground now? "Yes."

"Have you given up looking for him?"

"Of course she hasn't," Trace answered for her. "What kind of a question is that?"

"A valid one, I'm afraid, Trace. I spoke with the Andrews' attorney yesterday afternoon, after the report arrived from Welfare Services, and he says they will lean heavily on Carly's relationship with Danny."

"Carly's relationship with Danny is nothing short of perfect," Trace informed the lawyer.

"Of course, but the case worker did mention a concern about Carly psychologically substituting Danny for the child she lost. The Andrews have jumped on the comment, and they'll insist that kind of a relationship might be unhealthy for Danny, not to mention the fact that there is a possibility Carly might emotionally abandon Danny if her own son is ever returned to her."

The profanity Trace used to summarize his opinion of that was succinct and completely suited to the situation. If Carly had had the nerve, she would have repeated the word for emphasis.

"Not exactly Latin," Borell said, "but I can't say as I blame you."

"I would never do anything to hurt Danny. Never." Carly framed her words distinctly. "Why are they being so vicious? Are they so greedy they would destroy a child?"

"Personally, I think this new plan of attack is to counteract the case worker's negative comments on the Andrews."

"Such as?" Trace asked, scowling.

"The lack of warmth in their home, for one thing. For another, why they've never had children of their own, assuming they're capable. The judge would think twice about placing a child in a home where a couple had previously made a conscious decision *not* to have a family."

Trace raked a hand through his hair. "So you still think we have a good chance of winning."

"Yes...."

"I hear a but."

"But ... as your lawyer, I have to tell you that in custody cases, sometimes money is an issue." Borell took in the anger and frustration etched on his client's face. "It's ironic that Matt and Jenny's will was so ironclad regarding the disposition of the company, or you could buy Andrews off with stock."

At that moment a clerk stepped into the wide hallway and announced a half-hour delay in all previously scheduled cases. Borell took the opportunity to check in with his office. Knowing he would probably spend the time pacing, otherwise, Carly urged Trace to find them some coffee. The moment he left, Deirdre and Walker Andrews walked over to her.

"We'd like a word with you, *Mrs*. Holden," Walker said calmly.

"I don't think such a conversation would be ethical, Mr. Andrews." Standing between the two of them, an uneasiness that had nothing to do with the ethics of speaking to the opposition prickled along Carly's spine.

"A strange choice of words—" Deirdre smoothed an imaginary wrinkle from her immaculate suit "—considering your present situation."

"Exactly what *situation* are you referring to?"

"Your marriage, of course. Or should I say your *arrangement?*"

Carly's heartbeat accelerated. "I don't know what you're talking about."

"Come now," Walker said smoothly. "You don't expect me to believe you and Trace conveniently fell in love at first sight and couldn't wait to marry?"

"We know about your background," Deirdre added.

"My background?"

"Your divorce and custody suit."

Carly blanched. *Dear God! They were going to dredge up all the damning details of her divorce from Ken.*

"I wonder," Walker mused, "how a judge would view your behavior? An unhealthy attachment to a child so close in age to your missing son. It borders on the neurotic. Don't you agree, Deirdre?"

Stunned, Carly looked at the man in front of her and realized she had underestimated him. Unlike his pampered wife, Walker Andrews was a street fighter. "I suggest you leave before Trace returns."

"The indignant wife," he said. "Very effective, but wasted." He took a step closer. With Trace nowhere in sight, her back literally to the wall, Carly suddenly felt hemmed in. Pressured from all sides at once with nowhere to escape.

"How convenient that Danny required nursing. That must have fit your plan perfectly."

"What plan?"

"Money, my dear," Deirdre said. "Your plan to acquire money and position. Quite the little opportunist, aren't you?"

"No."

"Is Trace aware that you're hiding a shady past?" Deirdre asked.

"I'm not."

"Does he know you entertained lovers in the same house as your son?"

"That's a lie."

"Just like your phony mothering of Danny."

"I love Danny."

"He's only a substitute for the child you lost."

"No."

"The fact that you're willing to use a defenseless child to get what you want is sick."

"Sick!" Carly's eyes blazed cold-blue fire. "You give the word new meaning. Both of you are twisted. And before I would allow you to get your filthy hands on Danny, I'd do the rest of the world a favor and send you both straight to hell."

"Careful, my dear," Deirdre continued. "You really can't afford to antagonize us. But *we* can afford to be generous. We'll give you time to think about your mistakes. Time to change your plans before we're forced to disclose your sordid past. The burden of proof, as they say, will be on you."

With as much poise as her boiling rage permitted, she shoved Deirdre to one side and all but ran down the corridor.

She found Trace in front of a vending machine. "Are they ready for us?" he asked nervously.

Unable to speak, Carly shook her head.

"God, I wish we could get this over—"

"Good news," Nathan Borell said, joining them. "We've received a postponement."

"A postponement? Why is that good?" Trace asked.

"It will give us more time to address the concerns in the case worker's report."

"How did you get them to postpone the hearing?"

"I didn't. The request came from the other side not two minutes ago."

"If you lose Danny, it will be all my fault." *And you'll be alone*, she could have added. *That will be my fault, too.*

"What are you talking about?" Trace said, maneuvering his car onto the highway for Union City with one hand and loosening his tie with the other.

"I-I didn't tell Mr. Borell everything about my past."

"Don't tell me you're an ax murderer. I may hire you to take out Deirdre and Walker."

"I'm serious, Trace."

His eyes left the road just long enough for him to see the serious threat of tears in hers. "All right. What is it Borell doesn't know?"

She swallowed hard, not wanting to relive the most painful time in her life. But she had to prepare him for the damage his enemies were about to do. "I told you Ken was suffering the effects of the brain tumor even before we divorced."

"Yes," he said patiently.

"And his behavior was . . . unbalanced."

"Yes."

"When I filed for divorce, he filed a countersuit to win custody of Brian."

"And?"

"He accused me of being an unfit mother. Of taking lovers."

"No one in their right mind could believe that was true," he said derisively.

"Ken paid three men to swear they had slept with me while Brian was asleep in the next room."

Trace's head whipped around; he stared at her for a moment then returned his gaze to the highway. His white-knuckled grip on the steering wheel tightened, and he had to remind himself that Ken McShane had been a sick man.

"My lawyer was finally able to prove Ken had lied, but by that time the damage was already done. It was a nasty, ugly divorce, and it's all a matter of public record. I didn't tell

Mr. Borell, because I honestly didn't think it was important until today."

"It's still not, as far as I'm concerned. Anyway, you were cleared in court."

"But, Trace, don't you see? Deirdre and Walker could use this to influence the outcome of the case. What if the judge thinks, where there's smoke, there's bound to be fire? What if he thinks there's even the *slightest* chance any of the old accusations were valid? I couldn't live with myself if you lost Danny because of me."

"In the first place, Nathan will know how to handle the situation once he's been informed. In the second place, let's give the judge credit for some brains, considering his position."

"But, Trace—"

He pulled the car to the side of the road and shoved the gearshift into park. "Come here," he said, even as he pulled her roughly into his arms. "Now, listen to me. Nothing you can do, nothing you've ever done, could harm Danny or me. So I want you to stop worrying, do you hear me?"

When she didn't respond, he leaned her back far enough to be able to look into her eyes. "Do you hear me, Carly McShane Holden?"

"Yes." She sniffed, wanting to believe him.

"Besides, if you want to play the guilt game, you're not even in the same ballpark with me."

"Why?"

"Because I've never told Nathan that Matt and Jenny didn't go through a regular adoption agency to get Danny."

"But Mr. Borell was your brother's attorney. Didn't he handle the legal work?"

Trace shook his head. "Matt used another lawyer for the adoption, then never dealt with the guy again. I always suspected there was something not quite . . . I don't know." He shrugged. "Not quite right about the way Danny wound up a Holden."

"What do you mean?"

"As a child, Jenny had a heart murmur. In fact, her family has a history of cardiac problems. Except for Deirdre," he said with a sneer. "And she doesn't have a heart. Anyway," he went on, "a lot of adoption agencies, even private sources, turned them down because of Jenny's health. All I know is that Matt told me Danny had literally been abandoned on someone's doorstep. And knowing how desperate he and Jenny were to have a child, I wouldn't be surprised if the whole process wasn't a touch on the under-the-table side."

"You mean, black market?" Carly asked, not wanting to believe ill of the people Trace loved and yet hoping it was true, because that would make it just that little bit more likely that Danny was really Brian.

"No. I've seen the adoption papers—Borell even has a copy—and they're legal. I just think Matt and Jenny cut a few corners to get Danny as quickly as possible."

She didn't know what to say. He had just described a scenario that information and statistics indicated was the possible reason lots of missing children were never returned to their homes. Carly had even thought—hoped—such a scenario might be the case with Brian....

Trace saw the expression on her face subtly alter and knew what was going through her mind. He placed a tender kiss on her mouth. "Angel, I know that must sound awful, but I promise you, Matt would *never* have adopted a child from *any* source without first making certain that child was eligible to be adopted." He gave her another kiss, then eased the car back onto the highway.

"I-I'm sure you're right," Carly said. But in her heart she wasn't so sure at all.

Fate couldn't be so cruel, she told herself.

Still, the thought nagged her, whirling in her head and gaining impetus as they sped homeward. And as each mile brought her closer to Danny, she drew closer to the knowledge that she had to tell Trace about her suspicion that Danny might be Brian. But how do you say, *I think the child you've changed your life for—the child you're trying so desperately to hang on to—isn't yours?* And in the next breath say, *I think he's mine?*

By the time they reached the carriage house, she was a bundle of raw nerves.

Bridget smiled as they entered the living room, but the troubled expression on Carly's face prompted her to ask, "It didn't go well?"

"A postponement," Trace said, hanging their coats in the closet. "We'll be notified when they schedule another court date."

"H-how's Danny?" Carly asked, even as she walked toward the child's room.

"Fine. I gave him some of that stuff in the dropper like you said. He only ate half his oatmeal, then started acting like he was sleepy, so I put him down for a nap."

As Bridget left, Carly tiptoed inside and laid her hand against Danny's brow. He was definitely warm, but nothing to be alarmed about. But she decided that if the low-grade fever didn't respond to the medication by midafternoon, she would call Linc.

"Everything okay?" Trace asked when she returned to the living room.

"He's slightly flushed, but I don't think it's anything to worry about."

"Good." His arms encircled her waist, and he nuzzled her neck.

"I, uh... When you went for coffee, I had a confrontation with Deirdre and Walker."

"What happened?"

"You were right." Her hand rested on his shoulder, and she absently played with the point of his shirt collar. "I gave them the benefit of the doubt because family is so important to me. But now I understand how far they're willing to go to achieve their goal." She looked into his eyes. "I'm frightened, Trace."

"Don't be. As long as we stay together, they can't touch us."

"They're vicious," she said as he brushed her bangs back. "And they'll do anything, say anything, to get what they want."

"Hey," Trace said, gazing into her troubled eyes. "Those two really got to you, didn't they?"

They had. So much so that Carly realized her time had finally run out. She knew that if she didn't tell Trace everything, Deirdre and Walker would follow through with their threat to go public with her past. And Carly knew how easily facts could be twisted to resemble the truth. Even though she had finally been cleared of Ken's trumped up charges during their custody battle over Brian, some of her co-workers and so-called friends had assumed where there were accusations, there was guilt.

She *had* to tell him. She couldn't subject Trace and Danny to Deirdre and Walker's cruelty. And if it cost her everything she held dear...? It would be worth every tear as long as Trace and Danny were protected.

Carly tried to swallow the knot of fear in her throat. "Did . . . you know they suspect our marriage was a fake?"

"Can't prove a thing. Besides, it isn't."

Her knuckles grazed his softly-stubbly cheek, and she smiled sadly. "No, not anymore." He kissed her dimple. "They also think I'm only interested in Danny's inheritance, and that I'm obsessed with him."

"Obsessed? That's a pretty strong word, don't you think? Sounds to me like Deirdre and Walker are the ones who are obsessed—with power and money."

"They...they think that somehow I've convinced myself that Danny actually is my son. That he *is* Brian."

"That's ridiculous. The odds against such a thing are astronomical, to say the least."

"Those kinds of odds are nothing stacked against hope."

He looked at her as if she were speaking a foreign tongue. "Carly, what—"

"When I found out Danny was adopted, I checked his hospital chart and discovered that Danny and Brian have the same blood type."

Trace shook his head, trying to deny the idea forming in his brain. "You're scaring the hell out of me."

"Trace, you have to understand, ever since Brian was taken, *everything* I've said, done, thought and felt has been real to me only as it related to Brian. What will probably sound to you like a bizarre leap from logical thinking makes perfect sense to me."

"What sense? What are you trying to say?"

"That Danny *could* be my son." When he didn't answer, she added, "You said yourself that you always thought Danny's adoption wasn't exactly done through the usual channels."

"That doesn't—"

"And their birthdays are on exactly the same day."

"Stop it, Carly."

He held up his hands as if to ward off any more hurtful words. But he couldn't deny the conviction in her voice, the certainly in her eyes. "Tell me something, did this trip from bizarre leap to perfect sense take place before or after I proposed our arrangement?"

Carly glanced away, unable to face the pain she knew must follow. "Before." When she finally faced him, she was unprepared for the gut-wrenching agony reflected in his eyes.

Looks do kill, Carly thought, because the look in Trace's eyes was surely killing her. "Trace—"

He took a step back. "I couldn't believe my luck when you accepted my proposal. You were an answer to my prayer." A muscle quivered in his jaw; his expression was dark, cold. "No wonder you accepted so easily."

"No! I did not marry you because I thought I could get to Danny through you."

"Didn't you?"

"Trace, I married you because you needed me and..."

"And?"

"I needed you."

"Need? You didn't need me. I was a convenience."

"No, Trace. You're wrong. Please, listen to me."

"And hear what? More lies?"

"You want the truth? All right. Yes, I did think Danny might be mine. Yes, I deliberately kept it from you. And yes, I needed you. I still need you, Trace. You. Not because of Danny, because of you. I love you. Isn't that the only truth that counts?"

From the bedroom, Danny's wail demanded attention. "I'd better go—"

"No," Trace said. "I'll check on him."

So, Carly thought, the final insult. How could he think her love was a lie? Because he's been hurt, and the kind of soul-deep pain she had seen reflected in his eyes doesn't ask why, it just hurts.

"Carly?"

She turned to find Trace standing in the doorway. "Carly, come quick. I think something's wrong with him." She rushed into the bedroom and touched Danny's cheek.

He was burning up with fever.

Chapter 14

"A chess piece."

"You mean he shoved a chess piece down inside his cast and that's what caused the infection?" Trace said in disbelief.

"Yeah," Linc confirmed. "Crammed it so far down and so tight the carved edge cut the skin, and the rest, as they say, is history. He's got one helluva infection."

"But we watch him like a hawk," Carly exclaimed.

"Even hawks can't see everything, Carly. Relax. We'll cut the cast off, clean up the infected area and recast him. The three of you will be one big happy family again before the sun sinks slowly in the west." He patted Carly's shoulder.

She closed her eyes briefly and allowed relief to wash over her. "Thank God," she whispered. She clasped her still-trembling hands together in her lap. Were they a happy family? Would Trace be able to see past the pain she had caused and forgive her?

"Thanks, Linc," Trace said. "I mean it. I felt better the minute you arrived."

Linc smiled. "No sweat." He gave Carly a parting wink and turned to leave.

"Linc," she called after him. "Will you have them call me before they reapply the cast?"

He shrugged. "Sure."

Hands thrust deep in his pockets, Trace leaned against the corridor wall and looked down at Carly. "Do you think they'll keep him overnight?"

"Probably. They'll want to keep an eye on the infection. But we can..." She wasn't sure there was a *we* anymore. "He, uh, he'll probably be released tomorrow morning."

Head down, Trace nodded.

"We have to talk."

"What's to talk about, Carly?"

"For one thing, our marriage. For another—"

"We had an arrangement."

"It was more than that, and you know it."

"Do I? Yesterday I would have agreed with you. Hell, yesterday I would have extolled the virtues of holy wedlock from the top of the Transamerica Building. Today I wouldn't give you two cents for the whole institution."

"You're angry and—"

"Hell, yes, I'm angry." *And hurt. God, I'm hurt.*

"Trace, please, let me explain."

Just then the X-ray lab doors swung open, and a nurse wheeled out the gurney carrying an already sedated Danny. The nurse stopped the gurney long enough to satisfy them that her patient was indeed fine, then pushed on. When Carly gathered her purse and jacket to follow, Trace stopped her.

"You don't need to continue in your part anymore. The play is over."

"It's not a part. I honestly love Danny."

"I can live without your kind of honesty." *The question is, can I live without you?* "And so can Danny. Why don't you just leave us alone?"

Carly couldn't help but remember the last time they had been in the emergency room waiting together. The night she decided to marry him. The night her life changed for the better. The night fate stepped in and turned her toward her heart's home.

Now her heart was homeless, breaking.

And there was one last hurt to endure.

"I-I'd like to be present when they remove Danny's cast."

"Why?"

She swallowed hard. "To...look for a birthmark on his left leg."

"He doesn't have one."

"Brian does."

Briefly, Trace closed his eyes against the razor-sharp pain slicing his heart.

"Mrs. Holden," the nurse said. "We're ready for you now."

Please understand, Carly's eyes begged. *I have to do this.* She turned and followed the nurse.

There was a delay in removing the cast, but Carly couldn't face returning to the waiting room. She could have passed the time with some of the nurses, but she couldn't face idle conversation. She could have gone in search of Linc, but she couldn't face having to explain what a mess she had made of things. Instead she found a quiet corner all to herself.

Fate had a cruel streak a mile wide, she decided. And it knew just where and when to hit you the hardest.

The next few minutes, regardless of the outcome, would alter her life forever, and she was helpless to do anything but wait. No, she could pray. But what should she pray for? *Dear Lord in heaven, please give my baby back to me, and*

don't leave Trace alone. Even God couldn't grant that
prayer.

A gentle drizzle began almost as soon as Trace walked out
of the hospital. He didn't want to go back inside. And he
didn't want to go back to the carriage house. He wanted
Carly. And Danny.

He wanted yesterday back. Yesterday they had been together, fighting a common enemy, not each other. His heart
as heavy as the clouds overhead. Trace sighed, stuffed his
hands into the pockets of the trench coat and crossed the
street to a small park.

He ignored the rain misting his eyelashes and cheeks. He
ignored the curious looks of people scurrying past to get out
of the weather.

He ignored everything but the pain in his heart. That he
gave free rein simply because he had no choice. It hurt.

Trace tried to remember his life before Carly. He couldn't.
Had that life been so bad? *Just lonely.* He scrubbed rain
from his face. *So what? You've been lonely all your life.
You'll survive.* And he would. He always had. Alone. Even
his love for his brother hadn't changed that.

But his love for Carly had.

Put her out of your mind. And his heart? How did he get
her out of his heart? *She used you.* And what had he done
to her? Whose idea had this stupid arrangement been, anyway? She could have done exactly what he had expected her
to do and told him to hit the road. She hadn't. She could
have demanded the moon, and he would have paid the price.
But she hadn't. She never asked for anything. In fact, she
gave. Constantly. To him. To Danny. To Fitz and Bridget.
To anyone who needed her.

And oh, God, how he had needed her. How he still
needed her.

Need. Need. Need. Look where it's gotten you. You trust—you get hurt. You need—you lose.

But how could he lose something he'd never had? Everything he and Carly had, or thought they had, was based on lies. Wasn't it? All her smiles and loving touches—kisses and whispered love words were nothing more than pretense. Weren't they? She would do anything to be sure Danny stayed close until she could prove he was Brian.

Was the woman he had lived with, loved with, cried with, capable of such grand deception? And could he honestly say that, in her place, he would have done differently? Yes, she had deliberately kept the truth from him, but how could she have proved a suspicion that sounded more fiction than fact? Yes, he had trusted her as he had trusted no one else, but she had neither asked for nor insisted on blind faith. He had given her the attributes of an angel without allowing her the all too human errors she was entitled to. *And now you're angry because she didn't live up to your expectations?* Since when did love demand perfection? Since when did love offer trust in parcels, so much for this, but none for that? Love is, always has been, and always will be, all or nothing.

Was he so afraid to trust his heart that he was willing to settle for nothing?

No, Trace thought, he hadn't lost Carly. He had thrown her away. With both hands.

The carriage house was dark when Carly returned. And empty. She stood in the hallway for long moments, trying to absorb every last memory she could. Memories of Trace laughing, playing with Danny. Memories of Christmas, of lovers' sighs and whispered words. Memories of a life fate had handed her on a silver platter, then snatched away without warning.

Carly walked into the baby's room and turned on the light. She crossed to the crib and picked up the multi-colored dragon. A twist of its windup key filled the room with tinkling notes. On the nearby changing table sat a neatly folded stack of blankets she had washed only the day before. She left the dragon and picked up the stack of clean laundry and stroked the soft edge of the downy blanket.

"Packing?"

Carly whipped around to find her husband watching from the doorway. "Yes."

He nodded. "I, uh, couldn't...just wait, so I took a walk in the park across from the hospital." He had on a trench coat, the shoulders dark with moisture.

"It's raining?"

"Yeah."

"You'll get sick." *And I won't be here to take care of you.*

"And you're a worry..." The familiar banter died on his lips. "I'm fine." *Was. Past tense. Past Carly.*

"Danny—"

"Danny—"

"He's okay," Carly said. "Sound asleep when I left." *And went looking for you, but couldn't find you, and cried because I had lost you for good.*

"I know. I went back after I left the park." *Looking for you, but you'd already gone. I thought for good.*

"Did Linc tell you?"

He shook his head. And held his breath.

Her fingers curled around the blanket. "No birthmark."

Trace closed his eyes briefly, his heart torn in two. "Carly, I—"

"Don't," she said as he came toward her. The single word was filled with a multitude of emotions. *Don't offer pity. I don't want your pity. I want your love.* "I..." She tried to swallow the golf-ball-size knot in her throat. "Fitz can put me up for the night. I'll get the rest of my things tomorrow."

He walked to the crib and stopped. "You don't have to do that. I can sleep in here tonight." He motioned toward the bed opposite Danny's crib.

"No. Thanks."

They stared at each other, each waiting, hoping for the other one to say or do something that would end the silent torture.

Ask me not to go, Trace.

Don't go, Carly.

Neither moved. Neither spoke. The moment slipped quietly into the crowded void of missed opportunities and neglected chances. Outside, the drizzle became a drum-on-the-windowpanes downpour. Inside, hearts became can't-stop-the-pain empty.

"It's getting worse," he said.

"Yes."

They fell back to staring, until finally Carly couldn't stand another instant of the murderous quiet. Tears filled her eyes. "Will you tell him goodbye for me? I don't think it's a good idea if I see... I don't think I can..." She dropped the blanket and ran for the door.

He caught her before she could get away and turned her to him. "Isn't there something you want me to give Danny?"

She stared at him, her blue eyes filled with tears. "Like what?"

"Like...this," he said a heartbeat before his mouth took hers in a heart-to-heart, soul-to-soul, forever-to-forever kiss.

"T-Trace?" Carly whispered when his mouth finally released hers. Tentatively, she touched her hand to his cheek. His skin was cool and damp, and he smelled of rain. "Trace..."

"Shh." He kissed her into silence. "Just listen. I never wanted to trust you. Never wanted to love you. I'd gotten used to being alone. Alone was easy. No complications. Then one day I opened my eyes and found an angel in my life. An angel so beautiful and sweet she wouldn't let me go on alone.

"But I didn't believe she was for real." He smiled tenderly and brushed back her bangs. "And when she turned out to be merely human, I..." He swallowed hard. "I wasn't very forgiving."

"I should have told you about my suspicions from the beginning," Carly said. "If only—"

"You did what you thought was best. And you never intended to hurt anyone."

"But I did hurt you." Her fingers slid into his hair. "I'm so sorry, Trace."

"And I used your not telling me as an excuse to run from the responsibility of love. But I didn't run far before I discovered the truth."

"W-what is . . . the truth?"

"The simple truth is that there is no me without you. You're in my every breath, my every heartbeat. You're inside me, Carly. Deep in my soul. You're the other half of me, the best half. And somehow God in His infinite wisdom meant for us to end up together no matter how we began.

"Carly, I didn't trust what we had, what we felt for each other. It's not easy for me. I can't promise a miraculous change or everlasting and unquestioning trust, at least for right now. Life with me may never be a bed of roses, even when I've dealt with my fears. So I wouldn't blame you if you walked away and never looked back. But I *can* promise you one thing."

"What?"

"If you do walk away from me, it won't make any difference."

"W-why?"

"Because I'll come after you. I'll find you. Then I'll make you see what my heart knew even before my stubborn brain did. That needing someone is a natural part of loving. That I need you and always will. That life without you is no life at all. And that the only perfection is the two of us loving each other. Now. Always. I love you, Carly."

Her heart almost burst with joy. Life with Trace might never be perfect. But life without him was no life at all.

Epilogue

"Do that again."

"What? This?"

"Yeah. Just like that. Oh, yeah."

"You're so hard."

"And you're hands are so soft.... Just a little...ah, just a little lower.... Oh, yeah, that feels ... Oh, Angel, that's positively wicked."

"You're positively wicked."

"But you love every naughty inch.... Ahh, if you don't know how bad I am by now, you never will."

Standing on tiptoe with nothing but a bath towel wrapped around her petite frame, Carly ceased massaging her husband's shoulders. She gave his terry cloth-covered behind a wifely pat as her heels touched the tiled bathroom floor. "And if you don't finish shaving, we're going to be late to our son's birthday party."

"Danny's still napping. Besides, I thought you said stubble looked good on me."

"I did and it does. But tonight—" she kissed a spot between his shoulder blades "—I'm in the mood for clean shaven."

She turned and headed for the bedroom. Trace caught the back of her towel. "That all you're in the mood for?"

Carly clutched the towel to her and wondered what was considered fashionably late for a two-year-old's birthday party. "Trace Holden, don't you dare make us late."

"I'm only interested in making—" he took several love bites from the back of her neck "—love."

"Trace..."

"How about you? Interested?" His tongue slid up the nape of her neck to her earlobe.

"T-Trace...we don't...ohh...hmm..."

"Can't what?" His hand caressed her shoulder briefly before pushing her hands from the knotted towel. "Can't do this?" The knot fell victim to his eager fingers, and seconds later the towel lay in a heap about Carly's feet. "Or this?" His hands cupped her breasts and kneaded gently.

"We'll...oh, yes...be late."

"So what?" His fingers tugged at her nipples until they were deliciously hard, achingly ready for his mouth.

"So...ohh. That feels..."

"Good?"

"Wonderful." Carly sighed. "Did you...ahh...know I once had a fantasy sort of...like this?"

"You mean, you naked, me playing with you?"

"Yes. No. I can't think when you're..."

"Tell me your fantasy." He nipped at her ear.

"You were fresh out of the shower...and I watched you."

"Like the time you hid in the shadows in Danny's room?"

Carly spun to face him. "You knew!" she gasped.

He grinned. "That you were watching me? Yeah. And I loved it."

"Trace Holden, you should be ashamed of yourself."

"For what? Displaying my body for my wife's hot-eyed inspection?"

"No. For not letting me know you knew I was watching."

"Much more fun my way. Did you like what you saw?" He whisked the towel from his hips, then gently backed her up against the wall.

"I should tell you no." When her bare behind met cool tile she gasped, jerked forward and met Trace thigh to thigh, belly to belly, softness to hardness.

"But you won't." He trailed his fingertips over the soft swell of her breasts.

"No, I won't." A slow, sweet fire shimmered through her body, flowing through her veins like warm molasses.

"Did you like—"

"Yes." She arched against him, the raw hunger in her body ignited to a smoldering flame. "Oh, yes."

"Angel . . ." He took her mouth, filling her with the hot, deep strokes of his tongue, but he wanted deeper, hotter, tighter.

"Trace . . ." Carly struggled with a last bit of sanity. "We'll be . . . late."

"In about two minutes we'll be in paradise," he said, leading her to their bed.

Less, actually.

As always when they made love, the fire burned white-hot and soul-deep. As always, the flames of passion licked and danced across their joined bodies like living tongues of fire, the shimmering heat building until there was nothing left but the blazing pleasure, the all-consuming need to be in and of each other.

"Carly, Carly," Trace murmured, his hips rocking against hers in a slow, scorching rhythm that made her come apart in hot, languid fragments of exquisite pleasure. "Heaven made you just for me. You're so...sweet."

He had driven her to the brink of madness with his unhurried lovemaking, and now she wanted no more softness, no more teasing. No more waiting. She arched her back, bringing her breasts into electrifying contact with his chest. Then she bent her head forward and sank her teeth into his shoulder.

"Now, Trace." She licked the spot she had just abused. "Love me now. Hard and fast. I want to feel you move...deep...so deep...."

Trace, too, had reached the end of his endurance. The fire was too hot, out of control. "Yes, yes. That's it, Angel," he said, stroking her satin heat, feeling her meet each thrust as they went higher and higher into the flames. Until the heat burst inside them like a million suns showering them with a radiant pleasure so sweet it burned all the way to their souls.

Moments afterward, cradled in Trace's arms, Carly sighed her contentment. "You think it'll still be like this when we're old and gray?"

"Yeah. We may have to fan the flame a bit when we're eighty," Trace teased. "But we'll still be smoldering."

Carly laughed. "'Grow old with me, the best is yet to be,'" she quoted.

"Angel, if it gets any better, I don't know if I'm man enough to handle it."

She looked into his eyes. "You're man enough...and more."

"Your confidence is inspiring." His body stirred against hers, leaving little doubt as to just how inspiring.

She smiled and shook her head slowly. "You *are* bad. We have to get out of this bed, wake our son and prepare for our guests."

Carly never tired of the words *our son*. Even now, there were moments when she could scarcely believe Danny was finally and forever theirs. The judge's decision to uphold Matt and Jennifer's will had been one of the happiest days in Carly's life. That was also the day she had spoken the words *our son* for the first time.

"Can't they just serve themselves and leave us to our own private party?"

"No. Besides, you want to watch Danny open his presents, don't you?"

"I'd rather see the present you give me every time I watch you come apart in my hands."

Carly knew that if she didn't get out of bed that instant she would be lost. Another second caught between Trace's soft seductive words and his hard body would be her undoing. She pushed back the sheet, but he stopped her.

"Wait."

"Trace . . ." she warned, but her voice lacked conviction.

"I have something to show you."

"I've seen it." At his irresistible grin, she added, "And wonderful though it may be—"

From the bedside table he produced a folded document and placed it in her hand. "This, my know-it-all wife, is what I wanted you to see."

She unfolded the paper and began to read. Within seconds tears gathered on her thick lashes, then spilled down her cheeks.

When she lifted her gaze from the document and looked at him, Trace thought he could die that very instant, content in the knowledge he would never know a sweeter moment.

"T-this is . . . from a private . . . detective."

"It isn't much, Carly. But it *is* a clue to Brian's whereabouts. Small, but we have to be satisfied with small for the time being. Hopefully, this information will lead us to bigger clues, then bigger ones . . ." He captured a tear from the corner of her eye. "It may takes months, even years, but I promise you, we'll run down every clue, every scrap of evidence, no matter how small. And we won't stop until we find your son."

"Our son," she whispered.

"Our son," he replied, drawing her back into his arms. Back to the simple truth of their love.

* * * * *

SILHOUETTE·INTIMATE·MOMENTS®

NORA ROBERTS
Night Shadow

People all over the city of Urbana were asking, Who was that masked man?

Assistant district attorney Deborah O'Roarke was the first to learn his secret identity . . . and her life would never be the same.

The stories of the lives and loves of the O'Roarke sisters began in January 1991 with NIGHT SHIFT, Silhouette Intimate Moments #365. And if you want to know more about Deborah and the man behind the mask, look for NIGHT SHADOW, Silhouette Intimate Moments #373.

Available now at your favorite retail outlet, or order your copy by sending your name, address, zip or postal code along with a check or money order for $2.95 (please do not send cash), plus 75¢ postage and handling, payable to Silhouette Reader Service to:

In the U.S.	In Canada
3010 Walden Ave.	P.O. Box 609
P.O. Box 1396	Fort Erie, Ontario
Buffalo, NY 14269-1396	L2A 5X3

Please specify book title(s) with your order.
Canadian residents add applicable federal and provincial taxes.

NITE-1A

Silhouette Books®

SILHOUETTE'S "BIG WIN"
SWEEPSTAKES RULES & REGULATIONS

NO PURCHASE NECESSARY TO ENTER OR RECEIVE A PRIZE

1. To enter the Sweepstakes and join the Reader Service, scratch off the metallic strips on all your BIG WIN tickets #1-#6. This will reveal the potential values for each Sweepstakes entry number, the number of free book(s) you will receive and your free bonus gift as part of our Reader Service. If you do not wish to take advantage of our Reader Service but wish to enter the Sweepstakes only, scratch off the metallic strips on your BIG WIN tickets #1-#4. Return your entire sheet of tickets intact. Incomplete and/or inaccurate entries are ineligible for that section or sections of prizes. Torstar Corp. and its affiliates are not responsible for mutilated or unreadable entries or inadvertent printing errors. Mechanically reproduced entries are null and void.

2. Whether you take advantage of this offer or not, on or about April 30, 1993, at the offices of Marden-Kane Inc., Lake Success, NY, your Sweepstakes numbers will be compared against the list of winning numbers generated at random by the computer. However, prizes will only be awarded to individuals who have entered the Sweepstakes. In the event that all prizes are not claimed, a random drawing will be held from all qualified entries received from March 30, 1990 to March 31, 1992, to award all unclaimed prizes. All cash prizes (Grand to Sixth), will be mailed to the winners and are payable by check in U.S. funds. Seventh prize will be shipped to winners via third-class mail. These prizes are in addition to any free, surprise or mystery gifts that might be offered. Versions of this Sweepstakes with different prizes of approximate equal value may appear at retail outlets or in other mailings by Torstar Corp. and its affiliates.

3. The following prizes are awarded in this sweepstakes: ★ Grand Prize (1) $1,000,000; First Prize (1) $25,000; Second Prize (1) $10,000; Third Prize (5) $5,000; Fourth Prize (10) $1,000; Fifth Prize (100) $250; Sixth Prize (2,500) $10; ★ ★ Seventh Prize (6,000) $12.95 ARV.

   ★ This presentation offers a Grand Prize of a $1,000,000 annuity. Winner will receive $33,333.33 a year for 30 years without interest totalling $1,000,000.

   ★ ★ Seventh Prize: A fully illustrated hardcover book published by Torstar Corp. Approximate Retail Value of the book is $12.95.

   Entrants may cancel the Reader Service at anytime without cost or obligation to buy (see details in center insert card).

4. This Sweepstakes is being conducted under the supervision of an independent judging organization. By entering this Sweepstakes, each entrant accepts and agrees to be bound by these rules and the decisions of the judges, which shall be final and binding. Odds of winning in the random drawing are dependent upon the total number of entries received. Taxes, if any, are the sole responsibility of the winners. Prizes are nontransferable. All entries must be received at the address printed on the reply card and must be postmarked no later than 12:00 MIDNIGHT on March 31, 1992. The drawing for all unclaimed Sweepstakes prizes will take place on May 30, 1992, at 12:00 NOON, at the offices of Marden-Kane, Inc., Lake Success, New York.

5. This offer is open to residents of the U.S., the United Kingdom, France and Canada, 18 years or older, except employees and their immediate family members of Torstar Corp., its affiliates, subsidiaries, and all the other agencies, entities and persons connected with the use, marketing or conduct of this Sweepstakes. All Federal, State, Provincial and local laws apply. Void wherever prohibited or restricted by law. Any litigation within the Province of Quebec respecting the conduct and awarding of a prize in this publicity contest must be submitted to the Régie des Loteries et Courses du Québec.

6. Winners will be notified by mail and may be required to execute an affidavit of eligibility and release, which must be returned within 14 days after notification or an alternate winner will be selected. Canadian winners will be required to correctly answer an arithmetical skill-testing question administered by mail, which must be returned within a limited time. Winners consent to the use of their names, photographs and/or likenesses for advertising and publicity in conjunction with this and similar promotions without additional compensation. For a list of our major prize winners, send a stamped, self-addressed ENVELOPE to: WINNERS LIST, c/o Marden-Kane Inc., P.O. Box 701, SAYREVILLE, NJ 08871. Requests for Winners Lists will be fulfilled after the May 30, 1992 drawing date.

If Sweepstakes entry form is missing, please print your name and address on a 3" ×5" piece of plain paper and send to:

In the U.S.
Silhouette's "BIG WIN" Sweepstakes
3010 Walden Ave.
P.O. Box 1867
Buffalo, NY 14269-1867

In Canada
Silhouette's "BIG WIN" Sweepstakes
P.O. Box 609
Fort Erie, Ontario
L2A 5X3

Offer limited to one per household.

© 1991 Harlequin Enterprises Limited   Printed in the U.S.A.

LTY-S391D

Silhouette Special Edition

This April,
Silhouette *Special Edition* is pleased to present

ONCE IN A LIFETIME
by Ginna Gray

the long-awaited companion volume to her bestselling duo

Fools Rush In (#416)
Where Angels Fear (#468)

Ever since spitfire Erin Blaine and her angelic twin sister Elise stirred up double trouble and entangled their long-suffering brother David in some sticky hide-and-seek scenarios, readers clamored to hear more about dashing, debonair David himself.

Now that time has come, as straitlaced Abigail Stewart manages to invade the secrecy shrouding sardonic David Blaine's bachelor boat—and creates the kind of salty, saucy, swashbuckling romantic adventure that comes along only once in a lifetime!

**Even if you missed the earlier novels,
you won't want to miss**

ONCE IN A LIFETIME #661

Available this April, only in Silhouette *Special Edition*.   OL-1